IFWG AUSTRALIA DARK PHASES TITLES

Peripheral Visions (Robert Hood, 2015)
The Grief Hole (Kaaron Warren, 2016)
Cthulhu Deep Down Under Vol 1 (2017)
Cthulhu Deep Down Under Vol 2 (2018)

CTHULHU
DEEP DOWN UNDER

VOLUME 2

EDITED BY

STEVE PROPOSCH
CHRISTOPHER SEQUEIRA
BRYCE STEVENS

INTRODUCTION BY

PETER RAWLIK

A DARK PHASES TITLE

Cthulhu Deep Down Under Volume 2

All Rights Reserved

ISBN-13: 978-1-925496-99-4

Anthology Concept Copyright ©2017 Steve Proposch, Christopher Sequeira & Bryce Stevens

V1.0

IFWG Publishing Australia
Melbourne

www.ifwgaustralia.com

This collection is dedicated to Don Boyd

TABLE OF CONTENTS

INTRODUCTION

PETER RAWLIK

Cthulhu.

When a book includes that word, what is that supposed to mean? For some, it is meant to clearly convey that the volume in question will be directly related to the Cthulhu Mythos and chock-full of references to Lovecraft Country, Miskatonic University and its faculty, and the pantheon of cosmic alien pseudo-deities including Yog-Sothoth, Yig and, yes, Cthulhu. For others, it is more vague, setting the tone for a collection of tales that invoke the Lovecraftian without being bound by its setting and trappings. It might be more appropriate to use the word "Lovecraftian" or "Weird", or even "Cosmic", but these words don't have the same gravitas as "Cthulhu", which is why Mike Davis entitled his anthology *Autumn Cthulhu* and S.T. Joshi's anthology series *Black Wings*, has morphed into *Black Wings of Cthulhu*. This is not to say that Lovecraft can't be used to sell in the mainstream, as Ellen Datlow has shown in her anthologies *Lovecraft Unbound*, *Lovecraft's Monsters*, and *Children of Lovecraft*, but when it comes to weird literature nothing implies anti-anthropocentric cosmic horror more than the word "Cthulhu".

And I should know, I've been reading Cthulhu since I could read, since before I could tell the difference between Lovecraft and Derleth, since before there was little else to read but Lovecraft and Derleth and a few volumes by Brian Lumley and Ramsey Campbell, two authors that, having started with the same source material—the same inspirations—went in wildly different directions. That right there is one of the joys of the Cthulhu

Mythos: different authors can be inspired by and reinterpret and redirect things—the source material—in totally different ways.

The stories presented here in *Cthulhu Deep Down Under Volume 2* are a rare and heady mixture of talents, highlighting the diversity of direction that Lovecraftian fiction can be taken, and while some of these stories could be transplanted to other locales, some are uniquely Australian, relying on the landscape that Australia encompasses, or by the place that Australia occupies geographically—on the edge of the world, not far from the uninhabitable bleakness of Antarctica, and overlooking the Pacific deeps, some of the most remote places on the planet. Is it any surprise that writers in such places have unique perspectives, have adapted and adopted local myth cycles, have succumbed to the madness of the lonely, inhuman and inhumane Cthulhu? I hadn't expected such wonders, but in retrospect I should have, I should not have been surprised by the luscious, dark jewels that were sent to me to read.

In *Sleeping Dogs*, Kristyn McDermott gives us a protagonist named Ghost who has a most unusual and useful talent— the ability to find lost things, but, as she soon finds out, some things are better left lost, and for Ghost the horror might just be beginning. What is most interesting here is that the motivations behind Ghost's employers remain unknown, at least to her. This makes Ghost an unwitting pawn in the action and pits her mercenary drives against whatever concerns she might have for the wellbeing of the human race. This dichotomy creates a building tension—we like Ghost, we want her to survive, but do we really want her to succeed?

Where McDermott's story is firmly rooted in the Cthulhu Mythos, *Slither* by Jason Nahrung draws dread inspiration from Lovecraftian horrors and only hints at the existence of something terrible. Nahrung forces us to walk the line between confronting a horror, and the existential dread that is generated by something that creeps, seeps, slithers, even into the dark recesses of your brain.

Silvia Brown's *Melbourne Calling* echoes this same kind of concern. Haunted by what he thinks of as forbidden desires, a young man fights to keep his sanity only to be rescued by a kindred soul and a summer romance that drives the nightmares away. Only—as we older folk all know—romances are fraught with difficulties, which lead to doubts that can shake even the strongest of relationships. In the shadow of doubt the monsters come calling. To some, it might seem better to embrace the abyss and dive headlong into monstrous self-annihilation than to accept the angst-filled pedestrian world that haunts our teenage years.

Time and Tide by Robert Hood returns us to a more overt Cthulhu Mythos tale, one that should be applauded by the author's rather bold attempt to invoke the weird in a most unusual manner. We are told that the sense of smell is the most evocative of senses, but it is rarely used, and rarely used as effectively as Hood has here, to convey not only the preternatural, but a fundamental wrongness to the universe, an inversion of the natural order of things that has dire consequences to the residents of Mollymook.

Lee Murray's *Dead End Town* takes us back into the realm of personal horror, or perhaps personal apocalypse. Murray expertly avoids the tropes and trappings of Lovecraft, but at the same time mines the ichor and uncertain parentage that seems to accompany cosmic monstrosities and redirects them into a subtle but inescapable realm of body horror.

Where Murray's tale is subtle, Bill Congreve's *The Pit* is overtly Lovecraftian, and welcomingly so. A morality tale about the dangers of unregulated industry, Congreve manages to pay homage to Lovecraft's *The Shadow Over Innsmouth*, *At the Mountains of Madness* and *The Color Out of Space* without precisely referencing any one of them. It's refreshing to see a tale that roots itself firmly in the past, recognizes its origins, but isn't slavishly obsequious. It's reminiscent of a Delta Green tale or something that would have been at home in Ed Stasheff's recent anthology *Corporate Cthulhu*, but it is firmly rooted in the vast desolate landscape that haunts Australian nightmares.

Subtleness goes out the window in Jan Scherpenhuizen's *The Island in the Swamp* in which an aficionado of fringe theories sets out to debunk or prove a latest new-age pseudoscientific theory.

5

Either way he will improve his standing amongst his friends and family, unless of course things go horribly, terribly wrong, which of course they do. Here once again, the Lovecraftian *oeuvre* is evoked without actually delving into the trappings, though it might be thought of as Cthulhu through the lens of Clive Barker.

Where the Madmen Meet by T.S.P. Sweeney begins innocently enough as the tale of soldiers back from war trying to adjust, but as it progresses it veers directly into a sequel to one of Lovecraft's most infamous of tales. I will admit that while the first person narrative initially put me off, particularly because of the ending, I've come to realise that the horror invoked here doesn't end with death. Think about it, think about how this story is even possible, and then shudder, just a little. Then, think of the children.

The Seamounts of Vaalua Tuva by David Kuraria is perhaps the most ambitious of stories in this volume. There's hints of a zombie outbreak going on in the background, but that seems unimportant to the main action of the tale, which involves the protection of civil society amongst the Solomon Islands from seafaring warlords, amidst tall tales of an indigent tribe blamed for all sorts of ills. As things progress, details that seemed unimportant suddenly come to the forefront, and suddenly it is no longer clear who is in charge and what is legend. Lovecraftian without being pastiche, I suspect someone, somewhere, will adapt this into a rather gruesome and punishing scenario for a *Call of Cthulhu* home game.

Geoff Brown's *The Depth Lurker* is reminiscent of both *The Statement of Randolph Carter* and *Pickman's Model*, invoking the fear that goes with descending into the unfathomable depths of the Earth to encounter the unknown. Present as well is the dread that is derived from the most common of acts or objects once one has survived such acts, but can't quite shake the idea that horror is lurking just beyond the corner. In many ways *The Depth Lurker* is well paired with Bill Congreve's *The Pit*, for both rely in part on the isolation of the Australian landscape, magnified by descent into the darkness below. But where Congreve's hero rose to the challenge, Brown's protagonist must find a way to live with what he has seen—if you can call his solution living.

As I have said, luscious, dark jewels that I hadn't—but should have—expected, and all unique and vibrant interpretations of the weird, the cosmic, the Lovecraftian Cthulhu, even in his absence. They are, in a way, fitting successors to the weird traditions that spawned Joan Lindsay, Vol Molsworth, David Unaipon, and Ernest Favenc. I look forward to the day when my shelves run rampant with weird literature from what Dorothea Mackellar called "the Sunburnt Country".

Peter Rawlik, 2018

SLEEPING DOGS

KIRSTYN MCDERMOTT

Ghost has the start of a headache, the start of what she hopes won't morph into one of her colour-soaked migraines. Even if this job doesn't pan out, she hardly has the time to lay up in bed for a day or two with a cool washcloth over her eyes. She rubs at her temples. Squeezes her earlobes. Someone once told her that worked. Sometimes it does.

It's been at least a quarter hour, maybe more, since she was escorted into the room by the tall woman with the artfully expressionless face and asked — instructed, more like — to take a seat. Ghost doesn't reach for her phone to check her messages. She doesn't tap her foot on the polished wooden floorboards. She doesn't pick at the skin around her fingernails. She's been asked to wait, and wait she will. Patiently. Visibly. She suspects that might be part of the interview. She suspects there's at least one spy-cam somewhere in the room, feeding its sneaky live report back to whoever wants to see just how much patience Ghost is able to summon.

"More than you know," she whispers through unmoving lips.

The room is half-office, half-library, and the ultra-tidy desk before which Ghost sits would be long enough for her to use as a bed. It's made from a dark, reddish brown wood, most likely mahogany — most likely *real* mahogany, maybe even *antique* mahogany — that matches what she can see of the floor-to-ceiling bookshelves lining the walls, as well as the rolling ladder in the corner, and the exposed wood on the pair of lion-footed Georgian armchairs over by the window. Their flawless, cream-coloured upholstery must of course be the result of more recent renovations; no way could such fabric survive the ravages of almost a century unscathed.

Still, the room oozes wealth. This job should pay well.

Ghost waits.

Ten more minutes pass before the door finally swings opens and a woman in a modest but finely tailored suit marches into the room. Her hair is steel grey, cut into a sharp, chin-length bob, and her fingernails sport well-manicured French tips. She looks exactly like the sort of person who belongs behind that neat mahogany desk and, indeed, behind the desk is precisely where she sits herself.

Keeping a few paces behind, the tall woman who escorted Ghost previously closes the door before taking up a position at the older woman's side. "Ms Thurston," she says, "this is Ghost."

"Not your real name?" Ms Thurston's eyes are a blue so pale they're almost grey. She doesn't blink.

Ghost shrugs. "Real enough for me."

The older woman holds her gaze for a moment longer, then nods. By her right elbow, resting on a small stack of papers, is a polished green-black stone roughly the same size and shape as a boiled egg sliced in half. Ms Thurston picks up the stone and places it right in front of Ghost.

"Did you notice my paperweight?" she asks.

Ghost nods, not looking at the stone. Of course she noticed it, just as she noticed the empty in-tray where those papers had probably lain, *sans* weight, until five minutes before her appointment. Just as she noticed the Art Deco lamp with the inlaid mother-of-pearl shade, and the Montblanc fountain pen that likely cost more than a month's rent in the crappy Marylebone studio where Ghost has been living for almost a year, as well as the complete lack of framed photos or uniquely personal items anywhere in sight. It's her job to notice things. To see what others might overlook.

"Pick it up," Ms Thurston says.

"I'd rather not." Ghost doesn't know why she refuses. It's dumb, but she doesn't feel like even looking at the stone too closely, let alone touching it.

"Please."

Clenching her teeth, Ghost reaches out and takes the stone between finger and thumb, like it's something dead, or worse. Nothing happens. It's a little heavier than she expected, smooth and cool and polished so highly she can see her silhouette reflected in its surface, and now she really, *really* wants to put it down. The pressure in her head has intensified and she wishes she had a glass of cold water.

After a minute that feels like an age, Ms Thurston holds out her palm. Ghost drops the stone so quickly it almost bounces, but the older woman catches it gracefully. She opens a desk drawer and retrieves a small black bag—like velvet, but darker somehow, less *lightful*—then drops the stone inside.

"Our missing artefact is crafted from similar material," she says. "I needed to know how you would react before we proceed."

"Well, I won't be asking for a free sample."

She smiles, lips stretched thin. "In some people, it can arouse rather…covetous emotions. You, however, sat here for thirty minutes with scarcely a glance in its direction. A passing grade, Lavinia, don't you think?"

Beside her, the tall woman nods. "I believe so, ma'am." Her face has softened somewhat, relaxed, a corner of her mouth twitching upwards. Ghost reckons she would be the type to unravel delightfully after a few drinks down the corner pub, spilling crude jokes and cider until the early hours. Though she doesn't suppose she'll have a chance to find that out for herself.

"You're not as old I expected," Ms Thurston is saying.

Ghost swallows a sigh. She's short and has always looked much younger than her age—she was being regularly carded well into her twenties; sometimes *still* gets asked—and turning thirty last month didn't seem to magically gift her with the kind of face that signalled, *hey, I'm an actual grown woman, please take me the fuck seriously*.

"Is that a problem?" she asks, her tone carefully neutral.

"Merely an observation." Ms Thurston pulls a large envelope

from the stack of papers and slides it across the desk. "This is what we need recovered. It's an artist's impression, drawn from the memories of two people who've seen the object firsthand, albeit some time ago now."

The drawing gives Ghost the creeps. Sketched from three-quarter view, it looks like some kind of weird gargoyle, winged and crouching on a low pedestal, with an octopus in place of its head—if an octopus could have as many as a dozen or more tentacles writhing around its face. The creature's two hands—paws?—are resting on its knees, with huge claws curving downwards, and its body seems to be covered in scales. The pedestal itself is covered in squiggles that might be meant to represent inscriptions of some kind, but there's a question mark next to it. Ghost taps the page. "What's this about?"

"One of the gentlemen described a plinth with sigils. The other swore the figure was carved without a platform of any kind, but with markings underneath." Ms Thurston sighs. "They are quite elderly, you understand, in their nineties. Their recollections may be somewhat fallible."

"How long ago did they see this thing?"

"Approximately sixty years."

Ghost raises her eyebrows. "There's no one else?"

"Anyone else who claims to have laid eyes on the artefact is dead. It has been missing for quite some time." Ms Thurston leans forward, her hands clasped tight together. "Will you be able to find it, or not?"

In the corner of the page, the artist has scribbled *5"/12cm*. At least the thing is small. "Can I keep this?" Ghost asks.

Ms Thurston glances at Lavinia, who nods. "We've made several high res copies, ma'am. Print and digital."

"The original would be best," Ghost says.

The older woman regards her silently for several seconds. "We will need it back, once you're done."

"Of course." Ghost slides the sketch into its envelope. "So whereabouts is this thing anyway?"

"If we knew that, you wouldn't be here."

"I just mean, do you have a city? A country even?"

"We do not."

"Okay." Ghost gnaws on her lower lip. "You know I only find lost things, right? Not stolen, not given away and regretted, not belonging to someone else. The lost or forgotten, that's my jam."

Ms Thurston pushes back her chair and stands. "Oh, it is definitely *lost*."

"By you?"

The old woman laughs. "Do I seem so ancient?"

"You might look, ah, younger than expected."

"*Touché*, Ghost." She extends her hand for Ghost to shake. "Not lost by me, no. But the organisation I run has a claim."

The woman's hand is dry and warm; her grip is firm. Ghost likes that, but still. "I don't know if I can take the job," she says. "There isn't a lot here to work with."

"You might find there's more than you think."

"I'll let you know in a couple of days?"

Ms Thurston nods. "Lavinia will escort you out."

As Ghost follows the woman past the bookshelves, she feels it. A faint, familiar twang in her belly, like an elastic band pulled tight. She pauses. There, somewhere there. She reaches out, runs her fingertips across several nearby spines. *Twang*. That one, the dark blue. Blue as the darkling sky, blue as the collar on a four-year-old's first school uniform, blue as drowning.

"Was there something else?" Ms Thurston calls.

Ghost turns around, book in hand. "Maybe," she says, returning to the woman still standing behind the desk. "Maybe something for you. In here, I think."

The older woman glances past Ghost, making a silent exchange with Lavinia, no doubt. Then she takes the book and flicks slowly through its pages. When she finds the piece of paper, loose and lined, clearly torn from a spiral-bound pad, her face comes close to crumpling. But only close. She turns the page around, so that Ghost can see the little boat drawn in a child's hand, its sail a bold triangle coloured in blue ink. "My grandson's work. We were taking him sailing that weekend." Ms Thurston clears her throat. "Quite the party trick, you have there."

"I'm sorry," Ghost says. "I didn't mean—"

"No." Waving her hand in dismissal, even as she turns toward the window. "I've been missing it. Thank you."

Lavinia taps Ghost on the shoulder, ushers her wordlessly from the room and down the hall to the elevator. "Jesus," she says once they're inside. "You're the real fucking deal."

"I guess I am," Ghost replies, noting as she had when Lavinia had brought her up, the lack of names next to any of the buttons. Just floor numbers. Her mouth feels dry, but at least the pounding in her head seems to be retreating. "Tell me the truth, Lavinia. If I'd been...what's the word she used? *Covetous?* If I'd been covetous back there, with the stone, I mean...would I even have been allowed to leave?"

It's an odd smile that quirks the tall woman's mouth. Like a predator thwarted, yet somehow glad of it.

"But you weren't covetous," Lavinia says. "So you needn't worry about that."

In the lobby, she passes Ghost a business card. It's white, with a capital L written in a fancy black script, along with a mobile number and—

"A *Gmail* address?"

"You don't need to know who we are just yet."

"Okay." Ghost takes the card, tucks it into her back pocket. She stares out at the busy, oblivious street, waiting just a few steps beyond those glass sliding doors. There's a question she wants to ask, even though it already sounds stupid in her head. For some reason, she *needs* to ask it. "You're the good guys in this, though, right?"

Lavinia laughs. It would take a long time to get sick of a laugh like that, maybe even forever. "Seriously, Ghost? Who on earth doesn't think they're the good guys?"

When 3am ticks over and she's still wide awake, Ghost kicks off the blankets and rolls out of bed. Half a dozen steps carry her to the cabinet next to the sink where she keeps the Chartreuse, and she swigs a mouthful straight from the bottle. It's ghastly stuff, but she trusts it to give insomnia a solid punch in the guts.

She shouldn't have taken the job. It's too weird, even for her, and she doesn't have the slightest lead about the creepy little statue. Not even a whiff of intuition. She told Cassidy as much that afternoon, calling in while she waited out a sulky London shower beneath an awning several blocks away from her meeting with Ms Thurston.

You need to wrangle me out of this one.

They already wired a down payment. For expenses.

When Cassidy told her how much, as well as the additional finder's fee she'd negotiated for successful completion, Ghost slumped back against the wall. It was more than she'd been paid for any job before, more than she'd been paid for a year of jobs. Cassidy had earned her cut on this one.

Still there, G? Want me to bounce it back?

Fuck, no. Tasting the folly in her words even as she spoke them. *Tell them I'm in.*

Ghost takes a second swig of Chartreuse and grimaces. Across the room, stuck to the pinboard above her desk, the sketch from Ms Thurston mocks her. There's enough moonlight coming in through the window to illuminate the pencilled outline of the creature squatting—

—on the ground, head turned in her direction, tentacles writhing about a maw that opens—

Ghost blinks and takes a lurching step toward her desk, then laughs. The sketch is unchanged, the octo-goyle-thing still perched on its pedestal, looking off to the left through wide lidless eyes. She's tired, running a sleep deficit she feels like she'll never pay off, seeing trouble where there isn't any. Maybe after this job, she can rest. Go somewhere there's lots of sun and no lost things begging to be found.

go home

The voice a whisper more in her head than her ears, and Ghost swivels around to see a shadowy figure sitting on the edge of her bed. No, not shadowy—*dark*, as if no light can touch it, though she can make out the sheets tangled around it well enough. The figure stands, fluid and sinuous, taller than a human should be and thinner, willowy, one too-long arm stretching out as it slides

a pace in her direction and —

go home

Ghost hears again, *feels* again, and she stumbles back as the figure unfurls its elongated hand to reveal a sigil glowing so bright it hurts to look at: an eye cold and fathomless, reptilian almost but no, not reptilian, not anything that belongs on this earth. In a breath, the figure is right before her, that impossible hand on her chest now, pushing hard —

go home

— and now she is falling, icy water closing around her as she struggles to find the surface, but everything is dark now, an utter blackness that has never known the touch of light, and her throat clogs with mud and silt, and still she is falling

— falling, awake with a jolt. Gasping for air, Ghost rolls over and promptly falls again, a short drop this time from couch to floor but the landing is hard enough to bruise. She lies there, blinking in the grey morning light for a few moments, before registering the liquid soaking into her shirt and the sickly-sharp smell of Chartreuse filling the room.

"Fuck." Ghost spots the bottle under the coffee table, most of its expensive green contents now spreading over the floorboards. She rescues it anyway, wondering where the hell the cap wound up, and gets to her feet. The eye sigil is scorched onto her retinas and not even a tentative sip of Chartreuse can wash the taste of river mud from her mouth.

Go home.

Ghost shudders. Her phone's on charge by the bed but her hands are shaking so much it takes three attempts to send Cassidy a coherent message. *Need flight to Melbourne, Aus,* she finally taps out. *ASAP.*

Biz or econ? Cassidy responds in less than a minute.

Business, Ghost texts. *Tell Thurston I have a lead.*

It's only been seven or eight years since she was last here, but the city has changed so much Ghost has trouble fighting the dislocation that seeps in every time she takes a walk. Her sister

still lives nearby, nestled into an outer, *outer* suburban housing development with her husband and two little kids. Ghost has called her, once, without letting on that she's home. Jem would've insisted she come and stay with them and Ghost has a feeling it wouldn't be good to bring this particular job anywhere near people she cares about. They can catch up when it's over—if it's ever over.

She's been in Melbourne for nine days already, staked out in a hotel apartment just a tad more swank than she's used to, and no closer to finding the artefact than when she left. It's here, she *knows* it's here, but really, Ghost is talking needles and haystacks with no electromagnet anywhere in sight. She's been to the four addresses Ms Thurston supplied once the geography was narrowed down—places with some apparent connection back in the day, but all equally dead now. Three of them since demolished and replaced with new apartment buildings, the fourth a city shopfront housing a dumpling restaurant that Ghost has eaten at three times. Truly excellent gyoza, but nothing else of interest.

There have been no more dreams either, or visions, or whatever the hell it was that night in London, and no creepy voices in her head, and so she's gone back to first principles. Grid-walking the city with a daypack slung over her shoulder, slow and methodical explorations punctuated with frequent pauses to press a hand against an old brick wall, or the lattices of frosted glass that served as pavement lights for the ancient basements below, all the while keeping herself open.

Listening. Receptive.

Of course, there are a million lost things bleating out their presence in a city of this size, most of them barely even missed, and none of them the precise thing she's hunting.

Ghost's feet ache all the time. When she needs a break, like now, she grabs an extra-large coffee and finds a shady spot down by the Yarra River to scroll through Instagram hashtags for anything that might twang. She can't decide which is more painful—the blisters developing on her blisters, or the kind of artfully curated, perfectly framed Insta-lives that she will never come close to knowing.

#melbournelife   #melbournestreets   #melbourneyoufuck-rightoff

The last mouthful of coffee is cold but Ghost swallows it anyway, thumbing through a couple more screens as she gets up and shuffles over to the nearby bins. A kid on a skateboard jags her elbow going past and she almost drops her phone, scrabbles to keep hold of it before it hits the ground, and—oh. Oh, there.

The girl in the photo is blonde and thin, gazing up in mock fright with one gloved hand over her open mouth, and hovering above her right shoulder is the sigil that Ghost remembers from her dream. That same quasi-reptilian eye, with rays or something fanning out around it—she can't tell through the filter the girl has used if it's a framed painting or mural or what. It seems to glow, but that might be the filter as well. The caption reads: *Ever get the feeling your being watched?*, along with #theeyeshaveit and a cascade of other hashtags, including the ubiquitous #melbournelife. The date is more than a year ago, but Ghost likes the photo anyway and shoots the girl a DM—*hey, cool pic. where u take that? in melb now!!*—before downloading the image and sending it off to Cassidy. *Location needed*, she tells her. *ASAP*.

Surprisingly, it's the Instagirl who gets back to her first.

It's a stained glass window, not a painting, a small semi-circle mounted above the door to what is now a rockabilly clothing shop in one of the city's older arcades. And they're not rays that surround the eye, but tentacles. Ghost is in the right place, almost. She can feel it in her belly, a faint but persistent tautness. She takes a photo of her own; straight shot, no filter. Flicks it to Cassidy along with the address. *More info please*.

"Coolsville, hey?" The woman in the shop looks like she walked right off the set of early-season *Madmen*, except for the brightly coloured tattoos adorning her arms and collarbones. She's wearing red lipstick and a broad, infectious smile.

Ghost returns it, with interest, and steps inside. "I'm wondering if you can help me out."

"Sure thing, baby doll. Whatcha looking for?"

"I'm researching a book, actually." It's a well-worn line but one that usually works. For reasons Ghost hasn't been able to figure out, most people are super-keen to throw any number of minor favours in her direction if she tells them she's a writer. "It's about, ah, the weird side of Melbourne, the creepy stuff. A friend told me about this place."

"Oh, you meant the *basement*. They took it off the tour a while ago."

"The tour?"

"The Ghost Tour, you know. After the thing with that guy…"

"What happened?"

"He refused to leave. Like, screaming and wailing and throwing-a-tantrum refused. They had to get the cops in. Wound up in a nuthouse, I heard, but that's probably bullshit."

"Right." She catches a nearby dress between finger and thumb, appreciating the satin texture. Black with large colourful flowers all over, a thin little belt above a voluminous skirt. Pretty, but not her thing. "So, you reckon I could see this basement?"

The tattooed woman pauses for a moment before checking her watch. "What the hell, this place is a desert on Mondays anyway." She opens a drawer beneath the counter and pulls out a sign, hanging it on the inside of the door before ushering Ghost out and locking it behind them. *Back in 10, mother hen!*

"I don't want to get you in trouble," Ghost says.

"Yeah, because my boss is a total bitch." Grinning, the woman stabs a thumb into her own chest. "Can't get away from her."

She leads the way down a narrow flight of stairs and into a dim corridor. After a couple of steps, a light flickers on to reveal a large wooden door, its timber dark with age but fitted with a what looks like a fairly recent deadlock. Ghost takes a moment to orientate herself.

"So, your shop's right above here?" she asks.

"Yeppers." The woman unlocks the door and reaches inside to turn on the light. "The landlord lets me use some of it for storage, since I'm not allowed to do much fitting out upstairs." She rolls her eyes as she steps back, sweeping an arm in invitation. "Heritage issues."

The room isn't much brighter than the corridor outside, but it's three times the size of the shop above, cluttered with old furniture and stacks of boxes. Ghost feels the *twang* as soon as she crosses the threshold. She bites her lip, clenching her fists so hard, her nails dig painfully into her palms. It's here, the damn thing is *here*.

"You sense it, don't you?"

"Huh?" Ghost turns around, on guard.

"It's wrong, this room. No one likes to be down here for long."

"Except that one guy."

"Except him." The women opens a nearby carton and starts pulling out shoe boxes. "Have a gander while I grab some stock."

Ghost doesn't need to go far. There's a line of four filing cabinets on the far wall, drawing her in. She picks her way over and places her hand on top of the nearest, disturbing many years' worth of dust. But it's the next one along that really pings; her knees almost buckle as she leans against it, and the taste of muddy water coats her mouth. The statue was in the river at some stage, she can feel that, thrown into the silty depths only to be dredged up again by sheer stroke of luck—or perhaps not luck at all; perhaps it called out to be found back then, as it's calling to Ghost now, here in this forgotten old cabinet with merely a thin sheet of metal between them. She tests one of the drawers. Locked.

"Careful, hon, you might get tetanus. All that crap's been down here for God knows how long." The woman jangles her keyring. "Seen enough? I should get back upstairs."

"Actually, do you think I could stay here a bit? Soak in the atmosphere, jot down some observations." Ghost flashes what she hopes is a shy-but-winning smile. "You know, for the book."

"Yeah, maybe not. I shouldn't really leave this room unlocked."

"So, lock me in."

"Seriously?"

"I've been in worse places. Half an hour?" She switches her smile up a gear, places her hand over her heart. "You can search me before I leave, if you need to; I swear not to take anything except notes."

"Oh, I wasn't implying…" The woman looks flustered now, caught in a possible *faux pas*. "Half an hour, okay?"

Ghost waits for a minute or so after the deadbolt thunks home before slipping off her daypack and searching through it for the small leather case she keeps her lockpick tools in. The filing cabinet dates back several decades and likely hasn't been used in nearly as long, so it takes her more time than usual, and a lot more force, to work the mechanism open. Wishing she had some WD-40, Ghost finally coaxes it into turning. The first three drawers yield nothing of interest but there in the fourth, tucked behind some empty suspension files, she finds a small wooden box.

twang

Its edges are sealed with dribbled wax, once black, now crazing to grey in places, and about as heavy as you'd expect if it contained a small figure carved from mottled green stone. Ghost *knows* the thing is inside, knows it as much as she's ever known anything in her life—but still. The thought of lugging it all the way back to London, only to have Ms Thurston shake her head: *this isn't what we asked for; did you even look?*

Ghost takes out her folding knife. "Bad idea," she whispers, even as she digs through the wax around the slightly curved lid. "Bad, bad idea." She clears enough to wedge in the blade and lever it back and forth until—

"Fuck!"

The migraine hits without warning. Colours fracture and pulse in the centre of her vision, spreading rapidly. Her temples throb; a dull ache moves along her jawline. She needs to get out of here. Now.

The box is on the floor where she dropped it, and thankfully it isn't empty. She stares sidelong at the contents, peering through the edges of the aura that will pretty soon be all she can see for a while, and breathes a shaky sigh of relief. The statue is nestled into a velvety cushion, and seems intact. Ghost has no desire whatsoever to take it out and check. Sure, it's only her migraine that makes the tentacles around the creature's face look like they're writhing, that makes the symbols carved into its base appear to glow, but that doesn't mean she wants to touch the damn thing.

Ghost closes the box and shoves it deep into her daypack. Her fingers have started to tremble and she drops the pick twice while convincing the deadlock to hoist a white flag.

"Focus," she whispers. The colours have spread further; it's like looking through a psychotic kaleidoscope. At last, the bolt slides across and she fumbles her way out of the room and down the corridor, keeping one hand on the wall as she climbs back up those narrow stairs. Slim peripheral vision is all she has when she reaches the top, but she manages to make out the tattooed woman striding towards her—or the flared shape of her rockabilly skirt, at least.

"Hey," Ghost says. "Thanks."

"How did you get...?"

The woman's voice trails off as she backs away, backs right through the door of her shop as Ghost approaches, as Ghost shuffles past, down the arcade, touching two fingers to her temple and flicking a salute as she goes. "Don't forget to lock up down there."

On the street, the sun is too bright, the pain in her head throbbing, threatening to burst her skull into pieces. Trams rattle to a standstill at a nearby stop and Ghost makes her careful way onto the nearest in line. Any tram going north will take her close to the hotel, as long as she gets off in time. At least the colours are seeping away now, leaving in their wake the blurred and doubled vision that she knows will last an hour or two. She pulls out her phone and finds Cassidy's number, which goes straight to voicemail as usual.

"Hey, it's me. Tell Thurston I have it." She swallows, a sudden surge of nausea rippling through her guts. "And book a flight to London tomorrow. I want this done and dusted."

Fighting the urge to vomit, Ghost only registers the person who is sitting in the seat next to her when they make a grab for her daypack. She shouts, wrenching her shoulders around and trying the push the would-be thief away. He's a skinny guy, but strong, and his breath smells of sour coffee as he leans his weight against her, rough hands tugging on the straps. Jerking up an elbow, she catches him somewhere soft and hopefully fucking painful, and he lets out a short grunt before punching her. Hard. In the stomach. Gasping, Ghost reaches out with fingers arched into claws, determined to do some serious fucking facial damage, but the guy isn't there anymore.

"You okay?" someone asks and she nods, getting to her feet as the tram lurches to a stop. Her assailant is face-down on the floor, half-blocking the aisle with some dude's knee in his back, and Ghost climbs past, slides through the other passengers who move aside to let her pass, even as they're demanding to know *what happened?* and *why?* No one stops her, no one so much as touches her, and she goes as fast as her compromised vision will allow. Out of the tram, onto the street, squinting through the bleariness until finally she has her bearings.

Two blocks north, half a block west. The hotel. A quiet room. Ibuprofen.

Ghost shrugs her daypack higher on her shoulders, and hustles.

It's cold under the water, a cold so deep, so biting, it's almost tangible. Dark as well, but even so, she can see the slim, elongated figure swimming toward her. Swimming, or floating, she can't tell. Can't move either, can only wait, blood turning to ice, as it comes closer, closer, black against black, those long, long arms reaching out—

wake up

—and Ghost does.

Her head throbs and it takes several disoriented moments for her to realise the ringing she can hear isn't just in her ears. Only one person has the permissions to bypass her phone's Do Not Disturb mode, and Ghost's stomach is already churning as she swipes to answer.

"Cassidy? This better be the end of the world."

"Check your door, now. Via the peephole."

Cassidy's voice is clipped and strained. Ghost rolls out of bed and fumbles her way through the apartment. She pulled all the curtains before crashing but it's still daytime outside to judge by the thin lines of brightness sneaking past their edges, which means she can't have had more than a couple of hours' sleep. No wonder she still feels like shit. Ghost presses an eye to the peephole.

"Cassidy?" she whispers into the phone. "Why is there a neighbourhood watch meeting outside my room?"

"How many?"

Ghosts counts seven people, men and women of various ages, some in office clothes, some dressed more casually, and two who look like they've just rushed over in the middle of a gym session. An eighth joins them, a woman wearing the hotel's housekeeping uniform and brandishing a small card. A key, Ghost realises, as the handle turns and the door is pushed open.

"Hey," she says, pushing back. "Do not fucking disturb!"

The door only opens a few inches before catching on the security latch, and a hand slides around, fingers scrabbling. Ghost thumps the intruder, hard, and they withdraw with a yelp. She slams the door. Leans against it.

"What the fuck is going on, Cassidy?"

"Hold on a sec, I'm patching someone through."

"You're what?"

There's a click, and then that *someone* is on the line, their familiar British voice shouting over too much background noise. "Ghost, can you hear me?"

"*Lavinia?*"

"You need to leave now. Take the *essentials* and get out of there."

The door is opened again and this time two arms force their way through the gap, frantically grasping at empty air, while others outside pound on the heavy wood. Down the hall, an ear-splitting siren begins to blare a strident warning.

Ghost heads back to the bedroom, pressing the phone close against her head. "Is that a fire alarm?"

"Get to the pool deck. Fast as possible."

"Yeah, if there's a fire, I don't think the pool will help." She wrenches opens a curtain, blinking against the sudden light, and looks around for her jeans, her shoes.

"There's no fire, trust me. And the pool is on the roof. Stairs are down the corridor to your right as you leave your room."

"There's the small matter of the walking dead, Lavinia."

"They're not zombies, they're *covetous*. Figure it out."

The call cuts off. Fuck. Ghost dresses at breakneck speed. Snatches her daypack from the chair where she left it and makes a hasty check. Passport. Wallet. Box from the Watery Depths of Hell. As she jogs past the kitchenette, she grabs the small fire extinguisher from the wall near the stove. There are four different arms poking around the edge of the door now. She gives them all a bash with the base of the extinguisher until they retreat, then shuts the door so she can unhook the latch.

Ghost takes a deep breath.

Pulls the safety pin on the extinguisher.

And swings the door wide.

The chemical powder drives the milling hoard back far enough for her to make a run for it. She lets loose another lengthy backward spray as she sprints down the hall. Beneath the siren's bellow, she can hear coughing and spluttering, a confusion of voices that, for now, don't seem to be following her. Half way up the first flight of stairs—thank all the unknown gods that she took an apartment only three floors from the top—she bumps into a handful of bedraggled pool-siders coming down.

"You're going the wrong way," a guy, wide-eyed, yells in passing.

Ghost grins. "Forgot my towel!"

At the top, she pauses to get her bearings, and her breath. The fire stairs have brought her out at the end of the hall that leads to the pool deck, accessed through a pair of solid glass doors. She checked out the place on her first day and dismissed it as being of any interest. Out in the open with a spectacular view, but no shade sails or any other way to hide from the harsh summer sun, and full of people generally being people.

It's deserted now, though hardly peaceful, what with the

alarms still shrieking at high pitch. A pair of sunglasses left on one of the empty deckchairs sounds a small, terrified *twang*. They belong to Wrong Way Guy. Ghost hopes he gets them back. She finds a couple of damp towels and knots them together. Threads them through the D-shaped steel handles on the glass doors and ties off. They won't last too long against a sustained effort to get through, but it's the best she can do right now. At a loss, she slumps down in the slim shadow of a nearby potted palm, and pulls out her phone.

Cassidy answers on the first ring. "G, are you safe?"

"My poolside cocktail is missing but apart from that—what the fuck is going on?"

"You didn't read any of my emails?"

"I've been sleeping off a migraine since I got back to the hotel."

"Sounds about right."

"Don't start with me, Cassidy. I've had—"

"No, I mean, it really sounds right. That thing you found, it's not…it's not exactly what Thurston thought it was. It's worse. Or stronger—they weren't precisely clear."

"Cassidy…"

"The problem was, you stayed in one place too long. It's like a beacon, Lavinia said. It calls out, but it needs to be stationary for anyone to get a fix on it."

"It was pretty damn stationary down in that basement all those years."

"Did you break a containment ward?"

"What? No, I just…oh. Like a wax seal, maybe?"

"More than likely."

"No one said anything about fucking wards. This is some kind of slippery bullshit—"

"Agreed. Though they did seem genuinely sorry about it all; we should be able to negotiate a bonus. Undisclosed risks, and so on."

The fire alarm has finally been switched off. In the shiny new silence, Ghost can hear the squeak of heavy doors being rattled on their hinges. She peeks around the edge of the pot. Her stomach sinks. "Cassidy, my fan club has caught up. They might even have recruited a couple new members."

"Lavinia is less than a minute away."

"She's in the hotel?"

"Not quite."

And now Ghost can hear something else. A faint *thwop-thwop-thwop* in the air, growing louder and louder, closer and closer, a sound she can almost feel in her ribs. She gets to her feet, runs past the doors where a dozen or so people are pressing themselves against the glass, their mouths opening wide as they spot her, and around to the other side of the pool and the five foot concrete wall that surrounds the deck.

A helicopter rises up, bringing with it churning winds so strong they almost blow Ghost over. The side door is open, Lavinia crouched at its edge, dressed in tactical black. She waves, motioning for Ghost to move away, then drops down a ladder. Chains clatter against the wall. It doesn't look in the least bit stable. Ghost steps even further away.

"Cassidy," she yells into the phone. "You and me are gonna have words."

If there's an answer, she can't hear it.

Lavinia is also shouting something. She gestures toward the ladder, then points over Ghost's shoulder. Ghost turns to see that her unwanted entourage have worked enough slack into the knotted towels to make a sizeable gap between the doors. A lithe, lycra-clad cyclist is trying to push her way through. A man in a high-vis vest is sawing at the white fabric with a knife.

A *big* knife.

Ghost puts away her phone and reaches for the ladder.

The trick is not to remember that she's thirty-odd storeys above the unforgiving bitumen and concrete of William Street.

The trick, when her foot slips for the second time and she clings to her current position with eyes squeezed shut and heart pounding even louder than her head, is not to think of how few seconds she'll have to regret everything she's done in the last twenty-four hours.

The trick is to want nothing more than the very next rung.

In the end, it happens quicker than a jump-cut action scene.

Lavinia, grabbing her beneath the arms, hauling her up. Pulling off the daypack. Fastening her into a harness. Slamming a headset over her ears. Sliding the door shut as the helicopter banks away.

"It's in there?" Lavinia points toward the pack. Her voice, through the headphones, sounds ridiculously far away.

Ghost nods. Her mouth feels too dry for words right now. The woman unzips the daypack with gloved hands and reaches gingerly inside, like she half-expects something to bite. She brings out the wooden box, more of the wax flaking off at her touch, and raises an eyebrow. Ghost nods again. Lavinia takes a folded cloth from one of her jacket's many pockets—the same lush, impossibly black fabric that swallowed Ms Thurston's paperweight—and uses it to slowly, methodically wrap up the box.

Almost immediately, Ghost feels her headache lessen, the pressure in her skull ease, if only slightly.

Lavinia places her newly wrapped package into a heavy-duty metal box by her feet and spins the combination that locks it. Then she calmly retrieves a paper bag from another pocket, flaps it open, and vomits inside.

"Sorry," she says, once she's done.

Ghost shrugs. "I've seen worse."

"No, I mean—I'm sorry." Lavinia kicks the metal box.

"Oh. Well. At least you managed to come through." She swallows, wishing she had some water. "How *did* you manage it, though? A flight from London is well over twenty hours…" The tall woman is smiling. Ghost wonders if she should mention the smear of vomit on her cheek. Decides to leave it be. "You were in Melbourne the whole time. Spying on me?"

"Watching. There's a difference."

"You're gonna have to buy me a cider when we get back, and explain just what that difference is."

Lavinia laughs and extends her right hand. "You have a deal, Ghost." Her grip is strong. Safe. Ghost doesn't want to ever let go.

This time, Ms Thurston is already behind her desk as Ghost follows Lavinia into the older woman's office. Ghost has been in London for three days and has spent the greater part of those, as she had on the private flight over, sleeping the sleep of the jetlagged dead. Once the dregs of her migraine wore off, she skimmed through the curious, but now largely useless, info that Cassidy had sent her in Melbourne.

A secretive society of overly ambitious young men who, in the first half of the twentieth century, had headquartered themselves in the building where Ghost eventually located the statue.

Rumours of strange rituals. A sudden and unexplained death. Elder gods. *Elder gods?*

At that point, too exhausted to countenance such long-dead conspiracies, Ghost stopped reading.

Ms Thurston gestures for her to take a seat. "We are so very grateful for what you accomplished, and so very sorry that we weren't in a position to better prepare you. I trust the payment has come through by now?"

It had. Cassidy had texted her that morning about the unexpectedly higher sum. There had been several exclamation marks, and a dancing emoji.

"Lavinia still owes me a cider," Ghost says.

"I'm sure she will make good on that."

Lavinia doesn't smile exactly, but the corner of her mouth does twitch. "I fully intend to, ma'am. Just been a bit busy of late."

"Ah, yes." Ms Thurston picks up the large cardboard tube that's been sitting by her elbow and prises off one of the end caps. "As you know, the job you did for us wasn't quite what we thought. Locating the artefact was merely intended to be a trial run, a test of your abilities…and your fortitude."

"Sorry to disappoint you, fortitude wise."

"Not at all, Ghost. The stone from which it was carved has a very particular origin. Some people desire it; others—like yourself, like our dear Lavinia—are repelled. Most are neutral, though able to be swung one way or the other, in the right circumstances. We suspected that the artefact, being an idol, would enhance these effects. We didn't know that it had been amplified even further—a blessing of some kind, or a curse; we're still investigating."

Ghost folds her arms over her chest. "You don't need to tell me any of this."

"It's only fair that you be given all pertinent information this time." Ms Thurston extracts a yellowed roll of paper from the tube.

"This time?"

"There's one more job we'd like you to do for us."

"Is this one going to get me killed?"

"Possibly. But it's for a very, very good cause."

Carefully, the older woman unrolls the paper, which Ghost now sees is actually more like parchment, thick and creased and discoloured, and spreads it out on the desk. There are words in a language that Ghost doesn't understand, that she doesn't think anyone human is meant to understand, along with drawings that resemble the work of a deranged cartographer, and several scribbled annotations in English.

In the top right corner of page is one word: *R'YLEH*.

Ghost doesn't feel so good. Her mouth tastes of salted water, cold and unfathomably deep. She glances at Lavinia, who offers a barely perceptible shrug.

Who on earth doesn't think they're the good guys?

Ms Thurston leans forward. "Tell me, Ghost. What are your feelings about finding a lost city?"

TIME AND TIDE

ROBERT HOOD

Edited from Searching for Cryptonbury, *the cryptozoological blog of Douglas Oudemans Ormsham (searchingforcryptonbury.blogspot. com.au). The relevant entries have since been removed from public viewing on this site for unexplained reasons, but are reproduced here with permission of the original author.*

January 10, 2018, Mollymook, NSW, Australia

It began innocuously enough, a mere taint on the crisp sea-air. Now, two days later, the stench has become so unpleasant some residents have taken to wearing bacterial masks, even indoors. Tourists stay away. Outrage that the local authorities seem unable to locate the source of the strange smell has become a common topic of conversation, as the putrescent foulness of it is beginning to affect business, not to mention its impact on the township's oft-touted quality-of-life.

The main beach remains completely deserted. Once again, I walked down there this morning and as always saw only the pristine curve of the sand and the placid motion of the tide. Many have speculated that the beach must be, one way or another, the source of the trouble: some dead thing washed ashore. Yet the open vista offers no sign as to where it might be harbouring the offending carcass. The rocky headland at the southern end has been thoroughly searched by now, several times, as has nearby bushland, even though the strongest concentration is right in the middle of the beach itself. Breathing is unbearable in that spot, making it impossible to remain for longer than it takes to inhale once or twice, no matter how shallowly. Yet there's nothing there—nothing except a clean stretch of unblemished sand. The tangible sense of rancid presence is oppressive.

Heading away from the central focus of the smell, head down and dizzy with the foul odour, I found myself entangled with someone's fishing gear—the someone being a large slightly threatening shape named, I later discovered, Ezra Zabriskie.

"Careful, lad," he muttered, words issuing from his bearded face with apparent reluctance.

'Lad' is not an epithet that accurately describes me, but underneath his broad, cloth hat and straggling hair, Ezra could be aged anywhere from 30 to 80.

I apologised then queried the fact that, against the odds, he appeared to be planning to do some beach fishing.

"I've come here to fish every day for the past 40 years," he growled. "Won't be put off by no bloody fish-fart."

Good luck to him, I say. He's made of sterner stuff than I.

The circumstances of my coming to Mollymook presaged the possibility that I would find something strange in the vicinity, but a bad smell from nowhere wasn't what I'd anticipated. The surviving notebooks and activity logs of my great-grandfather, Dr Hugo Drakenswode, are filled with myriad accounts of his interaction with the unexpected and the strange, even the impossible. I peruse them constantly in my ongoing attempt to unravel the Mystery he spent his life seeking to expose. Generally, his writings are personal but distant in tone, rarely directed toward a specific audience. Therefore, I was surprised when I came upon the following note, hand-written, as is typical, but on a paper-scrap ripped carelessly from one of his notebooks. The note was remarkable in that it must have been penned when I was a child of 8 years or less—or even more likely, before I was born. Hugo Drakenswode died in 1981, at age 106, after a long debilitating illness. Yet the words contained an immediacy that suggested the letter had been composed much more recently than that.

Douglas,

Pardon my interference in your current activities—and forgive me too if receiving this missive comes as a sharp surprise. I do confess to having trouble keeping up with our temporal interactions, so it perchance may be that you have not as yet had occasion to speak with me since my passing.

None of that matters. You will come to learn more as time goes by. Right now, it is imperative you travel to the colonies, specifically to New South Wales in Australia, which I assume is still under British Imperial influence—I can't recall its exact status. What I do know is that in a place called Mollymook something of grave consequence is about to happen. I believe the town is situated on the south coast some 140 miles from Sydney and is to be developed some time around 1990 as a retirement-cum-holiday area. If nothing else, you might find it a pleasant break. Go there. Now. A reality loop or temporal break may soon be activated there. If so, you must use your insight to assess the situation and to end it. You should be on site by the 8th of January in the year 2018 at the latest.

In preparation, I suggest that you find and read my Journal entries for January 1913. They will explain the nature of my suspicions. I think it would also be prudent at this juncture to obtain, if possible, a copy of the fiction of an American pulp writer by the name of H.P. Lovecraft. I assume you have not heard of the man. He is something of a penny-dreadful sensationalist, but his view of reality contains more truth, I am beginning to believe, than at first appears plausible.

Above all else, however, take great care. I need you to give me a full report. Much depends on your judgement.

Yours
HD

Receiving such a message was not in itself as profound a surprise as you might assume. For one thing, I have indeed spoken to my great-grandfather since his death, under circumstances that put a considerable strain on both my credulity and my general state-of-mind. But that's a story for another time.

Enough to say that I took heed of what he wrote and immediately prepared to travel from Gate's Way in Queensland, Australia, where I was living at that time, to Sydney and thence to Mollymook. Unfortunately, I had no immediate access to the journal entry Drakenswode was referring to. Much of his vast archive had been lost a few years ago when his family estate in Britain, which I had inherited, was completely destroyed by "unknown causes"—though I believe it was some monstrous entity that was to blame, even if the official history says otherwise...But never mind what I think of that incident. The point is, all that remains of his writings is whatever I had with me at the time of the "accident", as well as the contents of a number of boxes I had re-located to New Zealand in a futile attempt to save my then floundering matrimonial situation.

So Drakenswode's admonition to read his January 1913 records could not be honoured, though I did locate a rather large tome of tales by Lovecraft. I had already heard of his work, of course, as he had certainly not fallen into the obscurity to which my great-grandfather would have consigned him. What to make of it was another matter. Surely Drakenswode did not suspect that Cthulhu himself had retired to Mollymook?

Though part of my mind whispered: "Stranger things have happened", I smiled ironically at the thought—and looked at my fellow occupants of the township with a suspicious eye.

January 13, 2018

I have no idea how long this can continue. I'm a stoic man, but even I cannot tolerate much longer the acrid putrescence tainting the atmosphere. The inside of my nostrils and throat feel as though they have been scoured with sandpaper and I have to force my lungs to work, as the body's subconscious reluctance to inhale grows stronger daily.

Today began unexpectedly cold and drizzly and got gloomier as the hours passed. Despite the tightly closed windows, the

Bad Smell was more oppressive than it had ever been, having escalated over the past few days. I hunkered down, blankets over my head, breathing in short, shallow gasps. By the time I staggered into the kitchen of my rented cottage this morning, I did not feel at all like eating breakfast. I forced myself to do so. A warm shower helped to revitalise my spirits.

As a result of this languid approach to the day, I got to the beach later than usual and found it taped off as for a crime scene. Police were searching the area. Activity was concentrated on a part of the beach I estimated was in the general vicinity of the Bad Smell's strongest concentration. A lengthy, gently flapping canvas enclosure had been erected there. That piqued my interest. Obviously, there was now something to see.

Curiosity impelled me onto the sand, oblivious to the situation, at which juncture I was bailed up by a policeman set to stop sightseers from contaminating the scene. I asked him what had happened.

"A death, sir," he said.

"An accident?"

"I couldn't say, sir."

"Who was it?"

"I'm sorry, but I cannot discuss a matter under investigation. I'm sure you understand." His tone suggested it didn't matter whether I did or not.

"Do you have some personal interest in this?" he asked, granting me a distrustful stare.

I smiled as though he'd made a rather quizzical joke and retreated from the beach back onto the grassed area. The usual group of idle residents had begun to gather. One was Tangerine Harken, a woman who lives a few houses along from my cottage. She wore her usual handmade hippy dress—colourful, with a loose weave—and tie-dyed smock. On her feet were sandals made of hemp. Her hair was black, long and loose, with a few streaks of grey, often lying on her shoulders like a shawl, as it was now.

Her surname—Harken—suits her well. She "harkens" to everything that's going on thereabouts and is very keen to talk about any topic that might arise. She blames the foul-smelling atmosphere on our "wantonly cannibalistic" society—all animals being equal to humans, aquatic life included—and our failure to pay proper attention to the world around us.

We first met when I found a letter addressed to her had been erroneously sent to my rented cottage. I took it to the correct address and when she answered the door said: "I think this was meant for you, Ms Harken. It was left on my—"

"I'm a married woman," she snapped.

"Sorry. Mrs Harken, then."

She took the letter and studied it with an ambivalent stare that might have been meant to convey anything from curiosity to disgust. "Yes, it's for me."

"Good then. Well, it was nice to meet you. No doubt we'll run into each other again."

I was about to leave when she stopped me by saying:

"Would you like to come in for some tea? My husband's not here. He died a few years ago...seven, to be exact."

"Oh, I'm sorry."

"I'm fairly sure it wasn't your fault. He ate too many hamburgers and took too many sea-lives—anything he could catch. When we take others' lives into ourselves, we eventually transform our soul into a spiritual wasteland." She paused for me to digest her words. Then added: "A shark took him when he was scuba-diving." She waved her hand in the direction of the ocean. "It's not a shark-infested area, so they claim it was just bad luck. *I* think it was revenge."

I didn't know what to say, so I said nothing.

"Anyway," she continued, "Tea?"

"Um, I—"

"I can't offer you dairy milk with the tea, though I have some soy."

"I always have my tea without milk, Mrs Harken."

"I hate being referred to as *Mrs Harken*, too. Call me *Tange*."

"*Tange*?"

"Short for *Tangerine*. That's my name. Everyone calls me *Tange*."

"Right."

"It rhymes with *Ange* as in *Angelina*. A few idiots persistently call me just that. Come on in! I'm not after a replacement husband, so you're safe enough."

I followed her in. Tange is the only person in Mollymook I've come to know at any depth. Our meeting was wonderfully fortuitous, in fact, as she proved to be a useful source of local knowledge — snippets she tosses in my direction when she isn't berating whoever it was had most recently committed some unforgivable crime against the Earth Mother.

Today, she waved to me as I returned from the sand, patting the wall on which she was ensconced. I sat next to her. For a while, we both stared across the beach toward the police activity, saying nothing. I eventually gave in.

"What's going on, Tange? Have you heard whispers?"

"Some." A sudden gust of wind swept over us, laden with a noisome reek so potent that everyone there gasped and turned aside, hands to mouth. All except Tange, who kept talking, oblivious to the potency of the stink and the shrieks of complaint. "I heard the dead person is Old Ezra."

"Ezra Zabriskie?"

"Who else? He's here every morning, fishing. Has been for... as long as anyone remembers."

"I spoke to him just the other day."

"He arrived early this morning, as usual, before everyone else. They say he discovered the empty beach wasn't empty any more. He went to investigate, bent to touch whatever was there, and now he's dead. Or so they say."

"Do you have any idea what exactly it was killed him?"

She scowled at me. "Maybe all those dead fish he's slaughtered. The spirits of the ocean are increasingly vengeful."

"Do you really believe that?"

She gave an impatient smile and turned away.

We sat for a while after that, in silence, while a miasma of complaint, gossip and general chatter from the other bystanders thickened around us. Out across the beach, behind the "crime-site" enclosure, the policeman I'd spoken to earlier stood guard, looking rather unimpressed and uncomfortable. He was, after all, closer to the probable source of the stench. I wondered if there was anyone on the other side of the canvas wall. No doubt Zabriskie's body was still there, along with whatever had killed him.

Tange started weaving theories about what this was about, all of which, unsurprisingly, involved the spectre of environmental catastrophe. Sadly, most sounded less like the ravings of a crazy person than they might have just a few years ago.

After ten minutes or thereabouts, three figures emerged from the Ulladulla District police incident van, which was parked on a fenced-off area of grass on the other side of the public carpark. One was a female police officer, from what I could see from this distance. Of what rank, I don't know, as I remain unfamiliar with Australian police organisational structures. The others were wearing archetypal lab coats: a man and a woman. All three had white anti-pollution face masks that covered their nose and mouth.

We watched them as they headed toward the canvas barrier. The hum of chatter, which had died off somewhat, was re-ignited. After five minutes or so, one of the scientists, the woman, staggered out from behind the canvas, pushing the flap aside in what amounted to panic. She staggered about five or six metres, collapsed onto her knees, tore off the mask and vomited. The others followed, obviously affected as well, but holding it in better. The police woman helped the first scientist up, while the other spoke loudly and earnestly. I couldn't make out what he was saying, but there was a definite edge of hysteria. Suddenly, he glanced back, yelled "Just stay away from it 'til we can get some hazmat suits!" Then he staggered toward the incident van. The policeman who'd been on guard came over and talked to the senior officer. She pointed toward the scientists. He nodded and went to help the other scientist, who looked worse than he had at first, off the beach. When the policeman returned, he took up a station much further away from the site. The senior officer came toward the crowd. During all this, the noise from the onlookers had fallen away to a low hum. Now they were completely quiet, obviously anxious to hear what she had to say. I noticed a tall, thin man push to the front, along with a photographer.

"Sergeant Sandros!" he yelled. "What on earth is over there?" He jumped down onto the sand to get closer to her. "Can you take us to it?"

She gestured him away. "Stay off the beach!" She spoke with some force and the man backed against the wall.

"The fact is," she said, talking to the thirty or so people that constituted the crowd, "some sort of toxic matter has appeared on the beach. It's killed one man, through contact we believe, and, as you have seen, seriously affects anyone who goes near it."

"Just what is 'it' exactly, Katherine?" the man interrupted.

"I'm sure you meant *Sergeant*, Mr Waldmar. Can we please manage some journalistic professionalism for once?"

He huffed.

"What it is, we don't know as yet." She spoke to the crowd. "It appears to be biological material, in an advanced state of decomposition. It's about ten metres in length, but appears to be part of a long-dead carcass. Of what, is hard to tell. How it came to be here, we don't know. It would all be very straightforward if not for the strangeness of its appearance and the unfortunate death of Mr Zabriskie—not to mention the reaction that affects anyone who goes near it." She paused. Waldmar began a question, as did a few others, but she cut them all off. "A formal statement will be made once we have something to report. A Hazmat team is on the way. In the meantime, everyone is ordered to stay off the beach, along the whole stretch, from here to Bannisters Point and further both ways. The Coast Guard has been alerted and will check the waters up and down the coast. More of this carcass may be anywhere, and accidentally treading on it could be fatal. We will be checking the beaches and the rock platforms, but until an all-clear is given, you must stay away. Thank you."

Questions swept toward her, bursting from Waldmar and others like a plague of locusts. The officer waved them off and headed back to the police van. Gradually the crowd began to wander away, especially when a police team proceeded to distribute themselves along the foreshore, erecting BEACH CLOSED and WARNING: HEALTH HAZARD signs at key points, and suggesting less than politely that the bystanders should disperse. Another sudden gust of wind coming off the sea, carrying the appalling stench with it, further encouraged a general exodus.

"I guess we might as well go," I said to Tange. I was beginning to feel nauseous.

Without looking at me, eyes on the flapping enclosure, she whispered to herself, "This isn't right."

"What isn't right?" I asked.

She looked at me, making her face into a comment on my obtuseness. With a toss of her hair, she stood and turned as though to proceed along the walkway. "I can't take the foul odour any more right now. I'll catch you later."

I said goodbye as she headed off. After a few long paces, however, she stopped and looked back. She stared at me, frowning, then came closer again. Very close. Her green eyes dug into my brain with the force of a migraine.

Raising her right index finger, she poked it at me without actually touching me. "I don't know why you're here, Mr Douglas, but I suspect...well, never mind what I suspect. But I strongly suggest you ignore that thing." Her poking finger left me and pointed toward the hidden secret on the beach. "Leave it be! You understand me?"

"Um, not really. And how did you know my name is Douglas?" *Douglas* is not the name I've been giving out.

"You look like a Douglas." She huffed. "Just forget the whole thing. It'll come to no good."

Then she strode away, turning right along the road and disappearing into the nearby streets.

January 16, 2018

The past few days have seen a gradual escalation in the adverse conditions plaguing the area. The smell is unbearable. I kept the usual fruitless vigil at the beach, sometimes accompanied by Tange, sometimes not. She seems increasingly edgy. Nothing much was happening, though the police appeared more and more agitated. I was told the promised Hazmat team had finally arrived by midday of the 15th, but nothing had been reported. I spoke to Waldmar the journalist at one point, but he knew little—and was extremely vocal in expressing his disdain for the police and their "blatant disregard for the sacred role of the Press in a so-called democracy". At one point, he let slip a rumour that one of the Hazmat team members had fallen terminally ill as a result of Whatever It Was on the beach, but he hadn't been able to confirm it.

"Someone's head's gonna roll over this," he muttered.

By mid-afternoon, I gave up, no longer able to withstand such direct exposure to the foul atmospheric conditions—in fact, feeling weak and nauseous, my mind a jumble of meaningless, unformed theories—and simply locked myself away in the cottage. As the evening engulfed the town like a sickly fog, I ate an unenthusiastic meal and went to bed. Sickened by the stench, I slept poorly, tossing and turning in a sort of shallow delirium. After waking from one vague but particularly grotesque nightmare for the third time, I gave up trying and headed into the lounge area. The house seemed darker than usual. I felt around for the light switch, found it and clicked it. Nothing. I flicked it up and down a few times, to no avail.

Suddenly a wave of burning nausea, like a gross tsunami, swept over me, so violently I staggered and collapsed onto my knees. As I did, my stomach heaved. I had no hope of holding it in; the masticated and partially digested remains of my meagre dinner burst out across the carpet. Again. And again. Once I had it under control, I glanced up. In that instant, I was struck by a sight so grossly weird it threw me back against the lounge. A huge eye stared at me through the window, even though I was sure I'd closed the blinds for the night. The eye was so large it took up more than the entire available space. It blinked once in the second I'd had to take it in before shock tossed me back onto the floor.

By the time I recovered and glanced toward the window

again, the grotesque vision was gone. The curtains of the window concerned were closed, though I swear they quivered, as though they had been rapidly pulled shut a moment before and had not yet settled.

I must have dreamed it, of course. Yet that phantasmal vision had been extremely detailed. One thing had been clear: it hadn't been a human eye. The shape was wrong, more ovoid, with what looked like multiple, and different-coloured, pupils. Parts of it were moving, as though the cornea was full of snakes.

I pulled myself together and slowly shuffled toward the window, less tentatively with each step. Though I was somewhat conditioned to accept weirdness thanks to my great-grandfather's notebooks, my actual interaction with the monstrous encounters he wrote about was minor, and I wasn't inclined to believe what I'd seen was real. It had to have been a dream, a mental eidolon. I reached the window and peered out between the two sides of the curtain. It was not completely dark out there; the street lights were on, providing patches of luminance, and from the vigorous movement of the foliage a decent wind was blowing — luckily from the west toward the coast rather than coming off the beach with its stink of rot. Needless to say, there was no sign of a monster. An unusual number of houses visible from that window had their lights on. And it was only about three in the morning.

As I stepped back, I realised the lights in my own lounge-room had come on without me noticing. I turned them off and went back to bed.

January 17, 2018, Mid-morning

In daylight, it all seemed even less likely.

With an eye the size of the one I thought I'd seen, any lurking creature would have been a Godzilla-sized colossus, and surely I would have heard its footsteps as it moved off. By the same token it would have left footprints (if it had feet) or scrape-marks (if it was some kind of serpent or giant cephalopod). In fact, it had left not a trace. The experience must have been delusory.

Confirmation of this came as the morning struggled on through the almost overpowering foulness polluting the air. Tange told me she'd suffered from terrible dreams as well, nightmare visions of grotesque creatures, some of which seemed so real she had for a while been convinced she was awake the whole time. Demonic horrors, sometimes monstrosities tearing each other to pieces or skinning human-like beings and ripping off their limbs. She wasn't the only one. Many of the usual crowd I talked to when we made our way to the beach had had the same experience—an uncomfortable, terror-wracked night full of unspeakable terrors. Some of them could barely find the vocabulary to describe what they saw, and several broke down almost at once, overcome by the memory.

"It's that bloody thing," one old bloke declared, with astute conviction, gesturing toward the quarantined area the police had expanded overnight. The canvas walls had doubled and now stretched some 80 metres along the beach. Moreover, it was no longer possible to get anywhere near the actual sand. All the amenities—the Beach Hut Café, the Surf Life Savers Club, the public toilets, and the kids' play area—were closed down. Crime-scene tape fluttered about everywhere, guarded with grim vigour by assorted sick-looking policemen. I later discovered that even the nearby motels had been abandoned, no vacationers having remained after several weeks of the Great Stench (as some wag had christened it). Mollymook was dying.

I tried to find someone in authority to get an idea of exactly what was happening on the beach. No one would talk to me, except to warn me away in no uncertain terms. Clearly, whatever this was about, it was escalating out of control. I knew I had to find out what it all meant, at whatever cost.

That night the nightmares were worse than ever.

January 19, 2018

Two days passed with little apparent change in the situation, apart from further escalation in the foulness of the stench and in the unbearable terror provoked by our own minds at night. It was almost impossible to spend any time near the beach. Even wearing masks and drawing breath from oxygen tanks strapped to their backs, few of the police could stand it for long. It was becoming clear, at least to me, that the smell was as much in our minds as it was in the air. I theorised to Tange that there might be some sort of sub-matter carrier of the smell, a quantum-level disturbance in the atomic structure of normal reality that simply by-passed what we perceive as solid matter. I expected her to laugh at me, to accuse me of insane fantasising. But she didn't. She became unnaturally quiet and visibly worried. Saying nothing, she strode away in the direction of her home, as was her wont.

Toward the end of the second day, nearly all of the residents that normally gathered in the vicinity of the beach, if only for a short time, had left town, unable to withstand the poisonous stink any longer. I understood why and suspected that Tange would follow suit. I hadn't seen her for more than a day. Did she even have a car in order to make her getaway? I didn't know. I determined to go see her at home tomorrow morning and find out.

From where I stood, across the park from the beach, I could see the police had mostly abandoned their vigil. A couple of uniformed figures stumbled about on patrol, enough to keep the curious away, if anyone might display the insane gumption to approach the sealed-off area. A dusky light lay across the grass and the sand, catching on the canvas walls of the enclosure, now perhaps 100 metres long. And what was that amorphous mass just visible over the top of it? I didn't recall noticing anything like it before. It was barely discernible, but it piqued my interest.

A sudden urge to run across the beach took hold of me. I began to breathe more deeply, pulses racing. The large forensic police wagon parked prominently to my left in the otherwise empty parking area seemed deserted, abandoned. I looked up and down the promenade and the beach, to check where the patrolling police were at that moment. One was some distance off, on my left with his back to me, walking slowly northward. On the right, if there was a patrolman, he was hidden from me by a clump of barely alive trees. Long shadows from buildings and a clump of taller trees lay across the sand. Should I try for it?

Before I knew what I was doing I'd wrapped another handkerchief over my nose and mouth, and was across the road and grassy foreshore, ducking under the police tape that silently and ineffectually blocked my way. I leapt down onto the sand. From behind me someone shouted, but I was so intent on fighting back against the rapidly worsening nausea that I couldn't, or perhaps simply didn't, register what they were saying. As I neared the closest entrance slit in the canvas walls, the pressure of the stench and the grotesque flashes of demonic terror that had been filling my dreams overcame me. I tripped and fell. Desperately scrambling to re-gain my feet, I crawled closer. I could hear someone shouting from behind me: "Stay back! For god's sake, mate!" and almost felt the vibrations generated by their rapidly approaching footsteps.

I pulled the flap of the canvas entrance aside…and saw it, saw what had appeared on the beach. It was huge. Alien. Demonic. That single momentary glimpse was too much for me. A wave of overarching dread, of cosmic insignificance and helplessness swept me out of myself. For a moment, a long agonising moment, I was somewhere else, floating in a vast, poisonous void and feeling the life being drained from me. I tried to scream, but couldn't get my lungs to work. Helplessly, I spiralled toward a seething pit of indescribable monstrosities…

I woke, trembling violently, screaming in terror. Faces without bodies hovered around me. I swore, threatened to attack them.

"Mr Whateley! Mr Whateley! You're okay. Safe. Please be calm."

Mr Whateley? For a moment, I didn't recognise the name, but

regardless I reacted to the human voice. A woman's voice. The disembodied hands holding me steady loosened somewhat as I calmed, and I remembered that *Whateley* was the false name I had adopted when I came to Mollymook, in order to keep my real identity secret.

"Where am I?" I forced the words from the aching wasteland of my lungs.

"In the forensic van. You'll be fine. At least you didn't *touch* the biohazard and we got you out in time."

"What is that thing?" I asked.

The woman glanced up at the doctor and attending policeman, and waved them away. I realised then that she was the officer who had addressed the crowd a few days ago: Sergeant Katherine Sandros. Without her cap, her reddish-brown hair fell loosely around her ears. She looked exhausted. "That was very stupid of you, Mr. Whateley," she said. "You could have been killed. Nearly were. So far I have lost two men to that...that carcass. Several others are gravely ill."

"Two dead?" I repeated numbly.

"Yes. Federal experts have finally been assigned to look after the problem, as I've convinced them it represents a significant danger to the public. And it's not too soon." Her voice lowered and she spoke the following words introspectively, talking to herself rather than me. "... though I don't see what they can possibly do."

"But what is it?"

She studied me for a moment. "More to the point, who are you, Mr Whateley? A journalist?"

I told her I wasn't. Just fatally curious.

"And very foolish."

I nodded, but then thought it might be better to tell her at least part of the truth. "Actually I'm a cryptozoologist." I paused. "I study reports of unnatural creatures."

She sighed. "Oh, I see."

I shrugged. "I know what you're thinking. I'm just another crazy nutter, on the hunt for UFOs. Well, I can tell you this: I've never found any evidence of extraterrestials. But heteromorphic creatures such as the Loch Ness monster, yetis, snakes so over-grown they could eat an elephant in one mouthful…That sort of anomaly is another matter entirely."

She was not appeased by my confession. But at least it gave her something more concrete to hold on to.

"Well, you'll have to satisfy your crypto-curiosity elsewhere." She spoke in a stern tone, hardened further by an undercurrent of fear. "This carcass is virulently toxic. It appears to be some kind of sea-creature, natural perhaps but so decayed it is still only vaguely recognisable. We're thinking it's a giant squid, as it appears to have tentacles. But it *is* unusually toxic, and even wearing hazard suits gives no protection." Realising what she was doing—that is, actually talking to me—she reined herself in. "Stay right away from it. If I see you here again, even thinking of taking a run across the sand, I'll arrest you and lock you away for the duration. You'll just have to wait like the rest of us to find out what it becomes."

"Becomes? What do you mean by that?"

She frowned. "Go before I change my mind!"

So, I went back to my cottage, where I flicked through some of the reference books I'd brought with me, without further revelation, until night fell and, once again, the nightmares galloped screeching through my sleep.

January 20, 2018

I woke with a strong sense of impending doom, a feeling that whatever was going on here was finally reaching a climax.

A violent storm had broken out overnight and though my clock claimed it was 10:04 am., it looked more like midnight. I peered out the window, the one in which I'd imagined seeing a giant eye. The trees thrashed about as though a wave of sentience had overtaken them and, in the thrill of this evolutionary high-point, they were determined to pull themselves from the restraining soil and high-tail it away. The sky boiled with anaemic clouds moving in every direction, also desperate to escape this dying part of the world in which they'd suddenly found themselves. I could almost smell their panic. But what I could no longer smell was the diabolical stench that had plagued the area for weeks.

Something had changed then, for the worse, I feared. Filled with a sudden urgency, I dressed and headed out the front door. Fighting my way against the storm, the predominant force of which, despite the seething clouds, was coming from the direction of the beach, I inched my way along the empty streets. Despite the unnatural darkness, there were no lights on—not surprising in this weather. I came across no-one living, only the figure of a man sprawled half hidden in a bush. I rushed over to him, and checked for a pulse. He was lifeless, with a look on his face that spoke to me of horror and utter terror. I left him where he lay.

As I approached the park area of Mollymook beach, I could see the police incident van, overturned and partially crushed under a fallen tree. Were any of the police personnel still here? I couldn't see any. Fighting against the wind, I staggered in the direction of the beach, seawater swirling through the air like rain, battering on me with an unnatural fury. Momentarily blinded, I tripped on something—one of the policeman, as it happened— and staggered to regain my balance. I checked his pulse, but he too was dead. What had happened here?

The air was thick with sand and water, and the winds became fiercer and more erratic as I approached the sea. However, once I'd cleared the surf-club building, I could make out the epicentre of the violent winds: it was where the police enclosure walls had been erected and the monstrous, once-hidden carcass had lain. The latter was so much bigger now—a gigantic amorphous mass, with multiple tentacle-like appendages, and a hideous mass of corrugated flesh that looked to be its head. It did not move except as it was tossed about by the winds and was clearly not alive. But the very sight of it, and the psychic emanations that sprung from it, made me falter and collapse to my knees on the grass. I remained curled into myself, eyes closed and unable to move.

I felt something grab my arm. Startled, I glanced around, for a moment afraid the monstrous creature had reached out to drag me into its maw.

"Mr. Whateley! What are you doing here?" The words were broken and the voice struggling to be heard, but I recognised it at once. "Get out of here! Now!"

"You're still alive. And still on the job," I managed, stating the obvious.

"Not for long." She had to shout over the fury of the wind. "It's going to get worse, and I can't take much more. I've sent my people away, those still living." She dragged me up. "Pull yourself together. Go!" She leaned in. "You were right. This is some preternatural phenomenon. But there's nothing you or anyone can do."

I could barely think. I just did what she told me to do, staggering forward, pushed by the winds. Debris torn from the trees flew around me, as though urging me along. When I glanced back, Sergeant Sandros was out-of-sight, hopefully as safe as anyone in the vicinity, so I kept going, my mind a whirlpool of questions: should I leave? Isn't this what my great-grandfather wanted me to witness? Surely it's why he sent me here? Did he expect me to make a difference against whatever forces were behind this chaos?

I'd reached the main road when a car screeched to a stop beside me—an old, light-blue Volkswagen Beetle. It says much about my state-of-mind that I didn't even cringe at its unexpected presence.

"Get in!" cried a barely heard voice. I bent to peer through the passenger-side window, wiping away the water still splattering down on the area. Tangerine Harken was in the driver's seat. Why was she still here? She should have left long ago. I opened the door and scrambled in.

"What the hell, Tange?" I spluttered. "Haven't you noticed what's happening?"

"Of course I have. We need to talk." Before I could answer, she accelerated the car away from the beach.

"I don't know how," said Tange, "but I think I caused all this." We were ensconced in her lounge-room, an old-fashioned, rather fussy space, with odd statuary more reminiscent of Morgan le Fay than Queen Victoria. Despite the chaos outside the house, she made us a cup of tea, and I had been quietly sipping away, while waiting for her to get to the point. So far, she'd been evasive.

"What? That's ridiculous," I said. "How could you be behind this?"

She ignored my question and instead asked her own. "Tell me, Mr Douglas Ormsham, cryptozoologist, what do you think is happening here?"

I was gobsmacked. "How do you know—?" I began.

"Don't ask questions! Just answer mine!"

"What's happening? Well, the obvious answer is: some unknown creature, washed onto the beach, is creating a toxic plague as it decays."

"Really? Is that the best you can do?"

"Well, I mean…" I stopped trying to gainsay her and made an effort to work through the confusion in my head, which was replicating the chaos outside the house. I remembered what Sergeant Sandros had said. *You'll just have to wait like the rest of us to find…*

"…what it becomes." I completed the thought out loud, filled with a sudden insight. "That thing on the beach is growing *into* something. It's *becoming* something, something bigger. It's not decaying. This is the *opposite* of decaying. It began decayed and is getting less so. I guess that means—"

"It's about to reach its true form, a living form."

"Yes, possibly, but what's that got to do with you?"

She hesitated and I saw that the unreflective energy that usually drove her had become suffocated by a deep uncertainty. When she answered, there was reserve, a sense of self-doubt, something I'd never seen in her before. "Like you," she continued, not looking me in the eyes, "I have a deep interest in strange phenomena."

"How do you know about my interests?"

"From your website and that one by the other bloke…the author. Stop interrupting me! I suspect we're running out of time."

I gestured compliance and she began her heart-felt story of anguish and frustration, of deep and deepening research, of a burgeoning belief in the sanctity of life, all life, and disgust at the way humanity insisted on wantonly working against the planet and its long-term well-being. Scientists and their well-founded warnings were stupidly being ignored by self-interested corporations and corrupt governments. Species were dying rapidly. Everything was being bent out of alignment. In every way, the future seemed bleak, not just for the guilty party— humanity itself—but for all life on Earth. Her anger grew so fierce she began to delve into less orthodox systems of thought. And that's when she found "The Book".

"What book?" I asked, feeling some urgency. She'd already fetched it in anticipation of this *tête-à-tête*, and now held it out for me. I took it. It was called *The Benevolent Deities: A New Hope* by someone with a name I couldn't begin to pronounce without having my mouth and vocal chords replaced by something less human. Clearly a pseudonym, yet the name seemed familiar in its construction, especially as I'd been reading Lovecraft's stories over the past weeks and the names of his fictional "Old Ones" were constructed of very similar groupings of consonants. The text itself was hand-written, though bound as a printed book. Quite possibly—hopefully as it happens—it was a one-off. While I flicked through the pages, Tange gave me her take on its contents. It quickly became clear to me that the author of the would-be grimoire had been familiar with Lovecraft's fiction, and had worked to re-tool that author's Cthulhuan monstrosities into something much more benevolent, something he called the E'ashalsinir—infused with a strain of universal good-will never evident in the pages of the Necronomicon itself.

"Have you read H.P. Lovecraft's stories, Tange?" I asked, interrupting her monologue.

"No," she growled. "Who's that?"

"He's a writer. He wrote about…oh, never mind. Keep going!"

According to her story, she became so desperate she began to practice reciting one particular summoning spell, a spell designed to draw into our reality an ocean deity from its own universe or sub-space hide-away or whatever it is they live in, believing it would help right the wrongs being perpetrated by humanity.

"I wasn't really serious," she said. "It was just a letting-off of steam, as it were. At heart, I didn't believe in it. It's ridiculous. But look at what's happened! Look at that thing on the beach! It can't be a coincidence. And there's nothing good to be had from its involvement in our problems. What am I going to do, Mr Ormsham?"

"I doubt you could have caused this." I held up the book. "This book is just plagiarised clap-trap, driven by the ignorant notion that Lovecraft—who originally invented all this stuff—was more than just an imaginative popular writer."

Disgust squirmed over her features. "From what your great-grandfather told me, I thought you were more open-minded."

That startled me. How did she know of Hugo Drakenswode? Chance? Then I remembered; she'd looked up the website.

Tange seemed to read my thoughts. "The website. But not only that. Remember the letter you brought to me, when we met? Well, it was from Professor Hugo Drakenswode, who apparently died several decades ago, as I discovered when I Googled him. I thought it was a scam. I only read on because he remarked that the person who brought the letter to me was in fact his nephew, Douglas Ormsham. He claimed to have detected a potentially dangerous temporal anomaly focused somehow around me. Though the Professor had no idea what form it would take, he'd sent you to investigate. He wanted to stress to me that I should trust you. That's when I looked you up online."

"You didn't think to tell me this?"

"He suggested I should keep it to myself until it became obvious something was wrong. All things considered, I decided to wait and see. That's why I *know* I caused this—and I know that thing out there is one of the E'ashalsinir." She scowled at me. "How can this Drakenswode write to me so long after his death?"

I said I had no idea, but he'd done the same with me. "He was...*is*, a remarkable man."

"So can you help?"

"I don't know." For a few minutes, I listened to the winds outside, aware at that moment they were calming down and that the Demon Stench, the smell of decay, was little more than a background ambience. Once again, I had to ask myself: how could the creature go from non-existence and gradually work its way up to life, going through a process of backward decay? Such an idea is rendered impossible by the Second Law of Thermodynamics, which dictates that everything moves from an ordered state to a disordered state, thus restricting Time's Arrow (as they call it) to a relentless entropic movement forward.

But—

What if, I theorised, when Tange spoke the enchantment that summoned it, little expecting it would work, the entity that entered our universe was not attuned to its physics, dying on entry, but bringing with it its own time stream, one moving in the opposite direction to our own. Is it possible the summoning of the creature created an intermingling of the two worlds' temporal states, though the incoming state maintained its integrity like a drop of oil in water? The creature then rotted away, doing so (from our point-of-view) backward in time as it drifted toward nothingness? Perhaps this phenomenon changed the stability of our Time's Arrow, from that moment of entry back to when the creature disappeared completely—a sort of unresolved temporal bubble. At this point, from our perspective, Time within the anomaly began moving forward again.

What if, unaware of these temporal shifts, and instead interpreting the "decaying" process as the gradual arrival of the E'ashalsinir that she summoned, Tange tried to send it back to where it came from, using an incantation from the book?

"Is there such a spell?" I asked her.

"Yes, yes, there is." I could see the mingled terror and confusion in her eyes. "So, should I try it?"

"I think you've already tried it," I replied, "but all it did was create another loop. I suspect you've been doing this over and over again for quite a while, never being aware you'd already cast the return spell—thus creating the escalating temporal anomaly that Drakenswode detected."

She frowned. "Sounds ridiculous—and the idea's full of scientific absurdities."

"Says the person who tried summoning a Dark God using a book written by some madman with an absurd name. Good motive, poor judgement."

Outside, through the raging winds, the gloom was rent asunder by a violent flash of lightning, instantly accompanied by a thunderclap that made Tange's house shake.

"So what do we do about it?"

I didn't reply, but moved toward the window and pulled the blinds open. The sight of what was out there chilled me to the bone. It was several streets away, yet visible even over the intervening trees and houses: a raging mass of tentacles taller than the tallest trees, eyes like exploding nebulae, winds and incessant lightning bursts sweeping around it. The carcass was no carcass now. It was alive.

"Now's the time," I said.

"What time?"

"The moment when you actually made the very first incantation, the one that brought the creature into our universe. See?"

I gestured toward the window, but she wouldn't approach.

"I should read the words before it's too late and force it back."

"You should do *nothing*."

"But if I don't send it away —"

"If you do, it will all just repeat."

"Are you sure?"

Before I could answer, the night filled with a roar, whether of anger or pain it was hard to say. It shook the house. A number of large trees along the street tore apart and fell.

"*Do nothing*," I said, hoping it was the right thing to do. "Come! Watch! You'll see what I mean."

We stood side-by-side. I could feel her tremble, reacting to the awesome, and profoundly terrifying, sight of the monstrous creature highlighted against a tumultuous sky. A swirling burst of light followed, causing pain right through my head, from my eyes to the back of my skull. Tange squealed. She grabbed me and I grabbed her, huddling together like scared rabbits under the hunter's spotlights.

Suddenly everything went quiet. Looking out the window, we watched as a whirlpool of dark clouds retreated into a pristine light-blue sky.

"Has it gone back to its own world?" Tange said.

"What we were looking at was its initial arrival, Tange, seen in reverse. After that it died—in some agony, I believe—and over the previous few weeks rotted away."

"So are you saying it's all over?"

"From our normal point-of-view, yes."

She had a look of desperate sorrow on her face. "But all the people who died...can't I bring them back? How can I live with the guilt of what I've done?"

"Give it time," I said.

I left soon after, aware much of her memory of the event was fading, as is usually the case in the aftermath of such otherworldly occurrences—or so Hugo Drakenswode reports in his journals. As I left her house, Tangerine Harken handed me The Book. I'd been hoping she would. "Don't forget this," she said.

"Thank you. Hopefully, this is the only one in existence. I'll keep it safe."

She looked at me with a quizzical frown. "Keep what safe?"

That took me by surprise.

"The Book," I replied, holding it up. "You just gave it to me."

Again, she regarded me with earnest puzzlement. "The Book? I haven't seen it before. Didn't you bring it with you?"

I smiled. "Never mind. Of course, I did. I meant, thank you for your hospitality."

"It's been a pleasure, Mr Whateley," she replied. "I'm glad the weather has improved."

Sometimes the universe can be kind.

DEAD END TOWN

LEE MURRAY

Uncle Bradley grunts. His eyes open wide, his mouth going slack, his fat tongue lolling between purple lips. He lets out a gasp.

I breathe through my mouth to block out the smell, not daring to gag. Moments pass, his weight pinning me to the sofa, then he pushes away from me, his lips twisted in contempt. I glance down, past the Salvation Army skirt bunched around my waist, as he staggers backwards, a silvery cobweb still tethering me to him. It dribbles from between my legs, a hideous white tendril snaking across the dark orange sofa cushion where it seeps into the stitching. I close my eyes, so I don't have to see while he pulls up his trousers. His zip buzzes. Still I don't move. Instead, I trace my fingertip over the scar on my lip, a pink welt extending from the corner of my mouth to my cheek. Uncle Bradley's backhand. Each time it reopens, it takes longer to heal.

"You really need to be more careful on that bike of yours, Kayla," my form tutor Mrs Arnott had said.

Like she even gives a shit. I haven't used my bike since the summer.

In the kitchen, the fridge door opens and there's the sigh of a beer tab.

Now. Pulling my knickers up and my skirt down, I tiptoe to the front door, push my feet into my gumboots, grab my sweatshirt, and slip out.

I take the back way, cutting through Henderson's paddocks to the forest. Henderson's dog barks when I pass, but I tell him to shut the fuck up and he stops. From there, I climb over the fence and head west towards the creek. Apart from the dog, no one sees me. I'm the only one who comes here. There's no track so it's tricky to get to, the beech trees leaning on themselves the deeper I go, their trunks squeaking where they meet above my head, the scratchy mānuka making a grab for my clothes. I breathe deep. The air is tangy, a mix of lemon and moss. I push on through the scrub, the bushes criss-crossing the backs of my arms with tiny cuts and grazes, little white lines that disappear if you lick them, only I don't, because when I get to the creek, I take off everything but my t-shirt and submerge myself in the water. The creek is shallow, barely coming to my knees, but sitting down with my back to the bank, the water swirls around my legs, rinsing Uncle Bradley's white rot off me. In seconds, my limbs are numb and dimpled, the flesh tinged blue-green, like a decomposing orange.

I sit there for as long as I can bear.

As always, I slip down, letting the water submerge me, allowing it to close over my face, inquisitive tendrils seeking out my nose and mouth. It would be a relief to let it stifle me. I will myself to do it, but something always stops me. I got as far as my eyes once, but, in the end, I was too chicken.

My teeth are rattling, so I crawl out and get dressed. Then I hunker on the bank, my back to a pūriri tree and my arms wrapped around my knees. It's getting dark, but I don't want to leave yet. I stuff my hands into my pockets, pull out my hand-powered torch and squeeze it rhythmically. The torch is small, but it keeps the shadows from crowding in on me, its friendly whirring playing bass to the trickling high notes of the water. In the treetops, the forest murmurs. Mum's people say it's the *patu-paiarehe* talking, the mischievous fairy creatures who live in the mists. The stories say they like to snatch little girls. They're like the Pied Piper, playing their flutes to lure people away. If it is the *patu-paiarehe*, their words are soft and mournful, like poetry.

I used to write poetry. *Before.* I've stopped now.

"Why is your writing always so dark, Kayla?" Mrs Arnott had said. For a woman of letters, she's pretty dense.

"Didn't you say that poetry's about self-expression?" I replied.

"That doesn't mean you have to be so morbid," she said.

What was I supposed to say to that? But she was right in a way, because Uncle Bradley kept recurring in my poems and it was as if I was giving him that power. Although, maybe stopping was playing into his hands too: because I made myself even smaller. Some days, I think I'm crumbling into dust, like a statue left to weather and getting rounder and blunter at the edges. Soon enough, I'll be smoothed away to nothing.

I'm a minor, so I have to go home. I scramble to my feet and start back. The forest doesn't want me to leave either, grey-green mānuka fronds grabbing at my sweatshirt as I scramble through the brush.

I open the front door to yellow electric light and the stench of cigarette smoke. Back from her shift, Mum is lounging on the couch watching *Game of Thrones* with Uncle Bradley.

"Where've you been?" Mum asks, leaning to her left to stub out her cigarette in the ashtray.

"Out," I reply.

Over Mum's head, Uncle Bradley smirks.

"Out where?" she asks.

"Just walking."

"She's been fucking that neighbour boy again, I reckon," Uncle Bradley says. I glare at him. If stares were kitchen knives, his face would be pulp.

Mum turns to him. "You mean Aaron from up the road? Kirsty and Wallace's boy?" She gives him a playful shove. "He's harmless. Wouldn't even know where to put it." She giggles like the girls from school.

Inside the pockets of my sweatshirt, I clench my fists. "I'm off to bed," I say.

"I brought you some chips back from the shop."

"I'm not hungry," I snap, moving towards the hall.

"Hey!" Bradley says. "You get back here and say thank you to your mother." He stands up. "Kayla!"

I stop.

"Well?"

I stare at a thin bit in the carpet, where the trample of too many feet have worn it to muddy threads. "Thanks," I mumble.

He points the remote at the TV, pausing it. "And you can say it like you fucking mean it," he snarls.

Mum leans forward and puts a hand on Bradley's leg. "It's fine, babe. She said she wasn't hungry. The chips'll be cold now, anyway."

"That girl is spoiled rotten, Leanne. After everything you do for her, the least the disrespectful little madam can do is say thank you."

"C'mon, Bradley. She's a just a teenager."

"She's a disgrace."

"Well, let's not let her attitude ruin our evening, shall we?" Mum says, taking the remote from him and flicking her eyes towards the hall. My cue to bug off.

I don't have to be asked twice.

In my bedroom, I pull the lock across. I bought it from Hammer Hardware and put it in myself with a borrowed a hand-drill and a screwdriver from the Wood Tech room at school. When he saw it, Uncle Bradley just laughed.

Mum's whole life is a fantasy, like thinking Uncle Bradley is the real deal. As if their relationship is something special. I squeeze my eyes closed and pull the duvet over my head, trying to get warm.

The thing is, Mum really believes it. Maybe she thinks she's in love with him. Uncle Bradley's not like my other 'uncles'. For starters, he's got a job at the sawmill. Shift work. Pretty decent money, too. Every now and again he gives Mum some of his pay packet, which makes her go all gushy with gratitude.

"Why do you have to make such a big deal about it?" I said once. I mimicked her voice: "You're so kind to think of us. So generous."

Her eyes narrowed and she grabbed me by my upper arm, pulling me into the bathroom where he couldn't hear. "Well, he *is* generous. You try making ends meet on a benefit, missy. Rent, food, electricity. Your school fees. It all adds up. And he doesn't have to help. It's not like he's your dad or anything."

That made me think about phoning WINZ because he's not

supposed to stay here all the time or she could lose her sole parent benefit. In the end, I didn't. It's not like it would've made a difference. Without Mum's benefit, there'd be no groceries, and anyway, everyone knows WINZ are as useless as tits on a bull.

The TV is still blaring next door when I fall asleep.

In the morning, I take the school bus and sit near the back with Aaron.

"Bags the window," he says, pushing ahead of me.

Ours is a friendship of convenience. Every day, we get on and off the bus at the same stop; have done since I started school. When you wait in the rain and fog with someone day in and day out, you get to know things. For example, I know that Aaron is gay, and he knows about Uncle Bradley. Not the gory details, but the general gist. It's not as though Aaron can do anything about anything, but it'd been a relief to tell him, and have him believe me.

"Anyone ever tell you, you look like shit?" he says when I slip in beside him, twisting my backpack around until it's resting on my knees.

"Yeah, someone was sick, so Mum picked up an extra shift at the Fish & Chip shop."

The bus roars, slowly picking up speed. Aaron nods. "You okay?" he asks.

I stare down the aisle. "I'm here, aren't I?"

He clutches at the straps of my backpack, leans closer, and whispers in my ear, "We should go, Kayla. Leave here. We could take the bus to Auckland." His eyes are big and round and hopeful.

"And then what?" I say. "Get lost in the big smoke? It's all right for you. You're already sixteen. You forget I'm only thirteen. When you're thirteen, they glue your face on every milk bottle in every supermarket in the country."

He rolls his eyes. "And take out full page ads calling for information about your whereabouts."

"Someone will start a Kickstarter."

"They'll call in a psychic."

"My mum will cry on TV."

Aaron grins. "Your mum would love that."

I smile in spite of myself. "I know."

"Think about it though, Kayla. You only have to survive two years. Auckland's big. I can help hide you. When you're sixteen, they can't make you come back. He won't be able to do anything."

"Two years and two months," I say, savouring the feel of the words in my mouth.

"So? It's not impossible."

I think about leaving Mum and how much it would hurt her. Uncle Bradley was right when he said that everything she does, she does for me.

Everything except see what I need her to see.

I pleat the fabric of my skirt in my fingers and shake my head. "If they find me and haul me back, Uncle Bradley will kill me."

Now it's Aaron's turn to look out the window. His breath fogs the glass an instant then disappears into nothing. When the bus has bunny-hopped over the potholes outside the Skelton's place, he turns to face me again. "What about your father?" he demands.

"What about him?"

"Why can't you go and stay with him?" He looks at me hard. Honestly, if he doesn't stop picking that pimple at the corner of his mouth, it'll never heal up.

"I don't know."

"What do you mean, you don't know? Just ask him."

"I can't."

Aaron stares at me like I'm the Prime Minister trying to evade a tricky question.

"Look, I have a father—obviously—I just don't know who he is."

"Seriously? You don't know anything about him?"

"I know he was a poet and a dreamer. Mum says he wasn't like other boys. He wasn't normal. His family wasn't from around here."

I pause.

"What?"

"Don't laugh, but she used to tell me the reason he couldn't stay with us because he was a *patu-paiarehe*."

Aaron scoffs anyway. "A fairy? A legendary creature from the forest? That's crazy."

"I know, right?" It is kind of sad. It's not like I'm a little kid who believes in fairy stories, but I like to think my dad was legit, that he had a real reason for not being with Mum and me. Before I started school, I had this picture book of Cinderella and in it there's a drawing of her meeting the prince in the forest. It's silly, I know, but back then I convinced myself that the prince was like my dad, and he was hiding in the forest, just waiting for us to come and find him.

The bus pulls into the bay outside the intermediate school. The doors sigh open and we all pile out.

Aaron stands up, shouldering his backpack. "More likely, if your dad split, it's because he didn't want to pay child support."

"Yeah," I say, but my heart says something else.

When we get off the bus in the afternoon, Uncle Bradley is waiting at the side of the road. He's never done that before. The back of my throat tightens.

I jump down after Aaron and the doors hiss. The bus pulls out, spitting gravel.

"Hello, Mr Sterns. Kayla's coming to my place today," Aaron says. "We've got an assignment."

Uncle Bradley lifts his chin. "Like hell she is. And who the fuck are you trying to kid? You're not even in the same class."

The bus labours down the road. Watching it go, I realise we should've got back on.

Too late now.

Hitching my backpack up on my shoulder, I straighten my back. "I'm going to Aaron's," I say. "It's all arranged. Mrs Waugh invited me over for afternoon tea."

Uncle Bradley cocks an eyebrow. "So, it's tea and cookies now, is it? I don't think so." Quick as ever, he steps forward and shoves Aaron full in the chest, sending him backwards into the road. Aaron stumbles, then recovers, moving off the road and onto the verge again. But now Uncle Bradley's bulky body is wedged between us. Aaron drops his backpack on the gravel.

In my head, I will him to go home.

He stands his ground. This time, when Uncle Bradley shoves him, he springs back like a piece of fencing wire.

"I'll teach you for messing with my stepdaughter," Uncle Bradley roars.

"She's not your stepdaughter and I'm not the one messing around with her," Aaron spits.

*No! Don't let on you know. He can't know you know...*I stare around Uncle Bradley at Aaron, praying for him to understand.

Uncle Bradley draws a line in the gravel with his toe. "You're right. She's a slut: there're probably half a dozen like you taking a turn with her behind the bike sheds."

"Bullshit!" Aaron shrieks, and my stomach sinks.

"No!" I shout, but already he's running at Uncle Bradley, his head down like a wild boar on attack. Uncle Bradley dodges the charge with a neat sidestep. Twisting, he punches Aaron full in the stomach as he come around again. Aaron doubles over and Uncle Bradley lifts his knee, slamming it into his nose. Blood spurts all over Aaron's t-shirt.

"Stop it!" I croak, my voice echoing over the paddocks. The sheep nearest the fence skitter away. But Uncle Bradley rounds on Aaron, punching him in the guts a second time.

Aaron goes down hard. "Run, Kayla," he chokes, his arms wrapped around his middle. "Get away from here."

"You run, and I'll kill him," Uncle Bradley says quietly.

I freeze.

"He's bluffing," Aaron says, getting to one knee, blood in his teeth. "If he kills me, the police will come after him."

"Is that so?" Uncle Bradley scoffs as he kicks out Aaron's knee. The action is swift and cruel, pushing Aaron back into the gravel. Uncle Bradley stoops, jamming his face close to Aaron's. "I could kill you and walk away and no one would even bat an eyelid. Not when I tell them how you've been fucking my stepdaughter, and when I called you out for it, you came at me."

"Except it's all lies!"

Uncle Bradley shrugs. "Question of perspective, isn't it?"

"Nobody'll believe you," Aaron says, but his face has turned as pale as butter.

"Of course they'll believe me." Uncle Bradley kicks him in the ribs with the toe of his boot. "My cousin's the superintendent of the local police." Grinning, he stamps on Aaron's leg. Aaron whimpers. Like a hedgehog, he curls into a ball, his skinny arms crossed over his head. Uncle Bradley kicks him again and again. In his back. His stomach. His head.

After a while, Aaron goes quiet.

"Please," I beg.

Uncle Bradley gives him one more kick for good measure. Then, panting, he wipes his hands on his jeans. He turns on his heel, grabs me by the arm and drags me back towards the house. I glance over my shoulder to where Aaron is a motionless lump on the side of the road and pray Uncle Bradley hasn't fractured his skull.

Afterwards, when he's finished his business, I run back to the bus stop to look for Aaron, but he's gone, His backpack, too. I'm about to head up to his house, when Mum turns into the driveway. If only she'd come home twenty minutes ago.

Slowing the car, she slides down the window and calls to me. "Kayla? Where do you think you're going?"

I fold my arms across my chest. "Nowhere."

"Well, what are you doing out here on the road?"

"Just checking the mailbox," I improvise. "It was empty."

Mum gives me a suspicious look. "Come inside, then. I bought some lamb chops for dinner."

I look towards the Waugh's house, and then trudge after the car, my gumboots scuffing in the gravel.

Aaron doesn't come to school on Wednesday. Or on Thursday. When he doesn't come on Friday, I ride past our stop, get off at Cooper's corner, and walk back to Aaron's place.

His mother opens the door. "Kayla."

"Hello, Mrs Waugh. Is Aaron okay? He hasn't been at school."

"You'd better come in," she says, opening the door wide.

I take off my gumboots and follow her into the kitchen. It's only four o'clock, but the amber pendant above the dining table is already on. I take a seat. The Waugh's sheepdog pads over and I give him a scratch under his chin.

Aaron's mother goes to the kitchen bench, where she's been cutting up a pumpkin. She picks up a knife and uses it to slice off the grey skin. "What do you know about what happened on Wednesday?"

I shrug and ruffle the dog's ears.

"Someone beat Aaron up after school. He wouldn't say who. I had to take him to A&E."

I pretend to be surprised. "Is he okay?"

She slices the pumpkin and places the pieces in a pot. "Yes. But he took the bus to Auckland first thing on Thursday. He's done with this place. His father and I weren't happy, but he's sixteen, seventeen in a week, so there wasn't much we could do about it." She stares at me hard. I want to tell her what really happened, but if I do, something bad will accidentally happen to Mum. Something bad could happen to Aaron's mum, too. Uncle Bradley knows where she lives, and Mr Waugh spends a heap of time down the back of the farm.

So I say, "There are some kids at school—"

"Yes, I know," she interrupts. "Bullies. A dead-end town like this—forcing people to pack up and leave just because they step to a different drum." She puts down the knife and sighs deeply. "It doesn't do to be different, does it?"

I shake my head. "No." The dog nuzzles closer. I give him another pat. "So where is Aaron staying? Does he have an address?"

Mrs Waugh scrubs away a tear with the back of her hand. "He knows our number here at home. He'll call us if he needs anything."

She gives me a piece of ginger crunch and a glass of Fanta.

Before I leave, she says, "You take care now, Kayla. Any

trouble with those kids at school, you know you can always come to Mr Waugh and me."

I know she doesn't really mean it. It's what people say to be polite, like asking 'how are things going' and not really caring about the answer. I smile and nod. "If Aaron calls, please tell him I said hi."

She rests a hand on my shoulder a moment. "Of course."

Aaron's dog follows me into the yard and down the driveway to the cattle grate.

"Go home!" I tell him.

His tail down, he heads back towards the house.

Mum will be another hour, so I cut across the Waugh's paddocks, then cross Henderson's to get to the edge of the forest. Henderson's dog is barking its head off at something in the bushes. His ears are cocked and the fur on the back of his neck is standing up. He doesn't even see me when I climb the fence. I step into the gloom. Today, I don't need the creek, so I wade to the other side and head further into the trees.

It's windy. High up where the branches touch, the bark squeaks. Through the rustle of the leaves and the gurgle of the creek, I hear a flute or a clarinet playing somewhere up ahead. It's faint, but there, the melody wistful and eerie, like an Adele song, the kind that makes your heart ache. For a second, I think it might be Aaron. Maybe he hasn't gone to Auckland yet. Maybe he stuck around to say goodbye.

Or to take me with him.

My heart racing, I speed up, plunging deeper into the beech trees, pushing aside the branches, grazing my hands on the bark. It's hard work, the wet ground sucking all the time at my gumboots. The mist rolls around me, cold on my muddy legs.

"Hello? Aaron?"

Three people step out of the trees. My heart stops in its tracks. I can hardly believe it. *Patu-paiarehe.* Tall and willowy, they have fair hair and brilliant diamond eyes. There are three of them, all dressed in skins.

"Kayla," they say, and I jump to hear their voices in my head.

I hug my arms to my body, my boots sinking in the soft mud. "You know my name?"

Their answer drifts towards me on gusts of wind. "We've been waiting for you."

The drawing of the prince from that old picture book flashes into my head and I can hardly breathe. They've been waiting for *me*? I'm almost too scared to ask. "Is my dad here?"

"Yes, yes, we know where," they whisper in my head. "We can take you."

"Take me where?"

"This way. Come."

I follow them further into the forest, clambering over rotting logs and ducking under fronds. Up ahead, the *patu-paiarehe* let the branches swing back and hit me.

"Hey!"

They giggle and smile. Well, they're known for being pranksters. I want to reach out and touch them, only they dart forward on their long legs, keeping just out of reach.

I hurry to catch them up. In the dim light, everything is shadowy and grey and my gumboots slip in the mud. Arms out, I tumble into a ditch. My hands break my fall, pain flaring in the webbing. I bite back a cry. A sharp twig speared me when I tripped. I lift my palm to my mouth and suck away the blood.

It's while I'm standing there, dealing with the cut, that I notice the barking. Somewhere in the distance, Henderson's dog is going ape shit. All at once, I realise how late it is. Behind me, the forest is so dark, the tree trunks are a blur. How did I even get this far?

"It's getting too dark: I'm going to need my torch," I tell the *patu-paiarehe*. But when I take it out of my pocket, they melt into the trees.

"Hey, come back," I call.

The forest groans about me, the shadows thick and dank.

"I don't know where to go," I say.

The *patu-paiarehe* don't answer.

The days go by. A week. I hear nothing from Aaron. No letter. No phone call. Not a whisper.

"You only have to survive two years," he'd said that last Wednesday morning on the bus. He'd made it sound so easy. Now, with no one to talk to, those two years stretch out in front of me like a dead-end road.

I'm in the kitchen doing the dinner dishes when Mrs Arnott calls my mother and tells her I'm getting behind on my schoolwork.

"What's this all about?" Mum asks when she gets off the phone.

"It'll be because that boyfriend of hers shot through," Uncle Bradley calls from the living room where he's watching the telly. I imagine his smug look and wish I could stuff the kitchen brush down his throat.

"Is that it?" Mum asks. "Is this about Aaron?"

"I guess so," I say and it's not entirely a lie. Since Aaron left, I've lost a lot of weight—I've had to put a safety pin in the waistband of my skirt—and lately I've been forgetting things. It's as if my brain's been getting blunter, worn down like a pencil.

The school makes me see a counsellor. With scraggly hair and big rimmed glasses, she looks like Professor Trelawney and asks me the usual things about what I want to do when I leave school, and if my falling grades have anything to do with the kids at school. I tell her no.

"And what about things at home?" she asks.

"They're okay."

"Just okay?" Through the glasses, her cheeks are an odd shape.

I shrug. "It's alright."

"It's just you and your mum at home, right?"

"Hmm." I don't mention Uncle Bradley. I can't, I can't mention him or something bad will happen to Mum.

Only, the counsellor must catch me pause because she says, "You know, anything you tell me is confidential, don't you? That means it's just between you and me."

"You can't tell anyone?"

"That's right."

"Like a priest?"

"Exactly."

I suck in a breath. Maybe I *could* tell her. Not because she can do anything, but just to be able to tell someone the way I told Aaron. Someone who's not going to pick a fight with Uncle Bradley and get herself beaten up and left on the side of the road. The knowledge makes me feel strangely light, like an old candy wrapper carried along by the wind. I'm opening my mouth to tell her, when she goes on, "That's how this works: unless you're at immediate risk, nothing you say here will get past me."

My shoulders slump. Unless you're at immediate risk. *Which means her lips will be flappier than a sheet on a washing line.*

The school makes me go see her a few more times, but each time I clamp my mouth shut, and after a while they give up.

Another day, I'm heading for the creek, when I find Henderson's dog lying up beside the fence. Rolled over on its back like its expecting someone to rub its stomach, the dog's ribs stick out under its ragged fur. Its head is lolled to one side, its tongue sagging from its mouth, covered in mucus. Looks like it ate some possum bait. Mr Henderson must've left it here to bury, away from the livestock. The flies haven't wasted any time getting into the carcass; thick white filaments lick out from behind the dog's eyes. I've seen maggots that got into a lamb once. Aaron and I found the wretched little thing in a ditch. It'd been dead a while because the maggots had eaten the entire body from the inside out. Its skin undulated in waves it was so full of the fat white worms. It was disgusting. Hopefully, Mr Henderson will come back and bury the dog soon. Poor thing. He barked a lot, but he was a good dog.

Backing away from the carcass, I swing my leg over the fence.

Mum's in the bath for one of her long soaks when Uncle Bradley gets me up against the kitchen sink, his hand pressed against my mouth. I'd let my guard down. Mum was home so I thought I was safe. He hisses in my ear to keep quiet while he fumbles behind me.

The water goes off, but Uncle Bradley doesn't stop. Mum's soaks can take a while.

I see the butter knife lying on the bench. Slowly, I move my hand, closing my fingers around it.

Suddenly, Mum comes out of the bathroom, her bathrobe wrapped around her, heading for the linen cupboard. "Silly, I forgot to get a towel." She stops, spying us through the kitchen. "What the hell?"

Hidden from her by the bench, Uncle Bradley flips up his track pants, flicks down my skirt and steps to one side. "I had to pin the little bitch down. She tried to attack me with a knife."

I shudder. The butter knife is still clutched in my fist.

"Kayla? What's going on?"

I stand up, my eyes pricking.

"I told you," Uncle Bradley roars. "You wouldn't listen. The kid has abandonment issues. Her daddy's not here and she's got it in her head that it's my fault."

"Shut up," Mum says, pushing past him to get to me.

"Mum," I say, warm tears welling. Gently, she takes the knife from me and drops it in the sink. A hand on each of my upper arms, she fixes me in the eye. "Look Kayla, honey, I know things are bad for you right now. I get that. Aaron leaving has brought up some things about your dad, but you have to understand, it has nothing, *nothing* to do with Bradley."

"I just want him to go," I whisper.

Uncle Bradley snorts. "What did I tell you? That kid is all kinds of crazy. Ever since I got here, she's had it in for me."

"Bradley, would you mind giving me a minute with my daughter?"

"Sure. No problem. See if you can talk some sense into her." He grabs his cigarettes and goes outside, but not without giving me a look.

"Sweetheart," Mum says, wrapping her arms around me. "This has to stop. You can't go around lashing out at the world or people really are going to think you're mad."

I try to tell her that wasn't like that, but she has to learn it for herself. It's like in *Beauty and the Beast*, where Belle has to choose to love the beast if she's going to rescue everyone from the witch's curse. If I tell her the truth about Uncle Bradley, it won't count.

"Mum please, just make him go," I gibber.

But she doesn't hear me, and after while I can't hear her either.

The next day, I don't go home. Instead, I get off the bus and go straight to the forest. Mr Henderson must have come and buried the dog because there's no sign of it by the fence. I tuck my school backpack into a hollow where no one will see it, stamp my feet into the gaps in the wire and climb the fence. I suck in a breath, inhaling the ripe smell of soil and leaves. The lush of the trees beckons me in.

I have to go a long way into the brush to find the *patu-paiarehe*. I hear their music at the creek, but it's an hour before I see them.

They hang back, lurking in the trees, laughing.

"I've come to see my father," I tell them.

"Yes, yes, we can take you to the place." They urge me forward, flitting in and out between the tree trunks. I follow them further into the forest.

After another hour, I glance backwards. The forest is dense black. It closes about me. This time, I've got no light to hold back the shadows. I'm wearing my school polo and the torch is in my sweatshirt. Maybe I should turn back. Go home. But which way do I go? If I'm going to get back to the creek, the *patu-paiarehe* will have to guide me.

They are the faintest silhouettes now. I feel my way forward, sensing them in the soft squelch of mud and the brush of the branches.

"Hey, slow down."

Out of reach, the mischievous fairies giggle like I've made a joke.

We keep going.

Finally, the trees part. Before us, moonlight glints off a limestone cliff. A dead end. Looks like we'll have to go back. But the *patu-paiarehe* point upwards and smile. I look up. Above us is an earthy overhang, the roots of a massive tree tangled and coiled in its underbelly. Something's moving up there.

I squint as spindly white vines spool from a slit between the roots, creeping outwards and waving to me the breeze.

My father came here?

The vines sway and undulate like the maggots in the lamb: disgusting but fascinating at the same time. Mesmerised, I watch the glutinous tendrils slide from the recess and curl towards me. Halfway, they strike out, a million barbed threads, grabbing me and pulling me upwards.

No! This isn't right. Why did they bring me here? This isn't where we're supposed to be.

The *patu-paiarehe* reply, "Yes, yes, we're here, we're here!"

But all I see is the fleshy curtain opening. A beak! And slithering from its yawning depths, a slick white tongue. I thrash and kick: the cords only tighten around me, the barbs digging deeper, lifting me up to meet that beak.

"Help me!" I wail.

The *patu-paiarehe* shrink back into the trees.

Grey slime drops from the beak. It seeps into my clothes, burning them away, searing my skin. I scream. A stinging acid gob falls into my right eye. With one sightless eye, I'm paralysed, helpless. I can only stare in horror as the beak drops further and further, its tongue roiling outwards to meet me, and all the while I'm rising, the vines holding me so tight I can barely tremble.

More foul mucus gushes from the beak, the oily slime smothering my face, and ruining my eye. It's a relief not to see it close over my face. My nose is left free. I breathe in bubbles of vile mucus and scream and scream into its insides, the sound going nowhere.

"We're here," the *patu-paiarehe* croon.

Yes, we're here, and it's feeding on me, its white coils reaching into my body, their barbed tips sinking through my skin to slurp up my insides.

The pain is searing white and endlessly slow. I can do nothing but endure it. I lay suspended and delirious while its ropey branches snake through my limbs, lifting my fingernails and burrowing into my bones.

For the first time in forever, I wish I'd gone home.

SLITHER

JASON NAHRUNG

The farmhouse sat, sagging on its stumps, its flaking weather-boards sun-bleached to the colour of bone. Rust seeped through the corrugated iron roof like bloodstains. The steps of the hand-hewn planks of the front veranda creaked under his boots.

He went through the homestead, room by room, but everything was as he remembered, pretty much. Someone had washed dishes and left them in the drainer. There was a stain on the living room floor near the telephone table. A heart attack, they said. His old man, stretched out there, still in jeans and button-up shirt and socks, his RMs by the front door, one hand reaching for the phone. Fighting 'til the end. Found, however many days later, by a neighbour, come to talk about a stray bullock.

He imagined tendrils, grasping the straining organ, squeezing. Reaching in through ears and nose and mouth, forcing their way down the throat, drilling through the chest cavity like hungry leeches.

Shaking, he retrieved a bottle of rum from the 'medicine cabinet' and poured himself a shot. Then he put the kettle on, seeking comfort in ritual.

He was still on the veranda when the neighbour pulled up in his battered ute, Red bouncing on a tether in the tray.

You sure you want him, the neighbour asked after the stilted condolences had been done with.

You bet.

Didn't think you'd have room for him in the city.

No words for that, just a hand on that boxy head, another

under the grey muzzle, feeling the vibration of the wagging tail, the wet licks on his fingers.

We're in no rush, you take your time, the neighbour said, rotating his battered Akubra in his gnarled fingers.

He wanted to ask, did you see anything…anything out of the ordinary? But all he said was: A couple days should do it.

Keep an eye on that storm, though. Gonna be a beaut. You wouldn't wanna get flooded in.

No, will do, thanks.

Good of them to give him a few days to say goodbye. Hard to believe it was finally over. He wondered what his mother would say about the SOLD sign on the gate. He wondered about those final days, those final moments, in the hospital, her lungs clogged with cancer. Had it been like drowning, like being pulled under? Or had the drugs eased her down, some kind of bath of unconsciousness from which she'd never climbed out?

And his old man here, clawing at the floorboards as he tried to call for help. Who would he have dialled? Not even the neighbour could've got here fast enough. Close enough to pick up the pieces, though.

He took Red out the back to his kennel and gave him tucker and fresh water, then went inside to get started. The sooner he was out of here, the better.

Tinder dry. Funny how words lose their meaning; though, to be fair, in his experience, the dryness rang true. Just another dating app waiting for the spark. A dry argument, indeed.

The grass crackled beneath his boots. The ground was cracked under the threadbare covering. Looked like it could tear open at any minute, an earthquake-style maw ready to swallow. He tried to avoid stepping on the worst of them, like cracks in the footpath; no point risking further bad luck. The creek was dry, too, reduced to a string of stagnant pools. It was a wonder the neighbour had taken the farm, even for the over-the-barrel price. But there were clouds on the horizon, a thick grey line of promise. The irony was not lost, laying his dad to rest in the face of the broken drought. It was the drought that had killed him, some said. Trying to fight all of nature by himself, they said. That rustle of whispers at the funeral, the old farmers and the next generation, not soft enough that he wouldn't hear. How's the city treating you, they wanted to know. Seeing right through the lies, that country BS detector turned up to full.

He hefted the rifle, the now unaccustomed weight dragging at his arms and shoulders, and pushed on.

Red jogged subdued by his side, nosing through the stubble. It was too hot for even the crows to give a flying fark, but something was watching. He could feel it, like the stares of the mourners over CWA teacups and pikelets. Penetrating through the drawling chat of weather and stock prices and government, banal fears for the future and wistful dreams of the rains of yesteryear. The gaze weighed on him now like the heat. Expectation, he thought. Anticipation.

It knows when you're alone, his old man had told him.

Bullshit.

His old man had been full of it, stories of wild dogs and ghosts and monsters, followed by that shit-eating grin when he saw he'd hit the mark. But not this time. When his dad had spoken about the slither, his breath rum-scented, eyes red from farewelling Mum, there had been no smile. Just urgency, a slurp on the glass, and that line repeated, more resigned: it knows when you're alone.

Something plopped in the creek. A lizard most likely, or maybe a turtle. The platypuses were long gone. He scrambled up the hill and sweat stuck his shirt to his back, his jeans to his thighs. His calves ached, his lungs burned, his face flushed boiling under the broad brim of his hat. Red's tongue lolled, the dog puffing beside him, head slung low.

Almost there, he told the mutt through gusting breath, his throat as dry as dust.

Finally, they slumped, him and the dog, in the cool shade of the old fig tree. The green dome spread above them, the ground underneath dotted with granite boulders like some kind of pagan cemetery. Up here on the ridge, the tree had survived his family's machetes and poison, fire and drought. It had seen their arrival and their departure. He found a flattish rock to sit on and drank, and poured water in his hat for the dog. He ate the lunch he'd brought and gave the leftovers to Red, who wolfed them down keenly enough.

From up here on the ridge, he could see all of his family's holding. Dry, yes, but beautiful all the same. Pulled out of his hands now with all the burn of a broken rope. The pain stung, no doubt about that. But he had to admit; his grip had always been tenuous. He was a farmer's son, but not much of a farmer. He traced the creek's sinuous path from up here in the hills, down across the flats, into a loose coil around the house. Brown paddocks as far as he could see, from mountain to the distant storm clouds roiling higher and wider. A hint of breeze gusted in his face, chilling the sweat, making him shiver.

Red lay, snout on paws, rheumy eyes fixed on him from under raised brows.

Let's do it, but the dog didn't move as he extricated the box from his backpack and pried open the lid with his pocket knife.

The ash came out in a cloud; much of it falling at his feet, but some the breeze took and wafted down the hillside. All the while he'd walked up, he'd been going over things to say, some fitting eulogy for the moment. But the dust came out and the words didn't, and he simply stood with powder on his boots and tears in his eyes and an empty box in his hands.

Red barked.

He looked around. Nothing. The wind getting stronger pushed along in front of the storm, a hint of wet earth on it. Leaves whispered, a hushed choir in a foreign tongue more conspiratorial than comforting.

He picked up the rifle, looked at Red. On his haunches now, tongue out, looking at him. A whine, a bark of curiosity, the dog staring over its shoulder and then back at him.

He couldn't take the dog to the city, back to his tiny apartment. Couldn't stand to leave the old fella here with the neighbour, either, and all those fucking young heelers of his. Drive the old fella mental, they would. Couldn't bear the thought of giving up his dog. His dad's dog really, the farm dog. He'd thought they could stay here together, his dad and the dog, but looking down the barrel at those brown eyes, thinking of walking home alone, the smell and sound of the shot, the sight of the dog stretched out and still...later. There'd be time for that later.

C'mon, Red, let's go home.

What a fucking lie. He had no home. They had no home.

Unseen eyes followed him all the way down the slope to the creek. From the scrub on the other side came the racket of cicadas, hacksawing into his ears. Red growled at every plop of puddle, at every crackle of falling branch; the grass whispered in the rising wind. And now a kookaburra mocked him, and it was too much. He and the hound all but ran that final stretch from the creek up the hill to the house, the storm wind biting at their heels.

The door slammed. He blinked himself awake, aware of his sweat-soaked shirt sticking to his arms. He gasped, his throat dry, his lips stretched thin. He sat up and ran his hands through his wet hair, pushing the fringe back from his clammy forehead.

Thump! He winced as the door slammed again. Grey light permeated the room, leaking in from the office doorway and the balcony beyond. A gust of wind chilled his legs, though he still wore jeans and socks. Something fluttered in the office. A bird? A snake? Or something else altogether, slithering across the floor?

Swearing, he stood, and tripped over an empty beer bottle that went spinning under the bed. The smell of spilled booze wafted up. Maybe that was why he had had the nightmare, that and the heat. Vague memories of a man on a horse, a bolt of shadow, the nag shying and the man falling clumsily, the crunch of head on rock, blood soaking into dry earth.

He grabbed the rifle from where it leaned against the wall and, peering into the murk of the office, worked the bolt. With the rifle at hip level, he hobbled to the door, looking for the source of the rustling. There. He sighed, uncocked the rifle and slid the safety catch forward, let the barrel tilt towards the ground. Papers scuttled across the floor as another gust rushed through, freezing the sweat on his body. Cursing, he limped through the office and pulled the swinging door shut with a firm whack. He leaned back against it, catching his breath as he scanned the shadows. Furniture, empty shelves, cartons, and the patchwork of loose papers still sliding listlessly in the breeze that sneaked through the cracks in the timbers. His hackles rose at the sound. Just papers, he told himself, blown from the desk because he hadn't sorted them out yet, hadn't shut the door. Christ, he hadn't shut the door. Dread washed through him like an ice-cold shower. He could see the foot of the bed from here. He'd been lying there, dreaming, with the door wide open. He trembled and looked through the window onto the veranda and beyond. He could barely make out the pointed hulk of the mountain in the storm shadow. There was an empty bottle near his boots at the base of the rocking chair, where he'd slumped when he'd got home that afternoon. So he'd had more than one drink. That didn't excuse his failure to make sure the door was locked. No, that was just stupid. He was lucky that nightmares were all that had visited him.

He checked the sky, where storm clouds had obscured the setting sun. He'd been asleep for maybe an hour. A whole hour.

A screech cut through the falling night, metallic and shrill, like a rusty blade being sharpened. Wide-eyed, he searched the direction it had come from, then sighed relief. The Hill's hoist turned again, giving another shriek of protest. A threadbare towel, pale in the gloom, flickered on the line like some tattered flag of surrender. He had to go, should've left already.

With the rifle propped in the crook of his arm, he stepped onto the veranda and snatched up his boots. Thunder grumbled like a starving gut and he stared out against the storm-wet wind and the certainty that eyes were upon him, watching from the darkest shadows.

His father had told him of the creature many years ago when, as a boy, he had trawled the paddocks without fear, imagining himself a soldier, an explorer, a hunter. At the time he had thought the legend merely a tale told to frighten him from the deeper holes in the creek and the more dangerous areas of the hills, where fallen boulders made hidden pits and the spiny vines of lantana bushes made the going treacherous.

His dad told him once that the slither had been left behind when the country's original people had moved on. Just why and how they'd moved on wasn't told; it had happened a long time ago, back when the homestead was just two timber rooms in a land without fences, when the hill paddocks had been choked with scrub and the flats had been covered in eucalyptus trees and wattle. Another time, he said it was a feral creature, brought by those early settlers, warped by its long, lonely life in the darkest hidey-holes of the bush.

As the house had grown, so the bush had shrunk, cleared and fenced to allow the cattle to flourish and the family to prosper. But that was all over now.

And the slither knew. And it would come. He knew it would. Just like it had come, his father said, for his great-grandfather, and his aunt.

Not that anyone had admitted that, of course, but over these past few days he had dreamed of them both. Of his great-grandfather and his great sorrow for deeds done of which no one talked; how easy it had been to lie on the ground and let the blood flow into the earth as the dark tentacles held him down, the body found only after the horse returned alone. And of his aunt lured fully clothed into the dam one hot night with her hands on her tummy, and the slither had wrapped her in dark bonds and pulled her under, and she had died cursing a man.

At the bottom of the hill he could still make out the dark line of the creek becoming ever darker as the sky's blackness deepened. The she-oaks whispered, their pine-like needles already bending and swaying with the approaching storm. Like a ghostly crowd, hushed in expectation of the coming spectacle. If any were taking odds, they would be against him, he knew.

The clouds spread like a stampede, curving out and around the mountain, then finally rolling over the top and sweeping down across the paddocks. The house groaned as the wind intensified. A piece of tin rattled and he wondered if he was losing the roof, if one of the sheds was coming apart. He imagined sheets of corrugated iron flying like scythes. He imagined the house unroofed, and him with nowhere to hide, staring up at the black sky and something darker still, reaching down through the hole where the ceiling had been.

He could smell the storm now, electric and icy damp.

A few large spots of rain spanged on the roof. Teeth chattering, he stepped back into the office and locked the door. The extension had been his mother's idea, tacked onto his bedroom when they'd lengthened the back veranda. She had died in a distant cancer ward and, somehow, they just never got around to painting the office. Times had got tough. He'd been in the city, working his first job. His father had fought the first of a string of droughts and then the floods that inevitably broke the drought before the cycle began again. Now the job was for someone else to complete, to take that vision and remould it as they saw fit. He shivered again. The thought of someone else in here, putting books on the shelves, maybe smoking or fucking…

A branch scraped against the guttering, the sound running an invisible claw down his spine.

He retreated to his bedroom to pull on his boots. Mementos of childhood surrounded him: model aeroplanes, posters, a cupboard which, on every visit, he would open just to stare at the toys and games inside, then shut the doors as though those memories could be so easily locked away.

It wasn't too late to leave, not if he hurried. There was nothing here he needed to keep, no one to leave it to. He eyed the hallway warily as he made his way to the kitchen, dodging his father's old recliner in the lounge room, that sheepskin rug he'd thrown over the dark mark on the floor.

The small, round kitchen table was littered with sympathy cards spilled from a carton, the white cards stark amidst the family photos and unwashed coffee cups, the empty stubbies of beer and dirty plates, the printout of the settlement of sale weighed down by a box of bullets.

He sat, rifle thunking on the table as he pushed it through the mess, and ran his hands through his hair. The branch banged again, an intermittent thump-scratch that seemed to reverberate through the whole building. The lights flickered and he felt his heart miss.

Then the rain hit, a massive downpour that roared on the iron roof. He could hardly hear the branch, could barely hear his own thoughts. The house moaned on its stumps; soot rattled in the chimney.

Outside the window the world turned suddenly bright. Thunder shook the house. A picture fell from its hook in the hall.

He stood, slowly, then grabbed the rifle and walked past the telly's blank face to the hall. It was lined with family photographs. They were among the last things he had to pack, just hadn't been able to bring himself to remove them. The black-and-white faces of his ancestors looked out from their shaded bush hats and a sole military uniform, reminding him of where he had come from, of the sacrifices made so he could live elsewhere with fluoride in the water, a shit-load of channels on the television and meals just a phone call away. And there, a gap, a brighter rectangle of paint, and on the floor below, a portrait lay on its face amid shards of glass. The hammering of the rain seemed louder.

He knelt, kept the rifle cradled under one arm as he reached for the portrait.

Ouch. He sucked the nick on his finger, and then more carefully turned the picture. It was of the three of them, staring out. God, he was so young. They all were. It was before his mother had got sick, before the drought and the markets had driven his father to the wall, before he had left for the city where the fates, if not less capricious, at least seemed more manageable...and more fun.

If he had stayed...he sucked his finger as he stared back at eyes now sightless, his own hardly recognisable with youth and naïve enthusiasm. If he had stayed...

The dog howled and he swore. How had he forgotten? But he knew how. He'd been gone too long, the time between visits stretching out further and further. Red hated storms; he should have brought him in before dark, when they'd returned from their long walk to the fig tree. Before he'd opened a beer and lay down on his old bed one last time.

Red whined again and he forced himself to stand, unable to resist the howl that somehow penetrated the drumming of the rain and the rush of the wind, the groaning of the house and the driving pulse of his own hammering heart.

The dog was chained up at his kennel. Outside, in the dark, with *it*.

Don't let it get you, his father had said. I seen it, after your mother died. It knows when we're alone. It knows when we can't fight back.

When they had found his father, he had looked scared, they'd said.

The dog was still howling, getting louder and louder, like a siren approaching.

Shut up! Shut up!

Might as well have yelled at the storm. More lightning crackled outside. Shadows leapt across the window, making him grasp the gun tight against his hip, the barrel pointing at the doors and windows.

And still the dog barked and howled.

Shut up, Red, you mongrel!

Thunder rolled through the house, pushing him back against the wall. Something snapped outside, followed by a metallic crunch and crack of glass. The rain swept across in waves. And now, in the troughs, when the thumping on the roof eased, he couldn't hear the dog.

Sweating, shaking, he advanced towards the door that led to the stairs. He swallowed, his throat and mouth dry, and coughed with the effort. Then he hit the lock and stepped back as he flung the door open, almost dropping the rifle in his frantic haste. Something white lay on the floor and dark splashes covered the landing.

No, he stammered, then sighed. Clothes. The wind had got into a load of laundry he'd left out, some of his father's clothes, and scattered it. He licked his lips as spittle returned to his mouth.

Red, he yelled. Where are you, boy? Can you hear me, Red?

No reply, just the rain and wind and groaning timbers.

The veranda was soaked. And then he saw the source of that

loud crack. The old jacaranda tree in the yard had fallen, the storm pushing it over by the roots. Incredible strength, but then, the ground had been so dry after so many years without decent rain. The downpour had probably soaked straight in and the weakened tree had toppled. That's what must have happened. Surely. The tree had fallen across the fence onto his car. For a moment his spirits sank at the thought of being unable to leave, but then he remembered the four-wheel-drive in the shed. Of course, the shed was down the paddock, towards the dam—the dam where they'd found his aunt, with her seaweed hair and staring eyes. The open paddock was now shining silver with pooled water, splashing and rippling with rain. Maybe in the morning…

Christ, he muttered. He'd be stuck here. Flood-bound.

Red!

He peered through the gloom. The house lights reached hardly into the yard at all and the trees swayed and groaned as though they might follow the jacaranda. Shadows twisted and flitted, and damp swept across his face and made the gun barrel shine like it was sweating. He stepped forward, feeling for all the world like he was six and back in his room, tiptoeing away from the bed, expecting that brush against his ankle with every step, until he could get to the light switch and vanquish the monsters of his own imagination. If only…

The steps were slick and he stepped on them hesitantly, desperately aware of the gaps, wishing he could turn and look into the dark space behind but also terribly afraid of what might stare back at him.

The slither is black, his father had told him, black and slimy, able to find its way in anywhere, with tentacles so rubbery you can't even cut them with an axe. And it knows when you're alone…

Down to the base of the stairs and his back was aching with the effort of holding himself straight. His hands were knotted on the rifle, fingers stiff and cold. He would have to walk out into the rain, into the dark. Had to get to the kennel, cut from the hollow trunk of a massive gum tree they'd used to make feed troughs. One of the old ones, so big it would take three men to circle it with their arms.

The clothesline screeched, slicing across his nerves. He stepped out, instantly soaked, instantly cold, and aware of his shadow at his feet vanishing at its waist in the darkness. He shivered and shivered, muttering to himself to stop his jaw from chattering.

Red, you bastard, where are you?

The muddy ground sucked at his boots. He squelched forward, peering through the rain that pasted his hair to his face and numbed his body.

He reached the fence, forcing his eyes to look up at the roof, into the yard, into the paddock…What if he turned and it was there, a dark, writhing mass blocking the stairs. What if it had snuck up behind him, was already on the landing? Or under the stairs, in the shadows, poised to grab his ankles as he climbed?

Oh God.

The dog was gone. The chain glimmered in the mud, the broken leather collar still attached. Were those patches of hair on the ground?

Red! But he knew it was useless. The dog was gone and he was alone. He turned and ran, falling to one knee as he tried to get back to the house, expecting all the time for the ground at his feet to erupt with slick, sticky tentacles. He sobbed as he clambered to his feet and ran up the stairs. He slammed the door shut.

Red, you bastard, he whispered through his tears.

A lightning bolt sizzled. Thunder cracked. The lights went out. He screamed.

He fumbled to the table, knocking boxes and papers flying as he scrabbled for the torch. Finally his stiff fingers hit the button. He flashed the beam around the house. Oh Christ, he couldn't use the torch and the rifle together. He needed both hands, to hold the weapon and work the bolt. And the torch…it wouldn't last all night. He had to make it to morning. They had to put the power back on. They had to. The slither loved the dark. Oh fuck.

The house seemed hot, so hot, the air as thick and heavy as a sauna. He could hardly draw breath, his chest was so tight, as

86

though the slither already has its tentacles around his throat and was squeezing, squeezing...

He retreated to the corner, so the table was between him and the rooms. The wind buffeted the wall like a beast, moaning and shrieking, making the timbers shudder against his back. How thick was the wood? Thick enough? And the floor? The house was on stumps. As a child he had played under there, making dust storms to suffocate his Matchbox towns until his mother had yelled at him to stop because dust was seeping up through the floorboards. Could the slither also seep between cracks that small?

What would happen when it came? Would they find him like his father, face a rictus of fear, a hand reaching for non-existent aid? Or like Red, just the signs of a struggle to show his passing, no one the wiser? Or maybe the locals would know and say nothing, for who would believe them? Oh Jesus, what had they done to deserve this? Why had it come?

Lightning crashed again, and the room filled with brilliant light. A shadow, outside on the veranda, peering in through the window? Or just the curtain, gusting in the wind?

The glass of the portraits in the hallway shone in the lightning, and then reflected his torch back at him as the light outside faded. Four generations on the wall, staring out from the darkness.

If only he'd stayed...

The front veranda creaked as though under a great weight. Something scratched at the door. The timber shuddered in its frame.

What would it do to him? Drag him out into the wet, down to its dripping, dark nest in some cave along the creek? Or, like a croc, drown him and tuck him away under some roots to wait for the water to soften him up? Or just tear him apart, limb-by-limb, and devour him hot and fresh right here? Christ, he was in the kitchen! How wrong was that?

Bang! The door flew open, smacked the wall so hard the pictures rattled. He dropped the torch, screamed, and fired.

The beam flashed around the room as the torch rolled off the table onto the floor. The rifle muzzle sparked red. Windows shattered. Wood chips flew from the wall. Again and again, fumbling with the bolt, sobbing, he fired until the gun clicked empty. His ears ached from the gunshots. Had there been a yelp amid the barrage?

He crept to the door. A dark shape lay on the veranda. For one insane moment, he thought he'd got it. Had put a red-hot round right through the fucker's oily head. But the lightning strobed and he saw the familiar muzzle, the glint of those dull eyes.

He backpedalled, slammed into the table, grasped for the box of ammo. It flew, spilling bullets like dice. His clawing hand seized one, just one.

Sobbing, he sank to the floor and stared out from between the legs of the table and chairs, the floor covered in papers jerking in the wind.

There was no escape. He could drive as far as he could, fly to a different land, but the slither would never leave him alone. Its shadow would follow him, its long, dark tentacles always groping to drag him back here. To the creek and the mountain and this house, and those eyes on the wall and the bed of his childhood. He fitted the bullet into the breach, tasted warm metal and gunpowder. The long, dark tunnel opened before him, and night fell with a bang like a slamming door.

THE PIT

BILL CONGREVE

Three Months Ago

Ken Greenfield dodged another shingleback crossing the highway. It was still early morning, he had left the pub in Penong before sunrise and the desert road was still damp from the predawn rain. Somewhere ahead was the turn onto Hart Ridge Corp's private road, and then he had another hundred and fifty kilometres of dirt through the Nullarbor Nature Reserve, across the Trans-Australian Railway, and through Hart Ridge's desert mining lease into the site. His appointment was at 11am, but, given the 400-kilometre drive, he thought they might be sympathetic if he was a few minutes late.

All for a site inspection so the Minister could give a press conference. The SA Country Fire Service hazmat crew didn't want anything to do with the place and, if anything at all happened out here, it would be a hazmat. Fire didn't cut it — there was nothing to burn and Hart Ridge had its own firefighters for the site itself. It was the Federal Minister herself who had forced the hazmat response role onto National Fire & Rescue, over the blustering of Hart Ridge's CEO.

A thud under the tyres of the rented 4WD dragged his attention back to the road. Now there was a dead shingleback amongst the live ones. Bugger. There were literally dozens of the lizards on the highway, one every fifty metres or so, but he still didn't want to kill one if he could avoid it.

Idiot things. Worse than sheep. And too slow on their feet to duck and weave. There had only been a little rain, just enough to wet the road. In the desert, that was enough to bring the lizards onto the road to drink from the ruts left in the blacktop by the endless road trains.

Then Ken noticed dead lizards among the live ones. Suddenly the majority of lizards were dead, smeared against the road, and not just in a single lane, but dotted across both sides of the road.

Some bastard ahead of him was swerving from side to side, killing the lizards.

Ken sped up, wanting to catch sight of the scumbag, but then he saw the sign for his turnoff.

'World's biggest and deepest open cut mine!' the sign screamed, as if it were a tourist attraction. Then, 'Entry prohibited.' Typical. Hart Ridge Corp were notoriously hungry for publicity, but hid themselves behind a few slogans and the blustering reputation of their CEO.

It wasn't a dirt road, either, but two lanes of blacktop with wide verges —in better condition than the highway that led past it across the desert; but the dead lizards continued, just the same, through the nature reserve and all the way until the artificial range of Hart mine tailings began.

Suddenly Ken didn't like Hart Ridge Corp at all.

An hour and a half later he was being ushered into the office of the site's security chief. "NFR's science advisor here to see you, sir."

Now the wrangling would start. Were these jokers going to let him do his job? Was he going to be escorted around the site by the security chief, not a foreman or mining engineer? So much for being allowed to do a site inspection and a risk assessment for any emergency services that might have to respond. It wasn't the first time Ken had been on the receiving end of such an attitude. Yet Hart Ridge Corp would be the first to complain if shit happened and they needed help. He would much rather be at home in Canberra, Ken decided, but then he chuckled, curious. From everything he had heard, this particular hole in the ground was huge.

"So tell me, Mr Greenfield," the security chief glared at him, "just who the fuck are NFR, and what makes you think you can walk in here and tell us our job?"

Ken answered the question with another question. "Why does the Minister want this now? That hole in the ground has been there for sixty years. Think of it as rhetorical. I like these things in the open," said Ken.

The glare was his only response.

"Now, down to business. You reckon with that hole outside you'll reach China? Or do you get to go through Hell first?"

No reaction to that either. This was going to be a long day.

Ten weeks ago

Ken had been in the boardroom twice before. Once after the Mount Isa job when NFR had helped Queensland Fire & Rescue pull thirty miners out of a collapsed mineshaft, and once to deliver a briefing about the impact of climate change on the frequency and severity of severe weather events and the added costs of insurance and building new houses to the required standards.

The walls were covered in dark green velvet wallpaper; the ceiling was light green with subtle lighting. It had all the necessary screens, projectors and workstations for a corporate boardroom, and even an old fashioned whiteboard for those who liked to stand and lecture, but it was the huge, solid jarrah boardroom table that Ken liked the best. It was the old-fashioned, dependable honesty of the wood that Ken liked; back home, entire pubs were built of wood like this, maybe not as hard as this jarrah, but just as dark and dependable. Even at a time ruled by corporate frugality, some things remained unchanged, and this table had been unchanged for fifty years. Take the high-tech corporate communications machinery away, and the room reminded him of the country pubs back in South Yorkshire. Just add beer-drenched carpet, the aroma of centuries of ingrained cigarette smoke, real ale and roast meat, and he would feel right at home.

He looked around the table. Some folk he recognised, others he didn't know at all. Not all wore NFR uniform. Then Deputy Commissioner Livings walked in and the meeting began. The Hart Ridge Corp mine was the first item on the agenda.

"Ken, I've got your report here. Thanks for going to so much trouble," said Livings. "Can you brief us on the main points? What are your feelings about the place?"

Ken leaned forwards on the table and looked down at his notes for a moment. He looked up. "The main points are size, isolation, and ego."

"Please explain that."

"You've heard that the thing is big. I've got some photos here, but they don't do it justice."

Ken flicked through the photos projected from his laptop to the screen at the head of the room. "This truck," he said, pointing to a speck on a track on the far side of the pit wall, "is twenty metres long, six metres wide and six high. Google Maps probably gives the best idea of the scale of the place."

Ken shifted to the satellite imagery and zoomed in. "Note the poor resolution within the Hart Ridge property. Out here in the Nullarbor Reserve, we can distinguish individual salt bush plants, but here —near the edge of the pit —the vegetation is just a blur, with a resolution of about ten metres."

"He's done a deal with Google, like the military of some countries." The speaker was a nondescript man of average height sitting with the Minister's department head. He hadn't been introduced.

"Possibly. That's partly what I meant by ego. You remember the old song, *Blue Sky Mine*? This is a bit like that. Hart Ridge Corp's idea seems to be that if they dig deep enough and wide enough they'll find something worth extracting. They might not know up front what that something is, but there *will* be something. They started digging for gold sixty-two years ago. It was Jon Hart's grandfather, Erasmus, back then. Now, the pit is twenty kilometres wide, and two and a half deep. The temperature at the bottom is close to twenty degrees Celsius higher than it is on the surface. All the machinery in the pit is climate controlled.

Right now, late autumn, it isn't too bad, a bit warm at the bottom, but that's all. But in summer, nobody can work outside in the pit. They pump out groundwater, treat it until it's crystal clear, pipe it fifty kilometres away and pump it back into an aquifer. The pipeline is underground—"

"Did they tell you about the pipeline?" asked the unnamed man.

"No. I saw the treatment plant and asked. They gave me the run around, so I researched it when I got back. It was built some decades ago, I don't know exactly when, probably the late seventies. I couldn't find any government approvals or environmental impact statements."

"1977, and there aren't any," the man said.

Ken continued. "Everything about this place is like that. Huge. Secretive. Getting information is like pulling teeth. They've dug out coal. The original gold is long gone, but they found more later. They've got big silver, lead and zinc deposits that they're currently working on two kilometres down along one of the pit walls. They've pulled out copper. The alluvial gravel they've pulled out covers half the dirt roads in South Australia. Parts of the place are radioactive; I had a dosimeter in my pocket when I went in, but most of what they pull out is dirt and rock, and that goes here." Ken indicated the range of mine tailings.

The unnamed man spoke again, "You mentioned ego. Do you think ego really explains this?"

Ken thought for a moment. "Perhaps it doesn't. Perhaps the pit is just a giant toy, and they're playing, like toddlers building sand castles at a beach."

"Grown men—" Livings began.

"And women. Remember, Hart's aunt ran Hart Ridge Corp for a decade." It was the Minister's department head who interrupted, one of the few who could interrupt the deputy commissioner.

"Of course. Playing like toddlers at a beach? With tens of billions of the shareholders' money?" asked Livings.

"But there are no shareholders," said Ken. "There isn't that level of accountability. This mine is the property of Jon Hart's family, they're funding it from their other mining enterprises, and we don't know his purpose. That's why it's so difficult to assess the risk the mine presents to the public."

"Could his purpose be something darker, more malevolent, do you think?" the unnamed man asked.

"Malevolent? Well, they're destroying the environment, but then they seem to be building a new environment. Who knows, his purpose could be anything."

The unnamed man was obviously fishing for something, but Ken didn't know what. The Minister's department head paid close attention to every word.

Two nights before

The railway line from Port Augusta to Perth passed forty kilometres south of the mine. The Indian Pacific passenger train, travelling from Sydney to Perth, reached the point of closest approach in the early hours of the morning.

At 2.31am, the driver saw a cloud of mist obscuring the tracks. That was rare on the Nullarbor, but it happened sometimes. She slowed the train and radioed ahead to Cook and back to Ooldea. The track was clear in both directions. The driver slowly accelerated the train into the mist. Instantly the stench of rotten eggs permeated the cabin. The driver remembered her high-school chemistry —hydrogen sulphide. She turned on the PA immediately. "Sorry to wake you up, everybody! I need you all to close your windows if they're open, and turn off your air-conditioning. Roll up towels and put them under the doors. Crew, go to your chemical spill kits and put on your charcoal P2 masks." She made up the advice, but it was common-sense. She braked and prepared to reverse, but by the time the train had stopped, the mist was clearing ahead. She accelerated, and the train nosed out of the bank of gas.

Ten minutes later, in clear air well away from the bank of gas, she stopped the train in a siding. A number of passengers and crew were ill, but alive. The crew conducted a roll call.

Six passengers were missing.

A day later, the right leg of one of the missing passengers—identified by the boot it still wore —was found ten kilometres north of the train tracks. Another part was found twelve kilometres from the tracks. Of the remaining missing passengers, there was no trace.

Satellite imagery showed the gas plume had come from the Hart Ridge Corp open cut mine, sucked up by a north-westerly gale blowing across the pit.

Now

The helicopter approached along the length of the artificial range from the south, with the wind behind it. The range of mine tailings was three hundred and five metres taller than the surrounding plain, tall enough to be called a mountain by all accepted definitions of the word —even in jurisdictions that measured these things in feet. It was nearly fifty kilometres in length, and was one-and-a-half wide. For most of its length, it ran due north-south. Where it reached the railway line in the south, it turned due east. Hart Ridge Corp had even built their own railway along the crest to bring the fresh tailings out to the end.

Someone had gone to a lot of effort to build this.

"Look at it. More money than sense," said Inspector Sophie Harding.

"What do you expect? That's Hart Ridge. Built by the Hart Ridge Corporation," said Ken. The range would be here long after its builders were dead. Not as long as the ancient features of the flat desert landscape it nestled on, but still long enough to be able to pretend. "They're doing it because they can."

Harding changed the subject. "When we get there, are you going in?"

"I always go in, Sarah. It's the reason I'm in the job."

"You're too important. I'm not sure we should risk it."

"Then I'll have to find another job."

Harding snorted, and turned again to stare out the window.

The final three members of the crew, Jack, Ahmed and Tina, sat behind them. Tina stared out the window, amazed but not impressed, Jack played with a Rubik's cube, Ahmed read a *Wisden's Almanac.*

As they got closer, the pilot lifted the helicopter up above the ridge. Ahead, the ridge turned west, at right angles, and then curved gently for another twenty kilometres. Nestled in the curve was the pit the tailings had come from. The helicopter slowed and dipped.

Ken spoke to the pilot. "Land near those logistics sheds there, at the head of the access road."

The pilot just grunted, and Ken realised that's just what he was doing. "Sorry. Bad habit."

The helicopter came to a soft landing beside two police 4WDs. The NFR crew jumped out of the helicopter, ducked under the spinning blades, and crossed over to the waiting SA Police Incident Management Team. Instead of joining them, Ken walked to the edge. The far side of the pit was visible in the haze, twenty kilometres away, just like the last time Ken had been here, except now the bottom of the pit was invisible, hidden below a roiling sea of fog.

Before, the floor of the pit had been visible two and a half kilometres below, the giant mining dump trucks crawling like ants on the tracks corkscrewing along the sides of the pit. There were two tracks for the trucks going down empty, another two for the full trucks coming back out. Then, the haze in the air had been dust from the massive rotary cutters searching through the rock to find the next vein of ore. Now, it was gas.

He heard boots crunching on the gravel and turned. "Didn't expect to find you here."

"Hello Ken." It was the nameless man from when he had given his briefing. The suit had gone, to be replaced by tan work clothes, boots, and a sun hat which completely covered his pale brown hair. Ken congratulated himself on remembering what colour it was; the guy was almost as invisible, almost as nondescript, now, standing under the desert sun, as he had been in the NFR corporate boardroom.

The man held his hand out. "Ray."

Harding wouldn't be happy.

Ken shook his hand. "Ray, what do you know about this place?"

Ray turned and looked out over the pit.

"Not enough. Not nearly enough."

"**W**hat detectors are we taking in?" Jack asked.

"Four-head—"

"Fucking thing'll never shut up!"

"So, acknowledge the alarm." Sometimes Ken thought he was talking to children. The truth was, these technicians would make sound decisions on their own. They only wanted him to confirm their thinking—or perhaps they only wanted to give him something to do so he could feel useful.

He took another look over the edge. Well, his superiors wanted him here, no question, and the Minister wanted his report, again for whatever that would be worth.

Ma'am, it's a big hole in the ground, he could imagine saying. He chuckled.

"Share it."

"Just thinking what I'm going to write in my report."

"You could start with it being a fucking big hole in the ground," Jack smirked.

"You read my mind."

Maybe they could achieve something, even if they only recovered bodies. Somewhere down there were two police officers and six miners, and nobody had yet found the missing tourists from the train.

"We know there's sulphur so bring the flame spectrophotometer. I'll bring the photo-ionisation detector so we can cross-reference and maybe identify something."

"Here's the plan," said Harding. She was the senior NFR officer at the incident. The senior cop, an inspector from Ceduna, had already given up trying to patronise her. "Just get going, or I'll send in another team."

"And SafeWork SA will put you in jail. It might be your incident, but it's my Hot Zone."

"That's a bloody big hole you've got in your Hot Zone."

"You've got nothing that can deal with it, buddy."

Ken chuckled at that memory as well.

"Share it."

"Can it!" said Harding. "Okay. Jack, you and Ray are one team. Tina, you and the dude are the other. Ahmed, you're with me. Jack and Tina, you're in charge down there, do you understand that?"

"Pardon?"

"I'm getting to that," said Harding. "Ken, this goes for you too, so listen up. Ray, think of it like the Navy. You might have the authority, but Jack and Tina are the helmsmen. You can tell them where you want them to go, but they'll tell you how you're going to get there, and even if you can get there at all. Understand? You're in two teams of two. Jack leads one, Tina leads the other. Stick together. Jack leads the crew. Ray, they will help you in every way they can, but they are in charge, and if you don't agree to that, I'll ask the good Inspector here from Ceduna to restrain you."

"I have no problem." Ray's voice was mild, as if he was truly unconcerned.

"Who are you, anyway? What training have you got?" Jack asked.

Ken knew that Ray and Sarah must have already spoken and worked things out as well as they could. Ray had obviously not given Sarah a choice about what he wanted to happen but had just as obviously not gotten his own way on everything. Harding had imposed limits.

"Military. I've had breathing apparatus and hazmat training with the Navy. I've shown your boss..." he indicated Harding, "... my credentials."

"Next question, what are we going to call you?"

"Ray."

"You don't get it. Ken here is the Science Dude. Who are you?"

"He's the Invisible Man," said Ken.

"Nuh. He's The Suit," said Tina, facing him. "I can just imagine you wearing one in downtown Sydney, blending in with all the other suits walking up and down the footpath, going nowhere but around corners, totally invisible."

Ken laughed and, for the first time, Ray looked disconcerted.

"But Tina, I am going somewhere."

"Not that we can tell." And the name stuck.

"**H**ere's the plan," said Harding. "We drive down the exit road until we start detecting the gas, or as best we can guess it. Ahmed and I will back up a couple of hundred metres and set up in clean air. Ahmed will do BA Control. He and I will suit up and be ready to come in as a backup. I want lower explosive limit readings every couple of minutes, understand? If we have to come and get you, we need to know if it's safe to drive in that shit, and we won't drive into it if there's an LEL reading. Take long duration tanks. You go down for one third of your air, and then turn around. You'll use more air coming up that hill than going down.

"Remember, this is a reconnaissance, a size-up. It might become a body recovery mission. We observe what we can, try to find the missing police crew and the miners who tried to get out.

"Communications. There's obviously no GRN out here. We'll use VHF channel 50. Hart Ridge has their own network. We will not use that. We'll make no attempt to monitor that. Understood?

"Now, take a moment. Look at the size of that hole. We're not going to finish this today."

And that was how the plan worked. They drove down the side of the pit in two Hart Ridge Corp vehicles, escorted by the police. The detectors identified the main contaminant as hydrogen sulphide, with sulphur dioxide and some organics mixed in.

"Have these idiots hit a volcano, or something?" Tina muttered.

They drove down until they reached the safe work limit for

hydrogen sulphide of ten parts per million. It wasn't rocket science. Ken simply held the four-head detector out the window and waited for it to alarm.

Then they suited up with twin air cylinders, did buddy checks of their teammate's equipment, and prepared to walk. They were halfway down the pit, the haze thin above them, a roiling cloud below, and the far side invisible.

"Like lemmings to the…dunno. Where's the cliff? Where's the ocean?" Jack said.

"Idiot." Tina punched him on the arm. This was the first time they'd worked together. Always the brotherhood, even if a few of them were sisters. Ken felt a little left out, even though he'd been with NFR for seven years.

"It's not a cliff, but you can jump off it if you like," Ken pointed to the edge of the road.

"I wonder if that's quicker?" said Jack.

"Any miners trying to get out would most likely have used the exit road, automatically. That's why the police drove down this way looking for them. If we go over the edge, the next road down will be the access road, not the exit. Besides, take a close look at that scree. Do you really want to slide down it in an FE suit? You'll be exposed in seconds."

"You're no fun, Science Dude."

They donned their facemasks, sealed their suits and began walking.

The mist thickened about them, until they could see only a couple of dozen metres in any direction. There was a vague yellowing tint to the greyness in the air, and they all had to constantly wipe a fine dust from their visors. The exit road disappeared into the mist behind them. The road had a very slight curve, like the curve of the horizon over the ocean when you looked at it from the height of a cliff. Above, the light was better, but the blue of the sky had disappeared.

Ken and Tina walked beside Jack. Ray followed close behind and to one side of Jack, as though he didn't want to talk. The rough-edged mine tailings, graded flat and rolled into the semblance of a road, scrunched dry and hard under their boots. There were well-defined wheel ruts several metres apart where the mining trucks had compacted the surface. The only colours were grey and brown, the walls of the pit blending into the dull white of the sky above.

"How'd it get so dark so quick?" said Jack, looking up, his voice distorted by his facemask and internal amplifier.

Ken used his ring finger and pressed the radio push-to-talk button in the glove of his suit. "What's LEL?"

"3.2%," said Tina, who carried the four-head detector.

Ken pressed the PTT button again. "Edging up. Something is flammable down here."

"But hydrogen sulphide is flammable," noted Ray.

"The Suit's got you, Ken," said Jack.

"No he hasn't," said Ken, turning towards Ray so that he could see him through his visor. "The explosive limit is way, way above the concentrations we're getting. There's something else."

"Might be methane from that coal seam we walked through."

"Methane's lighter than air. It would rise and dissipate, and there was no sign of it at the rim."

"They hit the coal seam decades ago," said Tina. "The methane should be long gone."

"Hydrocarbon though. There's cubic kilometres of it down here. Can't be anything else."

The conversation wasn't as spontaneous as it would have been without the portable radios. Only one person could speak at a time, and they had to finish before the radios allowed the next person to transmit, but this was still the kind of banter Ken loved. They sounded like a bunch of geeks walking into a volcano, daring the worst.

He checked the detectors he held. "Sulphur is edging up now, too. Also showing on the flame spectrophotometer."

"You sure somebody didn't just fart?"

Ken could imagine Harding trying to explain that one to the police. The spectrophotometer simply showed the presence of sulphur but not the actual chemical compound that contained the sulphur. Sulphur was in most nerve gases, but it was also in garlic and chili. The spectrophotometer couldn't tell if the Russians or the CIA were trying to gas you, or you were simply downwind of the toilet block in a Mexican restaurant.

"Bugger. LEL has hit 5%."

"Got it." Sarah's voice crackled in their ears.

"And, like you said, hydrogen sulphide is flammable."

"So are farts. Into the valley of gas strode the brave six hundred, er, four…"

The darkness came so gradually that they didn't notice until it was nearly complete, and they were walking in a still gloom their eyes could barely penetrate.

Ken sweated under the PVC chemical suit. It was like a loose fitting, heavy duty raincoat, but one which started above his helmet with a large hood and visor assembly. It was closed by a zip which started near his neck and ran down one side under the armpit and then across to his groin and down the inside of one leg to his knee. The gloves were built in, moulded to the suit, as were the boots. Even the zip was gas tight.

The soup they were walking through couldn't get in, but similarly there was no way for the heat his body was generating to get out, except for the tiny, one-way, exhalation valve where his waste air exited. He even wore his helmet and breathing apparatus under the suit.

The ground levelled out under their feet.

"Hey, we're at the bottom."

"Don't believe it."

Hardy joined the radio chatter. "You're probably on one of the staging pads. There'll be another eight of them ahead of you on the way down."

Shit, they weren't even scratching the surface of the pit. That's when it really hit Ken, the size of the place, the pointlessness of it all.

"We need a submarine to get to the bottom of this."

Jack took over, now businesslike. "My air is almost down a

third, check your gauges, people," he said. "Ray, do your stuff, this might be a point that people were trying to reach on the way out, or the way in. If they drove with the windows up and no air circulation, there's a chance the police crew got this far on the way in. Tina, SD, we explore this pad. Dude, take as many readings as you can get. Tina will help. And be careful everybody, somewhere here there's an edge, and we don't know where it is. Tina, leave your strobe light here at the start of the rise. We don't want to get turned around in this soup. Five minutes, and we go back up."

Ken started taking readings and making notes. He watched the torches flashing in the darkness as Jack and Tina quartered the staging area. The outside temperature was thirty-two degrees Celsius.

Then he slipped and fell to one knee. "Bugger!" He pressed the PTT button again. "Careful people, it's slippery."

Harding joined the discussion. "What's slippery?"

"The surface down here. Maybe they tried to settle the dust or something."

"That would have been yesterday. Shouldn't be anything in this heat. Wait…" A moment later, "The mine management says no."

Ken rubbed his boot against the ground. It didn't feel wet so much as slimy, like mud on a rock at the beach. "Maybe it's groundwater. We're a long way in."

The darkness, the goop in the air, the featureless, muddy, rocky surface reminded him of nighttime scuba diving. He half expected to smell the ocean.

"Got them. Oh shit!" It was Tina.

Ken looked around, saw a torch flashing, and trudged towards it.

The police car had parts of four bodies in it. One body sat behind the steering wheel, a police revolver in its hand. Two starred holes showed where bullets had punched out through the windscreen. Ken couldn't tell the gender of the corpse. Bones showed through its sunken flesh; its left arm was missing.

A thin layer of dust covered everything.

"Does hydrogen sulphide have narcotic properties?" Tina asked calmly.

Jack turned away and stepped a pace from the car. "Harding, we have the police car. We have four, repeat, four bodies, one of them in a police— "

Jack jerked, spun around, and slipped. "Shit, I thought I saw something. Bugger! Suit, what the fuck you up to? We stick together!"

Ken saw The Suit's torch flashing in the distance.

"There's more here," said Ray. "There's a body stuck in the door of a dump truck. Looks like he was trying to climb out... fuck! Something moved in the cabin."

Ken looked more closely into the police car. Both missing police sat in the front seat, their flesh so rotted that they were barely recognisable as male and female. Two other bodies sat in the rear, huddled together as though hugging. Ken couldn't tear his eyes away from the ruined flesh. It didn't look rotted, as if dissolved away by chemicals. It looked like it had been sucked, or eaten, off the bones.

Tina pushed him aside, reached under the dash and grabbed a Taser. She pulled a revolver from the ruined hands of one of the dead cops and pushed it at Ken.

"Something's moving out here!" Ken couldn't tell who that was. Thankfully they released their PTT button and freed the channel.

"Get out! Get out!" That was Harding. Ken heard an argument in the background. Harding wanted to drive into the pit. The police inspector from Ceduna—the Incident Controller—wouldn't let her. Then the channel was free.

Shit, they were on their own. Harding and Ahmed couldn't drive in, not with the potentially explosive atmosphere, and it would take them almost a half hour to walk in, and then what could they do? The police were just as helpless. They didn't have the equipment.

Ken looked at the revolver. He could hold it, but couldn't even get a gloved finger through the trigger guard.

Tina shoved him away from the police car, pushed her visor

up against his, and shouted, no radio, her voice distorted. "Use your pinky. Shove a pen in and use that. Anything!"

"Help. Red. Red. Red."

"Who was that? Roll call!" shouted Harding.

"Ken here."

"Tina here. Jack?" shouted Tina.

"Ray here. Jack was checking the body on the dump truck. Something dragged him through the window." The Suit's voice was cold, unemotional, unsurprised.

Tina pushed Ray back against a giant tyre, his FE suit hood thudding back against the rubber. "You know what's happening here, don't you?" She shouted, her visor against his, not bothering with the radio.

Ray didn't answer.

Jack's radio remained silent.

"Okay people, we're getting out. Re-form at the strobe," Tina, this time using her radio.

They ran, slipping and sliding on the surface, until the flashing green light was in front of them.

Tina grabbed Ken's hand and pulled. "Keep together. Let's go!"

She pulled ahead.

"Wait!" said the Suit.

"We're going, now!" Tina turned and punched him on the shoulder, shouting, again, no radio. "I don't give a fuck who you are, you're mine until we get out of here. Now move!"

Ken felt it then, too. He pressed the PTT button; Harding had to hear this. "Tina, stop! You left the strobe when we hit the flat coming down. Feel the slope under your toes." Now, the strobe pointed the way down into the pit.

"Something moved the light!" said Ray, also over the radio. The Suit was brandishing a machine pistol, which Ken didn't think he had found in the police car. "Plan B, straight up the slope, up the scree, until we're out of this goop. It's better for our air, too!"

"Fuck!" Tina jerked her foot from side to side. It was held by a wide, flat tentacle which slowly lifted from the slimy surface. It was wide and flat. It didn't have suckers, it had feelers. Ken could see them palpitating, flowing in the gas and dust like a millipede's legs. Muscles flexed under the surface as it settled against the thick PVC of Tina's suit.

Ray saw the tentacle too and ran, scrambling, up the slope.

Ken grabbed Tina, pulled her hard. It was like a tug of war with a football team, and the only person going to lose was Tina.

Another tentacle quested forwards, waving from side to side in the air. Ken shoved his little finger through the trigger guard of the revolver, held it with both hands, aimed and fired. The tentacle flinched, then quested towards them, drawn by the gunshot. Tina aimed the Taser at the tentacle holding her leg, and fired. The darts shot out and buried themselves in the tentacle. It flexed straight, knocking them both off their feet, and quivered in the air, colours madly flashing across its surface.

Tina grabbed Ken. Together they scrambled up the slope after Ray, two steps forward, one step back, sliding in the scree.

"Don't fall over, for fuck's sake!"

Rocks tumbled down the slope towards them.

"Go right!"

Then they saw Ray. Another tentacle had him. He calmly fired the machine pistol into it, kept firing until the gun was empty, then hacked at it with a knife. The tentacle held, dragging him down the slope. Ken saw the back of his suit tear open. Another tentacle joined the first, the feelers driving under the skin of his suit, encircling him.

Ken fired. No reaction. The tentacles had their prey.

Then Ray removed the face piece of his respirator, and with it his radio microphone. He looked at them and shouted. "Go! Tell them, the Hart Ridge CEO, they must act, now. Go!...Fuck but this stinks of the ocean!"

Ray stood, and drove one arm into his tattered suit, withdrawing another machine pistol and a grenade. He shouted, "Aaieh Shoggoth!" waved his arms, and ran into the tentacles, firing until the gun was empty.

Beyond him, Ken saw a looming darkness. He grabbed Tina's hand and dragged her up the hill.

Behind them, an explosion boomed.

A short time later

It had taken six hours for Ken to get back to Canberra. With him was Sarah Harding. The helicopter had whisked them back to Ceduna where they had boarded a government jet.

It took Ken most of the trip to come to terms with the actions of Ray, The Suit. Ray had bolted up the side of the pit, seemingly like a coward, anxious to escape. Then he had quite obviously sacrificed himself to ensure Tina and Ken could escape. It rankled, but the man had simply acted to ensure he could get his information out. When that was no longer possible, he had acted to ensure Ken and Tina could get out with whatever information they carried. Ken found himself wishing for the impossible, to know what Ray would have said had he been with them now.

"The only thing left to deal with is…" Livings looked up as Ken and Harding entered the boardroom.

Jon Hart, Hart Ridge Corp's CEO, was present, as was his lawyer. Also present were the Minister's department head — the Minister could never be present at something like this herself — Deputy Commissioner Livings and three anonymous men in brown and grey suits who could have been cousins of Ray. Two of them guarded the door; the other stood in a corner and surveyed the entire room.

Ken looked more closely. The one in the corner was a woman. Her suit bulged where it shouldn't. He almost laughed — equality only went so far. The men's suits were tailored to hide weapons, but they hadn't bothered tailoring the clothing for their female agent. Whoever 'they' were. He felt reassured at the armed presence.

The meeting was heated, and had obviously been in progress for some time.

"Good. You're here. Ken, the hazmat—"

Ken interrupted Livings. "It's more than just a hazmat, sir. Something's alive in there!"

"Ken, you will have time to write a full report later today, and I look forward to reading it, but for the moment I'd like you to concern yourself with the *hazmat*. What's the best way to deal with the *hazmat* in that pit?"

Ken looked sharply about the room. The Minister's department head smiled and nodded encouragingly. Jon Hart looked ready to sue everybody.

"I've had enough of this madness," said Hart, moving to get up. One of the suited men from the door moved to stand behind his chair, and he subsided.

"You all know what's in that pit, don't you. What's going on?"

Nobody spoke.

Ken looked about the table. He collected his thoughts and spoke.

"You've got a huge pit full of flammable, heavier-than-air, toxic gas. Hydrogen sulphide burns to form sulphur dioxide and water. All the organics in there, they're heavier-than-air as well, so I'm guessing propane and butane...Did you strike oil, Mr Hart? There's meant to be some in the Bight, if you go deep enough. They burn to form carbon dioxide and water. Turn off the groundwater pumps, and there will be even more water. Sulphur dioxide dissolves in water to form sulphurous acid. Now, you want my advice, you're going to have to listen to this next bit.

"There's something in that pit that kills people, and nobody knows what it is. The whole thing is on a scale even the military would have problems investigating, and even the military may have problems dealing with what we saw down there. Everybody we know about in the pit is dead. There. I've said it."

"Yes. Your suggestion?" The Deputy Commissioner was calm, too calm.

"Throw in a match," said Ken. "Burn it all. The combustion products have less climate change potential than the precursors. The acid is contained in the pit where it can be neutralised later. That deals with the hazmat. But initially the entire pit will be lined with sulphurous acid. That and the fire should deal with... everything else. And I'll stand on the sidelines and cheer."

Jon Hart's skin went grey. He began shouting incoherent

guttural sounds in no language that Ken had ever heard. Then his shoulders hunched and his suit bulged as if it could no longer contain him. Was this what a heart attack looked like? Beside him, Hart's lawyer looked concerned for a moment, then his skin also turned grey.

"Clear the room!" shouted the department head.

Ken pushed Sarah ahead of him towards the door; then he heard, quite clearly, the *pfhutt* of some kind of an air rifle, and the smack of a projectile hitting flesh. It repeated twice. Hart and his lawyer lay on the floor, their humanity oozing away into things with grey flesh and short stubby tentacles that didn't fit into the clothing they wore. Deputy Commissioner Livings pushed them ahead of him out of the boardroom and locked the door behind him.

"My apologies, I'm sorry you had to see that."

The helicopter banked and followed the artificial mountain range circling the southern side of the pit.

It had taken more than one match. The air force didn't have napalm anymore, so they used incendiary bombs and gelled ethanol with gasoline mixed in. The pit burned for a month. The media called it a volcano, and 'Hart's folly.'

Nothing survived. Even the giant mining trucks melted to slag.

Soon, the media would call it 'Hart's Lake.' Somehow, Ken didn't think Ray the Suit would mind.

THE ISLAND IN THE SWAMP

J SCHERPENHUIZEN

Frank awoke to a nightmare. The thing remained out of sight, its presence forever around the bend. Chanting filled the air, urging that monstrous being on. That thing he could only guess at by the shadows it threw upon the wall, like some unholy parody of Plato's metaphor of the cave, which was all man could know of reality. Now Frank knew more, more of reality—which was unreality—than he had ever hoped to know, or known enough to fear. He sank back in a faint. Momentarily he sought escape from this unending torture in the past.

That damn radio show was where it had all began, that damn stupid radio show, though maybe it wasn't so stupid after all…

Hi, and welcome to Purplevoid Studio, internet radio. An island of intelligence in the ocean of stupidity that is our blue planet. Maybe all of this spinning in space is bound to drive us crazy after a while, as we see the joke that was Obamacare unravel, while false flag operations facilitate the move to take away the guns that are our only guarantee of freedom from tyranny, and the masses remain distracted by the Hegelian antipathies of Left and Right and the illusion of choice they provide. Or could it be it's the fluoridation of the water, calcifying our pineal glands that blinds our ability to see? Or maybe you figure everything is A-okay. We're not here to tell you what to think, we're just here to present some 'alternate' views to what you'll get from the bought— sorry—I mean mainstream *media. I'm your host, Ernie Oakley, and we're coming to you from the West Coast of Hawaii.*

Today we have a real treat for you. Vernon Strang has an engineering degree from the University of New South Wales in Australia, which he

JSCHERPENHUIZEN

took out after abandoning his studies in archaeology, due to what he describes as the 'blinkered approach' of the academic establishment in that field. Nonetheless, he has continued to study strange and anomalous findings in his homeland, aided by his daughter, Stephanie, who has a degree in linguistics. Vernon has just released his first book, Beyond the Blindfold, which summarises over thirty years of study. In it he challenges much of what is believed about the original inhabitants of The Great Southern Land and the earth itself. Things that would amaze the average person but which our listeners here at Purplevoid will, perhaps, be more than ready to contemplate as true.

Welcome, Vernon, let's start off with a bit of background about you.

Thanks, Arnie. Well, I've always felt an incredible connection to the Original Australian people. We used to call them 'Aboriginals' but a lot of them aren't happy with that description so I'll be referring to them as the 'Original People'. They believe in reincarnation, like me, and I'm sure I've been one of them before, and a number of Elders have told me this is so. I've been accepted into the society of a number of different groups and been initiated. I've also been a frequent contributor of articles in publications run by them and usually written by them. So I'm about as embedded in their society as a white feller can be.

So what is the key to this acceptance?

Well, basically it's reversing what is, I'm sad to say, the common attitude to the Original Australians, and probably all indigenous groups that have come under European rule. That attitude is that white people have brought civilization and a better way of life to the 'natives'. They've brought education, knowledge and medicine to them, and their resistance to this enlightenment is where all their current problems stem from. They refuse to give up their superstitions, put on a suit and tie and become wage slaves like good Australian citizens.

But that's not how you see it.

No. I see a nation of sovereign people who lived an idyllic lifestyle and, basically, had everything worked out. The 'working day' of a person living their traditional lifestyle was four hours. They didn't suffer any existential crisis. There was plenty of time and opportunity to express yourself creatively. There was no war, no disease, no theft and no fear of death.

112

Woah, woah, woah. No disease?

That's right! Disease was imported by the Europeans. Original Australians had a diet that was perfectly suited to their metabolism. They had an extensive herbal pharmacopeia but that was usually only for infants and the elderly because the adults' immune systems functioned perfectly. And if they did get an infection, they had penicillin.

Penicillin!

Yep. Everyone thinks of Fleming as being the discoverer of penicillin, but it was Australian Nobel Laureate Walter Florey who contributed most to its development for use in medicine, and he found out about it from the Original Australians who used a mold that grew on one side of a certain tree to cure infections!

So why don't more people know about this?

Well, it doesn't fit in with the perception of Original Australians as being primitives. They have to be portrayed as inferior to justify the destruction of their lifestyle and culture.

So, it's a conspiracy!

If you like.

Hmmm, interesting. It reminds me of Michael Tsarion's description of how the British denigrated the Irish and destroyed their ancient monuments and culture as part of their justification for ruling that 'primitive race'.

Yeah, interesting isn't it. The British had a long history of this tactic by the time they got to Australia. My family's background is Irish, actually, and I have this sort of intuition that a lot of the 'transported felons' were actually Original Australian souls, reincarnated, being brought back to their homeland. We have to remember that the original inhabitants of Ireland and Scotland were also 'Aboriginals' who were displaced by Romans, Anglo Saxons and Normans. We meet these original people in Robert E Howard's stories of Bran Mac Morn, for instance, and I think, probably, at least some of those people's ancestors came from Australia, and certainly they had trade links with Ancient Australia.

Right, and this is among some of the more startling claims made in your book, that the Original People were a seafaring people with links to places like Egypt. Can you tell the listeners a little about that?

Well, there's a lot of archaeological evidence of an Egyptian presence in Australia. There's the Gympie Pyramid and the Gosford Glyphs. All of which are challenged, of course.

We don't worry about that at Purplevoid. We've had Michael Cremo on talking about forbidden archaeology. There's dozens of these anomalies out there.

Yeah, and there's also signs of a connection with Australia in Egypt. They've found marsupial bones buried around the Sphinx and eucalyptus resin is used in Egyptian mummies, and mummification is also found in Australia. And then there are the linguistic connections between Egyptian and Original Australian dialects, which my daughter Stephanie can tell you all about.

But none of this is officially recognised?

Well, we're getting there. The evidence keeps mounting and more and more people are coming on board, even within academia. We haven't reached the tipping point yet. Not that it bothers us. We've been pooh-poohed for twenty years, but what kept us going is that the Elders kept giving us more and more information, the longer we worked with them and showed them our respect and sincerity. They told us all these finds were genuine, so we just had to find a way to prove it.

Of course skeptics say, well if they know all this stuff and they want it known, why haven't they done more to publicise it? The fact is, too much of what they have said has been met with disrespect. And they don't give up their sacred secrets and hidden history easily. You have to prove yourself sincere. They give you a bit, and then a bit more as you prove yourself, and it can take a long time.

Anyway, I've just been shown something that will blow everything wide open, if I'm allowed to share it. This place is amazing. It shows a kind of construction that has never been seen in Australia before. It's going to rewrite history. But we have to be careful about revealing its whereabouts. These places are sacred and we don't want people stomping all over them and turning them into a tourist attraction. The Elders have said that if the wrong people go to this place, something bad is going to happen...to them.

Frank came alert again, jerked out of his memory, or dream, or wherever he had gone to escape his misery and terror. The stench of the sea was in his nostrils, seaweed and brine and the stomach-churning stink of sea creatures in a state of putrefaction. He was on his hands and knees, crawling toward the chanting, the smell and the glow where those sinuous shadows writhed. Aghast, he stopped in his tracks. What could possess him to draw toward such horror? Possess indeed. It was something unholy, or beyond any concept of good and evil, at least.

Though his mind recoiled from the idea of further advance, he had no energy to retreat and for the moment contented himself to simply halt his progress and rest; rest his body, and rest his mind with distraction. The present was too terrifying. He had been thinking of the radio show, that that was where it had all started. But it had really begun with Janine looking at him over the dinner table with that look in her eye.

Frank knew she was getting ready to bait him. His brother's wife had become easy to read in the five years he'd come to know her. He didn't entirely mind being baited by her, it was as close to flirting with her as he was comfortable to get, and who wouldn't want to flirt with Janine? She had the body of a swimsuit model and the face of a film star. She was also smart, if you discounted her penchant for mysticism. His brother Gerome certainly managed to do so, despite the fact that Frank was positively a New Ager in comparison. He guessed opposites attracted, though a guy would overlook a lot for a woman as hot as Janine.

"Did you listen to the podcast I mentioned?" she asked casually.

"Yeah," Frank grinned back.

"And?"

"It's bullshit!"

"You think?"

"What's this?" Gerome butted in.

"Vernon Strang. You know, I told you I listened to it on Purplevoid."

"What, the guy who thinks *homo sapiens* evolved in Australia? Not that it matters, as soon as you mention Purplevoid I know it's bullshit. I don't know why you waste your time with that rubbish."

"Well, it gives me something to listen to while I'm potting."

"Yeah, like you couldn't listen to the ABC instead of that right-wing idiocy."

"They're not right wing, they're libertarians, I think. It's not as if they tell you what to think."

"No, but the fact that they seem to favour right-wing flakes as interviewees is a bit of a tip."

"Strang is as left-wing as they come."

"Yeah, but did they get him on to talk about politics?"

"Not exactly…"

Gerome threw up his hands. "Of course not. As long as he's talking about the flat earth or aliens from the Pleiades giving the Aborigines their knowledge they'll like him. That's their bag."

"He doesn't propose the earth is flat."

"No it's a carrot shape," Frank smirked. "Long and pointy and flat on top." The brothers laughed together.

"What's so funny?" Janine said.

"It's from the *Illuminatus Trilogy*," Gerome said. "I keep telling you, you have to read it. Then you'll see there's nothing new about these guys and the nuts they get on. They're just recycling the same kinda nonsense Shea and Wilson lampooned back in the 70s."

"Yeah," Frank agreed. "If you want something to entertain yourself with while you pot, get that on CD."

"Okay," Janine said, cheerily. "I'm not a true believer you know, but I think it's entertaining and I like to keep an open mind."

"Yeah, well," Gerome said, "just so long as you don't keep your mind so open that your brain slips out."

"Which it would have to have done to believe these guys," Frank said. He sounded angry.

"Why does it bother you so much?" Janine asked. She looked like an angel in the candlelight. It was hard to feel anything negative looking at her, except for the fact that she could never be his.

"Because there's too much shit going down in the world and people should be doing something about it rather than being diverted by this sort of nonsense," Frank said. "People like Strang are just attention seekers. They thrive on the controversy and sucker people in to get them buying their books and going on tours to look at their phony 'finds', while honest researchers doing serious work are ignored."

"You're not a little jealous, are you?" Janine said, leaning forward, her cleavage rising up on her folded arms.

Frank raised his eyes to the ceiling, trying to focus his thoughts.

"What for? The guy is a laughing stock in intellectual circles."

"Yeah, but who cares about them, Frank? Who wants to be part of respectable circles? Copernicus wasn't, or Giordano Bruno, or Galileo. You want to just spout the wisdom of the day and preach to the choir and you're fine, but heaven help you if you're a pioneer."

"Yeah, bro," Gerome said, his voice dripping irony. "Get on board. Don't you know the paradigm shift to the flat-earth theory is reaching the tipping point?"

"Carrot-shaped-earth theory," Frank quipped back, but the light had gone out of his eyes and he avoided looking at Janine, whose silence seemed to mock his pose of insouciance.

The carrot-shaped earth, he wished life made that much sense. At least, then, the earth would have had a shape unlike where he found himself now, within the bowels of the accursed mound. He giggled nervously. The mound projecting from the island was a bit like a carrot top in shape, if you trimmed off the green bits, and, proportionally, as much of the structure projected down into the ground as did a carrot into the earth. Inside such a gigantic structure he was no more than a louse that had found itself inside a wormhole.

It was all a matter of scale, Frank supposed. Once he had felt like most humans, he guessed, a member of the prime predator species on the planet. Of course there were creatures with bigger teeth and even tusked beasts, which dwarfed humans in size, yet with man's superior brains and their technology all of nature had been tamed. Or so he had thought.

Now it was as if he had been a mite in a wormhole who had finally made his way to the surface and discovered the world of men, and tigers and elephants, and beings so fabulous and gigantic and powerful that his true nature was finally revealed to him. Except the mite was blessed with too small an intelligence to truly appreciate its own insignificance. Perhaps some higher power had blessed his own race with a similar kind of ignorance, which he had been foolish enough to seek to overcome.

Yet he had not been wrong about man ruling all of nature, for the beings that ruled here, beneath the mound, were not truly a part of nature. They were outside of it, above it, beyond it… he had neither the words nor the concepts to articulate what whispered in his heart in tones of dread and awe. He had craved a revelation, and now that one had sought him out, Frank cursed it, and he cursed the man who had led him to it.

Frank hated Vernon Strang. Janine loved him and he didn't deserve her love or the admiration of all the idiots who fell for his line; all the bleeding hearts who felt sorry for the Abos who were resisting the 21st century, being dragged into it kicking and screaming. If their culture was so damn fantastic, why had it fallen apart so easily? Even if Strang was sincere he was an idiot. Just because some old black folk who claimed to be Elders told him some stuff, he was going to believe them above all of the academic experts and scientists who said otherwise? The Gympie Pyramid and the Gosford Glyphs had been debunked more often than the Shroud of Turin, not that that deterred the shroudies. These types were impervious to proof.

Yeah, he was jealous of Strang. Frank had a brain. He had education. He could spin a convincing lie out of half-truths as well as the next guy, but he wouldn't do it even if it was what the public wanted, because he had integrity. He understood what that 'public wanted better than most, because he had been down that whole track of mystical searching about as far as one could go. Gerome had teased him endlessly about his gullibility, about the money wasted on visiting tarot readers and Mind-Body-Spirit festivals, reading *Nexus* and *Silver Chord* and everything from Alistair Crowley to Erik von Däniken and back. But too many seers had been proven wrong. He had been promised each time that he would discover something amazing, that he would get his glimpse of another world, but now, at the age of forty he had given up those roads. Strang had not.

And if Strang was not a fraud then he was even more to be envied. What if he really had been inducted by the Elders into some hidden knowledge? What if he had really experienced the amazing things that he claimed; the things Frank had always dreamed of experiencing? And these things were almost on his doorstep, not in Egypt or in the heights of the Andes. Strang had said he was going on another trip and, as usual, a small, select group was going along with him. A trip to explore, more thoroughly, the 'startling new find' he claimed the Elders were still holding back from making public. What if he were to call Strang, offer to volunteer, then he could examine the site himself. If it was a hoax he'd expose Strang, and get a bit of airtime for himself. He could picture himself now, masterful, erudite. He could marshal his own facts. Strang's crackpot ideas were spreading like wildfire, which would automatically create a market for a definitive debunking. Frank had hidden his own light long enough.

If he succeeded in debunking Strang, he would gain his brother's respect and Janine's, too, no doubt. And, if Strang had truly discovered something groundbreaking, then getting involved would be almost as good. Either way, he couldn't lose.

Strang was strangely easy to convince. The guy really wasn't on the planet, Frank decided. Not that he had promised much other than to meet. He hadn't asked for anything either. Frank guessed that would come once he'd taken the bait. Then he'd find out what being part of the trip would cost. He didn't have any time to consider it though. Strang said they were leaving in three days. Frank booked a flight immediately, packed a few things and left.

When he arrived at Strang's place, nestled in the bush in the hills above Ballina, he knocked on the door. A woman answered. She was tall and handsome, though unadorned by makeup.

"I'm Rose," she said. Frank felt odd. Rose reminded him uncannily of Janine, though she was a good ten years older and not quite the stunner, she had some of that same allure, a similar, slightly abstracted look, which intrigued and disarmed him at the same time.

"Vernon is around the back," she said. She walked down the veranda and led him through the lush garden full of tree ferns around the side of the house.

"It's beautiful here," Frank said, making conversation. "What do you do, Rose?"

"I make tapestries, and weave," she replied.

"So, you're an artist," he observed. Just like Janine.

"Yes," she smiled at him. "I like to think so."

"Maybe one day you'll be in the Louvre," Frank said.

"Sightseeing," Janine laughed. "Vernon's closer to getting recognition than I am, and he's worked long enough for that."

The sound of voices had already alerted Frank to the fact that there was some sort of gathering at the house, and as they reached the back yard he saw that a barbeque was in full swing. A man turned, tongs in hand, as if sensing their presence. He was tall and reminded Frank of some sort of bird, though his hair was more like a lion's mane, abundant and black, except for a little grey at the temples.

"G'day," Strang said simply.

Frank introduced himself. He wasn't sure if Strang heard. His gaze seemed elsewhere.

"No worries," Strang said. "Snag?" He held out a sausage.

"Put it in some bread for him," Rose laughed. She went to get a plate and a couple of slices and brought them back.

"Oh, yeah," Strang said. "So, you're interested in our work?"

"Absolutely," Frank assured him. Rose took the sausage and put it in the bread on the plate and handed it to the new guest.

A girl came up to Strang and took the tongs from him, "Let me do that, Dad."

"Yeah, no worries," Strang said. "Can't multitask," he said to Frank with a shy grin. "Probably bloody burn everything if it was left up to me."

Frank's gaze was still on the girl. She was even taller than Strang's wife and, if anything, even lovelier than Janine, who had become Frank's standard of beauty, though she had nothing of the dreamy demeanour of either his brother's wife nor Strang's.

"That's Stephanie," Strang said, "though I guess you know that if you follow our work."

Frank coloured with embarrassment, realising he was staring.

"Of course, I recognised her," Frank lied.

"Yeah, she's my right hand," Strang said. "Anyway, I can't promise you anything. There's a lot of people who want to see the site, but they have to be cleared by the Elders, like I told you on the phone."

"Yeah, no worries," Frank agreed. "But I'm really keen to see it. I'm willing to do whatever it takes to qualify. I've done pretty well in my business so I'm in a good position to help out."

He wondered what it would take. Strang had been cagey about the money side of things so far. It would have been easy to believe he really didn't care about it.

"Ah, that'd be handy," Strang said. "It costs a lot to do these tours and things, you know. We make nothing out of the books and articles."

"Really?" Frank tried to hide his doubt. "I would have thought with all the exposure you'd had lately you'd be raking it in."

"Doesn't translate into a lot of sales," Strang said sadly. "With the internet everyone expects everything for free. Makes it hard to do the work. Rose has had to support a lot of what we do."

"Oh? Well, I'll be glad to help out," Frank repeated.

"Thanks," Strang said. He slapped Frank on the back. "You want a beer?"

"Love one," Frank said.

"Stephanie, love," Strang said to his beautiful daughter. "Could you get our guest a beer?"

"Sure," Stephanie smiled. "I'd love to."

It was late. Strang and his wife had retired. The other guests had gone. Frank had drunk too much and didn't want to leave. Stephanie seemed to like him. They had certainly spent enough time talking together. They had much in common. The young woman appeared to be so much more down to earth than her father or Rose, who turned out to be Strang's second wife. Stephanie's mother had died of cancer when she was twelve. Strang had met Rose five years later. She was ten years his junior and more like an older sister to Stephanie than her step-mother. It was from her real mother that she had inherited her hard-headedness and, Frank suspected, her intelligence, for he was still disinclined to take his host seriously. He'd kept a lid on that pretty well, but it was late and the booze was taking its toll. He wasn't quite sure what he'd said but Stephanie showed herself every bit as sharp as he'd suspected, to his regret.

"I'm starting to think you have doubts about our work," she said.

"Well," Frank lied, "I'll be totally honest with you. While I find your research very fascinating and I respect your father's passion, I think there's a few leaps of logic there. A bit of a gap in a lot of the data, and let's face it, it does go against the main thrust of accepted science and history."

"I know what you mean. I'm more the methodical, analytical type myself, like you. But you have to understand that a man like my father goes about things the opposite way around. He has an insight and then he finds the facts to support it. He's a visionary. And he knows the truth when he sees it. He respects the Elders. For him, their words are like divine revelation. Even when they amaze him he takes it on board and he goes looking for the evidence to back it up and, you know what? He keeps on finding it. I know it goes against the main thrust of academic thinking, but it's almost as if his faith is rewarded. The universe sends the truth to him; it directs him toward the evidence."

For a moment Stephanie looked at Frank. Her eyes were shining. She was stunning in the soft light of the night. Frank leant toward her. She backed away hurriedly, alarm writ large in her eyes. Maybe disgust. God, he was twenty years older than her—what was he thinking! He pulled himself back.

"Lost my balance," he said, lamely.

Stephanie's smile didn't quite reach her eyes this time. "Well, it's late and you've had a bit." Was there a hint of censure in that remark? "We should retire. I'll get you a blanket."

Frank settled back on the couch, hot with humiliation. The girl had returned swiftly and held a light rug out to him.

"See you in the morning," she said. Then she was gone and the night was still. Frank lay staring out of the window, thinking of the young woman and how she spoke of her father, her face glowing like a convert's. She had the fervour of an acolyte. Strang was a visionary, she said. He would not be the first charlatan to hide behind that façade, nor the first to successfully adopt one and cultivate a cult following.

Sleep eluded him, and a koala began to scream out in the bush when finally he drifted toward slumber, as if all the fates conspired to ensure his lack of ease.

A day later, close to dawn they set off. Two dozen people took the trip, piling into three vans and a four-wheel-drive that took them into Queensland. Frank was surprised at how little cash Strang had asked from him. He wanted to think that he at least took a commission for the hire of the vehicles but it hardly seemed enough to pay for the petrol and food they would need. When Frank spoke again of his willingness to 'help out' Strang had just smiled vaguely and said, "We'll talk about that later when we need to."

They drove all day and the weather was hot though the sky burgeoned with clouds that taunted them with the promise of rain. After an overnight stay in Townsville they drove on past Cairns. Frank chatted desultorily to the other guests who were full of excitement at the prospect of being in on the find. Their enthusiasm irked him and the more he spoke to them the more he became convinced that they were as gullible a bunch as had ever been assembled, connected by nothing so much as their desire to believe. Yet he was careful to hide his dissent.

On the second day of the journey, though, he had fallen asleep in the muggy van and jolted awake in surprise to find that the vehicle had jerked to a halt on a dirt road. The bush was on his left, on his right the sea stretched on forever. The dusty ribbon of the track was the only hint of civilisation in sight. Everyone was disembarking and he hurried to follow.

Strang was standing with a small group of Original Australians, as he insisted they be called. Frank had never seen him seem so alert. So alive. As he spoke to these old dark-skinned people in their simple country attire his face shone with the same sort of fervour Frank had seen upon his daughter's face. Stephanie held up her hand as the others drew near. Apparently only Strang and his closest cohorts were entitled to approach these august personages without further instruction.

"What's going on?" Frank asked.

"Interview time," Stephanie said.

"Will there be any hypotheticals?" Frank joked.

"You'll see," Stephanie smiled again.

Frank felt strangely nervous. He was there on false pretences. What if they saw through him? But that was all wrong, he reminded himself. It was as if he had been infected by the aura of reverence he had had to endure from these dupes for the last two days. These old Aunties and Uncles, these Elders or Clever fellers or *wirijuns* or whatever they were meant to be, wouldn't have a clue about much of anything from the look of them. He was an educated man. He had a degree. He knew science. What did they know?

He looked out to sea and for a moment an overwhelming sense of his own smallness washed over him. Then Stephanie was calling his name again and he realised it was his time to meet the Elders. The Elders, that's what they were. All of a sudden his confidence deserted him. They didn't seem to pay him any attention.

"This is Uncle Billy," Strang said, in a tone that would have served to introduce the Pope.

Frank put out his hand to offer a handshake. Uncle Billy only glanced at his face for a moment. Slowly he reached up, ignoring Frank's palm and grasped the inside of his forearm in his warm dry hand. The grip was gentle but firm. He didn't shake. He didn't say anything. Frank searched for the old man's gaze, eager to show him by the steadiness of his eye that he was a man of honour, but the Elder showed no interest in any such fake evidence.

"What's he doing?" Frank asked, finding his voice with difficulty.

"Feeling your blood," Strang said matter-of-factly.

Uncle Billy dropped Frank's hand. He grasped his upper arm for one moment. Oddly it seemed like a small sign of comfort, though it had the opposite effect.

"Just go wait over by the van," Strang said gently.

Frank went and stood by the vehicle, watching thunderheads gather over the ocean. The rumours of rain the sky had whispered for days seemed ready to be spoken aloud. Everyone was returning to the vans, one by one. Finally Strang joined them.

"Come with me please, Frank," he said. They walked off a short distance together.

"I'm sorry," he proceeded, as soon as they were out of earshot of the others. "I'm afraid we can't take you with us."

"What do you mean?" Frank said, amazed.

"Sorry," Strang said again, "I told you we'd have to get the Elder's permission and they feel you shouldn't come."

"But why?" Frank protested.

"It's for your own protection," Strang insisted. "You have to have a certain mindset to learn some things, and you don't have it."

"But, but how do they know?" Frank blurted. "They didn't ask me anything about myself."

"Frank, they don't need to."

"Bullshit! So what did you tell them then? What did you say about me?"

"Frank, please," Strang ran his fingers back through his lion's mane. "Calm down. It's not up to me."

Frank forced himself to calm down. He knew what was going on, he realised at last. He was slow sometimes.

"Look, Verne," Frank said evenly. "I know this is a huge find and it's a big honour and I don't just expect you to share it with just anyone for nothing."

Strang looked at him with what seemed like real surprise. He was good, Frank thought, really good.

"I know you need money to do this work and you haven't asked me for nearly enough, but let me tell you how much I believe in you and in the work you're doing here, and let me tell you how much I want this. Just tell me, Verne. How much is it going to take?"

"Sorry, Frank," Strang shook his head sadly, "money has nothing to do with it. Some things you can't buy."

"Fuck you!" Frank cried. "Is this because I made a pass at your daughter? Is this some petty act of revenge?"

"You what?" Frank wasn't quite sure what the look on Strang's face meant, but it seemed to be comprised of equal parts disgust and pity. He just turned on his heels shaking his head and walked away.

"They're never wrong," Frank heard him mutter.

I must have lost the plot, Frank thought. Strang was a fake, so why was he so desperate to go on the trip? How much would he have been willing to pay to see his phony find? Yet, he wasn't really sure it was phony, was he, because if he was, why would he feel genuinely rejected? He had never really stopped being a believer, deep down inside. That was why he was in love with his brother's wife. That was why he looked forward to their debates; why he listened to those idiotic programs like Purplevoid so avidly, even while he kept up a running commentary on what was wrong with them, because he was hoping that they would prove him wrong. Hoping that they would say just one thing that would be his entry into that world he had always known was there but was somehow closed to him. It was the realm the Elders seemed to walk in and yet they would not let him follow, because he was unworthy.

But he had come this far and would not turn back.

Of course there was another explanation. Maybe he hadn't hidden his doubts as cleverly as he'd thought? Maybe they didn't want someone finding their fake and debunking it? Maybe he should just stick with plan A? Frank decided he was chronically confused. He didn't know whether he wanted it to be a fraud more than he wanted it to be real. Presuming there was something to see out there and they weren't all just heading off to have an orgy or take psychedelics. Either way, Frank had to know. He would follow them at a safe distance.

At least they were sticking to the coast. Frank reasoned that this way he could not get lost. Still, he feared, maybe he was losing the plot. They were in the middle of nowhere. If he turned an ankle or was bitten by a snake there would be no one to help him. Maybe he was ill. It was as if an odd fever was upon him, a kind of insanity. Yet there was no quitting from this path, no matter how unwise it might seem. Frank kept after the group, hanging well back, spying on them through his field glasses. The sweat clung to his body, the thunderheads grew darker, but refused to release their bounty upon the earth. The world stayed hot and dark while lightning played out over the ocean.

His pack was well stocked with rations but he ate sparingly. As night fell he saw the party make camp. There was no orgy. There was quiet laughter and someone sang with a voice of haunting beauty, which carried to him in the emptiness of the night, interrupted only by the occasional sounds of surf and the rumble of distant thunder.

Laughter floated to him across the distance as well and an incredible sadness and longing welled within him. He settled down to sleep as close to the others as he dared. In fitful dreams he heard the singing all night and imagined that he heard other voices. Fears flitted across his mindscape like wallabies bounding through the night. Visions played in his head of strangers stumbling upon him and driving him away at the point of a spear.

The morning was so overcast that the sun did not wake him and when he arose there was no one in sight. The camp was deserted and the campfires cold. Frank rushed on, careless now of being discovered, terrified of being abandoned out in the bush. He reminded himself that he was on the coast and could retrace his way with ease, if need be.

It seemed that he had lost track of time. This was madness. Surely it would be better to go back. Strang had been cagey about how long it would take to reach the site. All Frank knew was that it was on the coast. They were meant to be gone a total of two weeks, but Strang would not say how many days would be spent marching and how many on site. Frank thought about turning back but the sun had been hidden all day and there was no way of knowing if it was one hour to dark or five. He decided to press on up the coast until night fell and then persist until he came upon the party. They would stop to camp and he would find them. He would hear their laughter and singing and see their fires and he would set the alarm on his phone so he did not sleep past dawn again.

The day seemed impossibly long and a state of trance seemed to creep over him by slow degrees so he no longer knew if he walked half asleep or dreamt that he walked. Finally he found himself walking in darkness and did not know how long it had been so. How had he proceeded so far without consciously monitoring his progress? How had his feet carried him safely without the assistance of his mind? Where were they? How could anyone possibly miss them? Surely they were not so much faster that he had not caught them yet? Could he have passed them somehow? Exhausted, he lay down to sleep at last. The clouds that had pressed down on him all day, blocking out the sun, persisted, and hid the stars from his sight. The heat was oppressive. The only thing he could count on was a series of nightmares to disturb his sleep. Enough, he decided, in the morning he would turn back.

Frank's eyes snapped open on a sky full of stars. He had never seen a sky like it before, and it was easy to imagine he was lying up there among them rather than staring up from the earth, until the aches in his body reminded him of reality. The clouds had finally departed without delivering their promise, unless this was a dream. If so the Pleiades was part of it and he recalled how Strang had spoken of the Elders' claim that their ancestors had come from there. The seer had also spoken of the UFOs inscribed among the infamous Glyphs at Gosford. It seemed harder to scoff at them now. Faced with the immensity of the universe and its million blinking eyes it was only too easy to conceive of other beings in the Pleiades; to believe that, just as he lay staring up into the heavens, a myriad of strange intelligences, upon a multitude of earths, stared back at him. Yet, with what intent? The thought shocked him and made him shudder, for it felt more like an insight than a fancy.

Frank mocked himself. He was catching Strang's disease, the pathology of the visionary: to take one's imagination for inspiration. Was that how it had begun for ol' Vernon? With nights like these, staring into the immensity of the heavens as he camped out with his 'Aunties' and 'Uncles'?

When Frank awoke it was to see the dawn, bright and ruddy in the sky where a few vagrant clouds had taken up residence. He felt different, as if a fever had indeed gripped him for the last day or so, but now had finally passed. The desire to pursue his mad quest any further had departed. It was time to surrender, go back. After a quick breakfast of energy bars and a few sips from his canteen he began to retrace his steps. His march was not more than a half hour commenced when he came upon the camp. There was a little inlet there and he could not believe he had waded across it the previous night without realisation. How deep had his fever been? The coals of the campfire were still warm. Mangroves grew along the creek and the ground was mud rather than sand. His own tracks were clearly observed going over the creek and back, but there were no others. That meant that the party had not proceeded beyond the creek. Examining the area around the camp he found more subtle traces of tracks leading inland, away from the shore. Strang had said nothing about that. But then again, he had wanted to keep the location of the place secret.

Heart beating faster, Frank gave up all thoughts of return. High dunes rose up beside the inlet and he climbed to the top of one. From there the ground sloped away gently into the distance. The creek from the inlet wound upstream through wetlands, where clumps of mangrove rose from fields of reeds. About three kilometres away an island projected out of the reeds and in its midst sat a mound which seemed as if it could hardly be natural.

Frank slid down the dune and headed back to the path that wound itself alongside the stream. This was a bad idea, he thought. The sky disapproved also. The legion of thunderheads had flocked back as if a fool like him did not deserve to see the light of day. And now they delivered, finally, as if things were not wet enough underfoot. Wetlands were well named from a descriptive point of view, he decided, but from an emotional point of view swamp, bog and quagmire all seemed like better descriptors. He had a tent but nowhere to pitch it. Unless he went back. Yet the elements could not be allowed to conspire to keep him from his goal. He pressed on. He found the creek. He found mangroves. He found a snake and feared that crocodiles might find him, for something large was moving out there. The beach suddenly seemed the best bet, anywhere, in fact, but that damnable bog. Yet it proved as elusive as the island. Exhaustion threatened. At last he found a rise and was relieved to find himself quitting the swamp. On all fours he crawled to the top of the rise. Somehow he managed to get his tent up and crawled inside.

Frank saw Strang and his group on the island in the wetlands. They cavorted drunkenly, chanting and singing, while fires flamed high into the night under the blazing stars. He saw Stephanie naked, prancing like a nymph. Something slithered in the swamp. No, he didn't see it, he told himself, it was all a dream. Vaguely he was aware of the rain beating against his tent. So he dreamed.

When he awoke there was no more rain. Crawling from his tent he saw the island again. He was on a dune to the south of it. About the same distance as he had been when he left the coast. It should not take long to reach it, however, the same thought had occurred to him the day before. He would not reach the island if it did not want him to. Somehow he knew this now. Frank laughed quietly to himself, "Strang's disease," he laughed, "Yes, I'm a visionary, that's me."

Still the mound called to him. His yearning had brought him

this far and now, chastened, he would be allowed his glimpse of that which he had always hoped for, his final unassailable physical proof of the numinous, *fascinans*, *mysterium* and *tremendum*.

He stumbled down the dune and plunged into the swamp. The clouds held back. The curtain of rain remained drawn aside. He wondered where Strang was. It seemed, once again, he had lost time. But then he was at the island. He hardly believed it as he trudged up the slope out of the boggy reed-clogged water. The mound rose up before him. The size of the structure had not been apparent from a distance, but it was enormous. He staggered toward it, his legs weak, as much with fear as fatigue. He searched for his phone. It would be a sin to return without a picture of it, but the battery had died. How long was it since he had left the van?

The outer wall of the mound was ten feet high and covered with soil and grasses. No opening was apparent. Frank began to walk the circumference. The sun came out. He looked around for a sign that anyone had been there recently. If there had been any evidence the torrential rains of the previous night had washed it away. Vaguely he wondered about the Strangs, the Elders, Uncle Billy, and the people who had been on the bus. Now and then he thought voices were on the wind. Yet if they were on the island they stayed hidden from sight. A maddening vision formed in his mind of the elusive party circling the mound just ahead of him, by design or manipulated by the gods, so they remained just as the numinous had always been: so close but out of sight.

Unless…were they on top of the mound? Frank decided to climb it. Who knew what he might find up there, or what he might see. The sides were only slightly inclined but plenty of handholds offered themselves. Rough stones protruded from the dirt and the tufts of grass were firmly embedded. Frank was fit and strong for someone his age, but the trials of the last few days had taken their toll on him. The climb was difficult but he reached the top. A grim smile crossed his lips as he hauled his weary body over the lip. The feeling of satisfaction was short-lived, however, for the tuft of grass he grasped gave way, and he tumbled backwards out into space, landing with a crash back on the island. There was a blinding flash of pain as his head hit the ground and, for the moment at least, Frank Clarke knew nothing of pain.

When finally he awoke once more, the stars blazed down upon him again. He feared his fall had done some major damage. Nothing felt or looked right, and he had never felt so sick. The stars seemed too bright and close and the heavens seemed rearranged. It felt as if the world was less substantial, as if one might float away, but there was nothing pleasant about the sensation. As he climbed to his feet the feeling of decreased gravity made it hard for him to keep his balance. He thrust a hand out against the mound wall and a section swung in, as if some hidden lever had been activated. This must be a dream, he reassured himself, though a dream had never felt so physically real before.

The light from these strange heavens was so bright that the carvings on the massive stones that lined the doorway were easily discerned. Frank goggled. They could have been Celtic, or Egyptian. They could have been Aboriginal. *Original*, he corrected himself. For some reason he could not articulate, he had a new respect for Uncle Billy and the others. The markings grooved deeply into the stone were beautiful, but disturbing. What was it about them—the whorls and rings and crosses—that suggested such disparate influences, yet an uncanny commonality? He could not comprehend them. Whatever they were, they were not fakes, and as far as he knew, they were his discovery.

A dizzying sense of excitement swept over Frank. This was sensational. If only his phone's camera would function. Who would believe him without proof? He had to make this new find, *his* find, known. His newfound respect for the Elders did not extend to keeping their secrets. This was a discovery of huge significance. It would make him famous. Suddenly Frank's reverie was disturbed by a new sound. He heard voices, chanting again. Did it emanate from within the mound? As he put his head inside the entrance, the sound grew louder and a faint glow greeted his eyes. Strang? The others? Frank cursed. So that was why he could not find them. This was not his find after all.

What could they be up to? The vision of Stephanie, naked, flashed before his eyes again and it felt like the memory of something seen more than the recollection of a dream. He found himself moving along the passageway, which sloped down toward the interior, his hand feeling the wall, which was covered in the strange runes. The chanting was louder in the passage with its odd acoustics. The passage continued to slope down through an eccentric series of twists and turns and Frank began again to think that he must be dreaming, for it seemed that time stretched and he walked for days, deeper and further, and yet he came no closer to the glow which always seemed around the next bend, no nearer to the sounds which always seemed further ahead.

Finally it occurred to him to look behind and he saw that the same glow that was always ahead, also lay to the rear, behind whatever twist he had just quit. It was madness to continue where he was going. He was trapped in a nightmare and could expect to encounter nothing here. He had been so intent on exploring this amazing new place that he had not bothered to think of why it might have been built, or by whom. A vision of the strange stars in the sky above the mound recurred in his mind. The runes in the doorway and those that his fingers had traced on his journey became superimposed on them, and he had another intuition that this place was a neither temple nor tomb, but a prison of some kind, a trap for a monster, or a god, or something in between.

He turned now, at last, but it seemed the floor sloped down again and that could not be so. How could he know where he was if his senses could no longer tell up from down? A sob broke out in his chest. It was tempting to lie down in the passage and refuse to move, but how long before that became intolerable? He crept on, choosing a direction randomly, no longer pondering whether it was descent or ascent, forward or reverse, fearing that somehow the physics in this place abolished such distinctions. Yet some progress was being made, for a new scent filled the air, like seaweed, ozone and the ocean, and a sound like the crashing of waves or the surge of surf into some vast underground cavern.

Frank about-faced, reluctant to approach that sound, that stench, and hurried away, but the sensations only grew louder and stronger the further he fled until he thought, somehow he had made a mistake and ran back the other way. Again the sensation repeated itself and he stopped in terror and sank down against the wall behind him, which seemed as damp and unpleasant as the interior of a bowel. He sobbed again, and, straining his ears against the dark symphony of the 'surf', heard a new sound, like a slithering, a shuffling, as of something huge and unimaginable.

Straining his eyes toward the glow at the right end bend of the passage he saw weird sinuous shadows play against the wall. He rolled to his knees and prepared to scramble to the left, only to see the same sight at the other end as if there was a mirror there. An incoherent prayer escaped his lips, to be replaced by a scream and in the echoing silence that followed the slow progress of the thing from below came inexorably on.

Janine was putting the finishing glaze on a vase in the potting shed. She had had enough of music for the time being. She couldn't play Joni Mitchell or Van Morrison again. Even *Astral Weeks* could only stand so many listens. She couldn't hack the ABC either. Her mind didn't need any more improving. Time for her guilty pleasure, she thought. Purplevoid radio. She'd already downloaded the podcast and had been saving it for the right moment. This was it. Finding the MP3 in her Purplevoid folder she clicked on it. A new interview with Vernon Strang. She was keen to hear of his progress since the last interview, where he'd mentioned a find which would re-write history.

Vernon, last time you were on, you mentioned a startling new find, something that, once recognised, would require the re-writing of the history books.

Yeah, well, that's right, Ernie. But, unfortunately, the Elders are saying that it's not something we can share with the general populace.

Hmmm. That's going to cause credibility problems, isn't it?

Ha, mate! If I was worried about my credibility I wouldn't be appearing on your show.

I feel you, my friend, I truly do.

Strang continued. *Let those who have eyes to see, see, and those with ears to listen hear…*

Just to play devil's advocate for a moment, Vernon, did it ever occur to you that, if this find is really so important, that maybe it would be worthwhile sharing anyway? I mean, from one point of view, as much as we might respect the Elders, their viewpoint isn't scientific.

Well, is that true? I mean, just because it isn't derived from research in a laboratory…Experimental method is what proves theory, right? So, when for 40,000 years the Elders say, if you do something we tell you you shouldn't do, something bad will happen, and you do it anyway, and it happens, that's a pretty large body of evidence.

So you're saying it would be dangerous to go in the face of their advice.

Mate, it wouldn't be worth my life.

Janine felt she had done enough for the day. She finished up what she was doing, and went to the trough to wash her hands.

Frank awoke in terror. He had suffered a terrible nightmare. The memory of his ordeal in the passage was etched in his mind and he doubted it could ever be erased. Yet where was he now? If the monstrous shadows and the ghostly lights, the sounds of shuffling and the stench of the sea had all been some fever dream, what was real? The island in the swamp? The mound? All he knew was that he was in some unpleasant, dank, dark place. He risked a glance to the left. The glow was there. His heart started to pound. He glanced in the opposite direction. The glow again, as cheerless and haunting an illumination as could be imagined.

As if in answer to his fear the stink of the sea began to creep back and the chanting recommenced. The slithering began once more and the shadows returned. This was what had happened last time, and he had sat waiting, waiting for whatever approached to come and claim him, for there was nowhere to flee, even if he had not been paralysed with fear; until, eventually, he had passed out in terror. So why had the things not come for him? There were only two possibilities. Something held those creeping terrors from turning the corner, some barrier, or—and the thought was so bizarre he could not imagine why it would occur to him unless it was another of those 'insights' that had plagued him of late—the things desired his fear more than his flesh, if they craved the latter at all.

So what was he to do? Though he may be safe from being rent for the moment, he would starve if he remained where he was. If he went forward, however, he might find another branch tunnel, ahead of the section of the maze the creature would not, or could not, pass. It was the most slender of hopes, yet more than he had felt before his faint. Afraid that, if he did not move now, he would never find the courage, Frank forced himself to his feet. He set off toward the right, needing to choose one direction.

He feared he dreamt, after all; that he had merely dreamt a dream of waking within a greater dream, for again he experienced that uncanny sense of time displacement and the glow and the shadows seemed to retreat before him. While it had seemed that there was a corner to turn, he never reached it, as if the walls were morphing as he walked and the corner remained the same distance ahead. Yet the sound of chanting grew stronger and the stench of the sea and even the unholy sounds that accompanied the movement of the writhing shadows, as if he truly was nearing something.

I'm being tortured, Frank thought, *I'm being played with like a cat plays with a rodent or a bug. It's feeding off my terror.* For Frank was indeed drowning in horror. He feared, in fact, that he had simply gone mad, for reality was refusing to play by any rules he had ever encountered. Time and space were plastic here, and seemed guided by some unimaginably cruel alien will with the express purpose of frustrating and tormenting him.

He remembered what the Greeks had said about vengeful gods, *whom they would destroy they first make mad.* An involuntary giggle escaped his lips.

"Show yourselves," Frank screamed. "Show yourselves, I'm not afraid of you!"

This was no mere bravado. He *was* no longer afraid, so they must have truly driven him insane, for terror was the only sane response to this nightmare world he found himself trapped in. Yet, if they wanted his fear, if they fed off his misery, then they had no more use for him now. The game of keeping out of sight had reached its end. Yet the Old Ones had not finished with him, nor would they be until he was drained of every ounce of energy he could produce. Frank knew this.

The chanting grew, his heart began to pound once more, the blood beat at his temples and the shadows moved closer. Time stretched and space with it, until it seemed that either he shrank or the passage grew with the increasing effulgence, and the thing that cast the shadows hove into sight. And then Frank learned that there were levels of madness, and levels of terror, and he had been initiated into an entirely new level of hell.

MELBOURNE CALLING

SILVIA BROWN

Kew Asylum, 1987

The events I am about to recount occurred a year ago. So much has changed since, I am no longer sure of the purpose of this exercise, whether it's closure I'm seeking or one more chance to look into the alluring abyss. In truth, these words I write are my last chance at freedom. I must prove to them that I am whole when I am not. I must prove that the monsters no longer haunt me.

I used to wish I could be like everyone else, but I've never been able to be anything but who I am.

"It's just a phase," was my mother's verdict. She looked at my father, expecting confirmation that every boy my age goes through such a thing. Clueless, he shrank his shoulders while she fussed over me, her hand on my forehead, checking my temperature. As if fever was a symptom of being queer. But my cheeks were burning hot for a very different reason.

"You'll be late for training," Dad said, giving me a cue to get out.

Returning to my room took what little I had left in me. I felt insignificant, every step on the stairs a task. My room was a junkyard. Grandiose piles of everything I had ever wished for loomed over my head. A sleeking tentacle ventured out from the depths of my closet as I reached for my cricket whites. The slimy extremities stretched all the way to where I stood, seeking me out in a threatening yet familiar way. I closed my eyes and counted to three like the psych had suggested and the vision went away, leaving a path of slime all over my shoes. Yuk. My mother waited at the bottom of the stairs and walked me out of the house before waving me goodbye.

Ferndale Park, our training oval, was a couple of blocks from our home in Glen Iris. Cricket was my father's idea of a good time and I had nothing against it, but watching the game at home didn't mean I wanted to join the school team. Not even remotely. I wasn't built for the outdoors, with fair skin rapidly turning a bright shade of pink, and freckles that multiplied by the thousands. As I dragged my cricket bat on the pavement, I didn't see our neighbour's decadent houses in Valley Parade, but a desolate landscape; a vision of what was to come should the beast in my closet rise from its dormant state, and doom and sudden death become a more desirable prospect than my parent's oblivion.

"Get out of the way, carrot head!" I heard Connor O'Brien behind me before he pushed me. I let go of my bat as I fell and Connor picked it up, laughing with his mates as he left me behind, my knees badly scratched from the fall.

Such an interaction was by no means new, but somehow it got to me a bit more than usual and I just sat there, feeling hopeless, while O'Brien got smaller and smaller in the distance until I could no longer see him.

"Are you alright?" Someone helped me up.

I blushed as the reason I kept going to practice materialised in the flesh right by my side. Captain Josh Teague. Six foot three, an A-class player and student, Josh was someone everybody looked up to. Even me.

Josh started stalking me not long after that. Day after day, he'd follow me home after cricket practice and stand by the fence, looking up to my window, before continuing on. But I wasn't there. I'd been watching Josh for months as he grew taller and fitter, his voice deeper. From the moment he took notice of me, everything changed. The stalker became the 'stalkee'. After getting home, I'd sneak into my father's old shed to spy on him until he was gone.

One day I got home and he wasn't behind me. Both relieved and disappointed, I assumed the chase was over and lay down on my beanbag in the shed. Pencil in hand, I turned the pages in my notebook. Recollections of the creatures that lurk in my visions when I feel at my lowest came alive on the pages. Drawing took the edge off these monsters, allowing me to, somehow, own them. A blank page stared back at me as I tried to recall what I saw earlier, but something wasn't right. I felt observed. Paranoid, I expected my darkest thoughts to take monstrous shape and swallow me whole...until I saw them. Josh's blue eyes stared at me through a crack in the wooden wall of the shed, giving me a fright. He came in, temporarily blinding me as the light came through behind him.

"So this is where you've been hiding?" He looked around and I grew self-conscious. The stained beanbags, the crinkled pages on my comics, the appalling state of my boom box. And what was that smell? God.

"It isn't much," I said. What the hell was I apologising for?

"You kidding? It's grand," he replied before making himself at home.

We spent weeks pretending to read comics and listen to music, stealing glances at each other while I filled my notebook with Josh's features. The unbearable tension between us drove me nuts until I couldn't take it anymore.

"You have to stop pretending," I said, hesitant.

Josh seemed humoured at first, before he realised I was serious. Without warning, the drums and guitars hit in unison—*London Calling*—The Clash's apocalyptic angst reflected my own.

"You're right," Josh said, and my heart sank. His pose shifted, his confidence nowhere to be seen. Hammering downbeat chords enfolded us. "You're all I'll never be," he said. "Shit, that came out wrong. I...I wish I was more like you. You come as you are. You don't pretend you're something you're not, and you shouldn't have to." Then he leaned forward and kissed me.

It was tentative at first, his lips pressing softly on mine. My skin prickled and something took us over. Our kiss grew deeper before disintegrating into smaller atoms until it was no more. The moment lingered as we opened our eyes to a brand new world. Us.

After our first kiss, we took every opportunity we had to be together. When school camp was announced, I was reticent to go but Josh sweet-talked me into it. He described nights under the stars, sharing a swag in the middle of the outback. As if the school would allow that. *A place to reinvent ourselves,* he whispered in my ear.

How could I resist?

We packed our bags and stole hair products from our mothers. Our wet hair was the perfect playground for the strong gel as we sung out the chorus, and *London Calling* soon became 'Melbourne Calling'. Mirrorless, my fingers dived into Josh's middle length hair, straightening it forward, while he spiked up my own. We experimented, until our upper-suburban haircuts resembled those of our idols: John Lydon. Glen Danzig. We were ready.

A run-down town in the outback was the chosen destination for the camp. On the first night, Josh and I sneaked out from our dorm and into the bathroom before we headed into town. We stripped off our uniforms and changed into our Salvos clothes— tight jeans and black leather pants—and styled each other's hair. I replaced my collared shirt for a second-hand 'God Save The Queen' find. We giggled as we stood by the mirror, showing off our new personas. We were no longer the product of privileged trash. We were free.

Silence spread throughout the complex before the crickets started to cry out their warnings, but we didn't listen. We were high on pheromones, our brains flooded, our bodies straightening as we shared the confidence of those who faced the world together. We were bold, two proud punks, in love.

The town didn't expect us. Most businesses closed after sunset, and the empty streets seemed to change Josh's state of mind. His hand slipped from mine, purposeless. Was that all I was to him, I wondered, a chance to prove himself?

Hurt, I walked on, picking up speed as my head spun with overwhelming thoughts I didn't care to push away. Self-doubt consumed me as I approached the steps to the only store with lights on, a vintage shop. As I stood there our eyes locked. Josh's disheartened pose disappeared as he read my mood, or so I hoped. He frowned, concerned, picking up the pace towards me, before I turned my back on him and crossed the shop threshold.

A collection of dolls welcomed me, their faces partly broken. Looking closer I noticed the spaces between the wreckage, the artisan work beneath. Intricate threads were holding the ceramic in place, covering up the darkness. My gaze had lingered on them for way too long, spooking me, when I heard the clanky little bell on the shop door ring. Warm fingers found their way between my own, and Josh stood, close, right behind me. As his head leaned in towards my neck, every inch of my skin ached. As his breath, and then his lips, explored uncharted territory, I moaned, barely holding my balance. My hand accidentally hit the stand in front of me, sending one of the ceramic dolls onto the floor, breaking it into smithereens.

"Shit!" I cried, but Josh didn't flinch. He turned me around and pushed himself against me. His hands worked their way under my shirt while his tongue conquered my upper neck, my ear. Electrical impulses made me jerk back, leaning on the stand while he continued his ruthless offensive. My head turned to the side to catch my breath. An old, speckled mirror on the wall reflected Josh's determination and my struggle.

"Who's there?" The voice made us jump back to the real world: the vintage store, the hot summer night. We couldn't see the owner of the voice. High shelves stood between him and us. We straightened ourselves, our clothes, trying to appear normal while our tight pants told a different story.

Josh's eyes sparked as he opened the shop door—"Don't worry old man. We're leaving!" he called—then closed it. He took my hand, dragging me to the side of the store, insisting we stay low to avoid being seen.

In a moment I realised his intention. He led me towards the front of the store and opened the little trap door that led into the window displays, facing onto the darkened street.

Inside a soft chaise longue embraced us as Josh's soft kisses filled places inside me I never knew existed. Our tongues were intertwined when the music started. It was almost a whisper at first, buzzing in the background, but growing louder as an invisible hand pushed the volume to max.

"Can you hear that?" I mouthed, pointing to my ear. Using the distraction to take in much-needed oxygen. Josh nodded, sitting back. He reached under the chaise longue, digging out an old Walkman, with headphones, that was playing our song. Josh's smile widened, made ecstatic by the discovery, while I wished I hadn't said a word. Our moment was gone. I looked at Josh, pointing with my head toward the trap door that led back into the store. But he sat there instead, absorbed in our musical find, an object replacing the attention I previously had to myself. Suddenly angry, I left him behind to drool over the device, and made my way back into the store. The mirror I saw earlier reflected my frustration, mocking my ruined punk hair. I am a fool.

I removed the doorbell to avoid alerting the owner and stepped out into the street. Fresh air tingled on my skin, drying sweat. My fingers tapped impatiently on the store window, but Josh didn't look up. His open hand was extended. WAIT?

"Wait for what?" I yelled, and pounded my fist on the glass.

Josh smiled at me as he lifted the vintage headphones over his head. He sat back on the chaise lounge as he did so, daring me to react, defiant. Damn you, Josh Teague.

A blast went off as the headphones snapped onto his ears. Flesh exploded. Glass and wood shattered. I spun my face away from the window, shards flying in all directions, digging into my exposed skin.

Ears ringing, I sat back in the street, covered in glass and blood. When my eyes could focus again I saw the broken window, the ruined chaise longue, and what was left of Josh, the pointy end of a shotgun still levelled at where his head had been.

The old man behind the gun looked me in the eye, seemingly indifferent to the loss of life and property. Soulless, he proceeded to reload the shotgun, and then point it right at me. His boots crushed glass as he walked slowly towards me, past Josh's sprawled body, to where the Walkman lay—still playing—on the floor. The old man's partly hidden features became more obvious as he moved into the light of the store window. His human face fell into a mass of feelers from the lips down, miniscule tentacles lurking in all directions.

Music roared in my head, past my temporary deafness. The Clash. "Fuck off!" I yelled as the volume increased, piercing my ears, until I couldn't bear it anymore. I closed my eyes, held my head, and wished for it to stop, for everything to come to an end.

The tape stopped with a click.

The nurse announces visitors and I put my notebook down, exhausted. Josh's mother stands by the door but she can't bear to look at me. Her perfect makeup covering the paths of tears only visible up close.

"He would've wanted you to have it," she mumbles, approaching me.

The Walkman sits on the bed, right where she left it. A modern set of headphones has been rolled around it. Torn, I calculate the damage it would do if I were to push it onto the floor. But there's no use. Josh is all I can think about. His cheeky smile. I'll do it for him. My hand reaches out. I can feel Josh by my side as I set the headphones on my ears. He dares me, 'chicken'.

My fingers push play and The Clash takes over my senses, a song I've avoided for too long now. No visions of fantastic monsters haunt me as I weep. Deeply buried emotions resurface like calm waves smoothing the rugged sand of my soul. Sketches of us, our courtship, my father's shed, every treasured moment, going through my mind. Melbourne Calling. I smile.

Colin

What the hell? I jump, taking the headphones off my ears. There is no one there. The muted music keeps playing in the background. I put the headphones back on and focus. Listening. Lyrics. Bass. Louder.

Colin!

Josh? Hands over my ears, I close my eyes. Trying to concentrate as if that will increase my ability to hear his voice. The tape stops with a click.

I open my eyes and darkness surrounds me. I've been here before, after the blast, but the voices brought me back. Nurses. My parents. Only this time no one is calling out for me. They have given up.

I am lost in limbo and I am not alone. I can feel the others, their bodies sharing our doomed confinement. I can't move. I think I am going to be sick.

Then I feel him, Josh's warm fingers threading their way between my own. His body standing close, his voice whispering in my ear: *I missed you*.

The music starts, louder than ever before. We sing each word from the top of our lungs and Josh tightens his grip on my hand as the chorus rises. Melbourne Calling. Ecstatic, I give in. Falling into the abyss.

WHERE THE MADMEN MEET

T. S. P. SWEENEY

The door to my house was open. This wasn't unusual in itself. I have a pair of teenagers, and both could be careless enough to forget to lock up properly. It was the middle of the day, and Danielle and Jonathan should have been at school. Jon had been caught skipping class a couple of times recently, though, and was just brazen enough to bring a girl home while I was supposed to be at work. There were plenty of logical reasons to summon up a twinge of anger at that point, but all I could feel was dread. I crept to the door, the hot summer sun suddenly oppressive. Every step was harder than the last, and by the time I reached the end of the path my heart was hammering against my ribs. I grasped the door handle and edged the door open the rest of the way, praying that the old brass hinges would not squeal.

A man sat on the couch in the living room, dressed in old maroon footy shorts and a grey singlet that showed off a sun-darkened, heavily muscled body. Dark brown eyes stared at me, crinkling in the corners, and his thick, scruffy beard was unable to hide a crooked grin.

I screamed.

"Nice to see you too, sweetheart," my husband said as I threw myself at him.

"How…?" I managed to choke out, tears flowing as I clutched him to me. "How can you be here?"

"They flew us home early…" Tom trailed off as his arms encircled me, crushing me to his chest. "It doesn't matter. I'm back now."

I shifted around on his lap, bringing my face in line with his.

"I'm back," he repeated, stroking my hair, tucking it behind my ear. "I'm back, Steph. For good."

He kissed me.

My head was swimming. I had not seen my husband in almost a year. Tom had been deployed — supposedly to Afghanistan — but there had been almost no communication in the intervening months; just a few letters here, a rare call there. The only constant in our lives had been that he would need to disappear sometimes and I would need to trust he would be okay.

And now he was home.

"How?" I asked again.

"Shhh," he placed a finger over my lips, and the grin that had made me fall in love with him was back on his face. "Later."

He kissed me again, harder this time. Hungrier.

"I missed you." Tom smiled up at me from the bed.

"You missed this, you mean." I cocked my hip, emphasising my nudity.

"Absolutely," he laughed, running his fingers through his beard. "But that wasn't what I meant."

I tied my hair up into my usual ponytail and changed the subject.

"What is that thing growing on your face, by the way?"

"It's a bit hard to shave regularly where I was, love." The smile slid from his face as he spoke. "Hard to do much of anything human."

I felt his mood darkening.

"Well I bet you're feeling pretty human right now," I said, sauntering over and laying down next to him with as much exaggerated sex-appeal as I could muster.

"You have no idea," he said, his voice oddly cold. He didn't look at me.

"Hello?" Jon's voice rang out from the front of the house. "Mum? Why is the door open?"

"In the bedroom," I called back, scuttling under the sheet and pulling it above my chest. At the last second I threw it over Tom, as well.

"Mum, why are you in bed…" he trailed off as he saw Tom, his school bag dropping from his shoulder onto the floorboards with a thud. I could see the thought process ticking over in his mind as he went from wondering why I was there, to why there was a strange, bearded man in the bed, to realising exactly who that strange, bearded man was. It was oddly satisfying to see my own reaction from earlier mirrored in our son.

"*Dad!*" Jon shouted as he hugged his father. I felt my eyes well up again as it really hit home that Tom was back.

"Good to see you too mate." Tom roughed up his son's hair. "I swear you've grown a foot since I saw you last."

"I've been…" he paused and stood up from the bed, his mind finally catching up with what he was seeing.

Jon blushed. Tom did too.

"Oh come on you guys," my son covered his eyes and backed out of the room, almost tripping over his school bag. Tom went even redder. I burst out laughing.

"We should probably put some clothes on," I managed to get out between giggles.

"Probably," Tom laughed, cheeks still flushed.

"Yeah you probably should," called Jon from down the hallway.

"**D**ad's next," whispered Danielle. She looked lovely in her dress, bought especially for the occasion. She was bouncing up and down in her seat, unable to contain her excitement.

"Quiet," Jon elbowed his sister. He'd somehow found time to loosen his tie.

"Sergeant Thomas Lilyman," the Governor-General paused for an uncomfortable second, clearing her throat. "…152 Signal Squadron, Special Air Service."

I rolled my eyes.

Tom stepped onto the stage in full dress uniform. I felt such pride seeing him up there.

"For your bravery in service to your men, your regiment, and your country," The Governor-General held forth a felt-covered box. "We, the people of Australia, thank you."

Danielle gripped my hand. I squeezed back; feeling the unfamiliar weight of the strange gold bracelet Tom had given me that morning shift on my wrist.

"For your actions defending the lives of innocent civilians against the assault of anti-Coalition militia," the Governor-General announced, "it is my honour and privilege to award you this: the Medal of Gallantry." She leant forward, pinning the medal to his chest.

The crowd began to politely applaud. Jon rose to his feet, but Danielle pulled him back down before I had to. It was a sombre occasion, though I could not help but smile as my husband turned around.

He stood there as the cameras flashed—I had to assume they were from the army, as the ceremony was not being made public—and smiled, slightly. His eyes made contact with mine, and I realised the smile was a lie; as fabricated as the insinuation that he and his men had been serving with the Signal Squadron instead of one of the combat units. Then, as quickly as it happened, he looked away from me, smiling that fake smile at our children instead.

I shuddered. Something was not right. Not right at all.

"We need to talk."

Tom did not look away from the television. "What about Steph?"

"About what happened over there," I had sent the kids out to see friends so Tom and I could be alone. He had been fine the majority of the time in the couple of days since the award ceremony; but there was still a certain distance there, and I could not shake the feeling that he was hiding something.

"Sweetheart," he turned, smiling at me. I could feel the wariness coming off him. "You know the rules—I can't talk to you about work."

"I don't need to know the details of your adventures in 'signalling', I leaned forward in the old recliner, resting my chin in my hands. "But I do need to know what happened that makes you so unhappy to be back here with me and the kids."

I regretted it as soon as I said it.

"That is some passive-aggressive bullshit," Tom snarled as he stood up from the couch.

"I'm sorry, but you haven't exactly been making it easy," I tried to soothe him, but I'd put my foot in it already.

"What, exactly, am I guilty of here?" he paced over to me and grabbed the remote, jabbing a finger at the power button.

"You've been quiet, distant. Sometimes you seem fine and everything is great, and then five minutes later you're staring off into space and I don't know whether to hug you or lock myself in the bathroom."

He froze on the spot and stared. "You think I'm going to hurt you?"

"Oh god, no, Tom, not like that," I was backpedalling now. "I'm just scared for you because you look so hurt; so angry. I just want to know what is happening in your head."

"I need to go for a walk."

I reached out to him, but he turned his back and strode away.

It was three in the morning.

The kids had come home earlier; Danielle first, dropped off by my sister and bubbling over with excitement that quickly disappeared when she sensed my mood.

Jon came in a couple of hours later, smelling of cigarettes and booze, not expecting anyone to be awake. I knew he was waiting for me to tear him to shreds, but I honestly didn't have it in me. He went to his room, mumbling about how late it was.

I sat there in the dark and at three in the morning my husband came home.

"What are you still doing up?" He sounded tense.

"You walked out before we could finish talking earlier," my voice was a harsh croak; I hadn't spoken in hours. "I needed to talk to you and you've been gone for hours."

He walked over and sat next to me, grabbing my hand. So gentle compared to earlier, much more like himself.

"I'm sorry," we both spoke at the same time, the words tumbling out. Tom snorted and I couldn't help but smile.

"I didn't think you'd still be awake," he said after a little while.

"Where did you go?"

He hesitated; it obviously wasn't the question he had been expecting.

"I need to tell you something," he said after a long moment. "You're probably not going to like it."

I nodded, knuckles white where I gripped his hand.

"I've been seeing someone."

My fist was flying at his face before I even realised it, a left hook just like my dad had taught me.

Tom, the utter bastard, slapped my hand away with his forearm before it could connect. Then he had the temerity to laugh.

"Not like that, not like that!" He grabbed my wrist, gently, before I could try to deck him again. Bloody training. "I'm not cheating on you, Steph, I swear. Shit, when would I have had the time?"

It was a good point.

"Then what?"

"A therapist, in the city," his voice turned serious; earnest. "She was over there with us."

I just stared at him. I had known Tom for most of my life, and this was the last thing I ever would have expected him to say.

"At first we thought it was just bullshit, you know? But after a few visits we all realised that she was really helping. She moved back here when we did and said we could call on her at any time."

"So you saw her tonight?"

He looked away, cheeks flushed, emphasising his smooth shaven cheeks. "I was so angry and my mind was spinning. I—"

"What, hon? You can tell me."

"It was bad, Steph."

I drew him toward me on the couch and wrapped my arms around him. He was shaking.

"That medal is a joke, you know that?"

"That's not true, Tom."

"It is, believe me."

I held him, feeling him shudder against me. Finally, he pulled away and looked at me.

"You're not mad?"

"No I'm not mad," I smiled at him and reached up to stroke his face. "In fact I think it's good for you. What is this doctor's name?"

"Olmstead," he replied. "Doctor Marion Olmstead."

"The doctor will see you now."

The pretty receptionist gave us a smile and wandered back to her desk. My eyes lingered on the necklace she wore; dark, reddish gold of a very strange, almost unsettling, design. It looked oddly similar to my new bracelet.

"Ready, sweetheart?" Tom looked at me as he stood up. He was smiling, a gesture that would have usually calmed my nerves, but not today.

I nodded and stood up from the leather chair, throwing the magazine I had been thumbing through onto a table. Briefly I wondered how the Army could afford to pay for its soldiers to attend a therapist who worked in these kinds of surroundings— all glass and brushed steel, and a prime waterfront location.

The elevator gave a soft chime as the doors slid open—no ground floor offices here—and Tom pushed the button for level six with the confidence of someone who had been spending more time here than at home of late.

Tom held my hand and squeezed it. I squeezed back, heart thumping in my chest.

The elevator doors slid open again, framing Doctor Olmstead.

"Welcome Thomas, Stephanie," Olmstead said, a cool little smile on her face.

She was younger than I had expected, not much older than

myself, if I had to guess. She was a plain woman, slightly pop-eyed and with a blotchy complexion no amount of makeup or expensive clothing could disguise. Still, she was not the horrible monster I had been expecting, and I felt myself relax slightly.

Olmstead led us down the hallway to a room at the end, exchanging pleasantries with Tom. All the offices were built of opaque glass, with unlabelled doors, making me wonder if anyone else worked on the floor.

"Please, make yourselves comfortable while I set up," the psychiatrist ushered us into the room and closed the door.

"Have a seat, Steph," Tom suited action to words, making himself at home on a black leather couch, the twin to the furniture in the lobby. "She won't keep us waiting too long."

"What did she mean by 'set up'?" I tried to keep the sense of unease from tingeing my words as I sat down next to him.

"We do a lot of video sessions," Tom placed his hand on my knee. "It helps, you know, with my condition."

It was easy to forget, with how strange he had been the past couple of weeks, that this was all happening because he was sick.

I leant over and pecked him on the lips, feeling his hand squeeze my knee in response. The doctor chose that moment to return.

"No issues with personal contact, at least," she said, closing the door behind her and dimming the lights. "I assume there has been no problem with your sex lives?"

I coughed and blushed. It wasn't that I was embarrassed, but the question took me by surprise.

"It's just fine, thank you," I murmured, hating the fact I sounded prudish.

"Is it, Stephanie?" She sat down in the chair opposite us, crossing her legs and peering down her nose at us through rounded glasses. "Thomas has indicated otherwise in our prior sessions."

I shot Tom a look and he did not even have the good grace to appear embarrassed.

"Do not blame him, Stephanie. The truth is everything within these walls, even when it is uncomfortable." She paused, smiling thinly. "Especially when it is uncomfortable. Everything depends upon it."

"It is hard to have a discussion about the truth when my husband is here talking to you, and yet he cannot tell me anything about what is troubling him."

Tom winced. "Steph, you know I can't—"

"That is not the issue right now, Stephanie." Olmstead leant back, steepling her fingers. "But let me assure you that all truths are revealed in here, even those once hidden."

I raised my eyebrow, "I find that hard to believe."

"As I find it hard to believe that everything is fine when you have only slept with your husband once since you have been reunited, despite almost a year apart."

Tom at least looked away this time. I might have hit him otherwise.

"But perhaps we do not need to discuss that right now," Olmstead continued. "You have issues of trust. Let us see about addressing them first."

She tapped a few times at the tablet resting on the arm of her chair. The lights dimmed, leaving the room in darkness for a moment before a large flat screen that was recessed into the wall hummed to life. The lights came back up to a dim glow, seemed to flicker, and then finally died completely.

Grainy, off-white tinted footage began to play, accompanied by heavy breathing that crackled with static. It took me a moment to realise what I was looking at; or, more specifically, who.

"Isn't this classified?" My voice was a whisper, as though someone might overhear. My husband's face stared at me from the screen, bearded and dirty. His eyes seemed to glow with a feverish light, courtesy of the night vision camera.

"Of course it is," the therapist responded, "but, as I said, there are no secrets here."

Tom's eyes were locked on the footage, staring at his own face like nothing else existed.

"There's a BMP and twenty grunts sweeping down the ridge towards the beach." Tom's voice was a harsh whisper.

"What are they doing?" The camera turned to another soldier:

Greg Fells, one of Tom's troopers. "Going for a swim?"

"Dobbo says there are civilians down there," Tom said, referring to Slavko Dobric, another one of his men. We had known Slavko since high school, and he and his wife Hannah had been my closest friends for a very long time. "He reckons it's some sort of religious ceremony, lots of dancing around fires and chanting—maybe a rival sect?"

"Rival sects don't last long coming out in the open like this, especially not this close to a major town." The voice seemed to emanate from the camera, but I struggled to recognise it. "Besides which, there aren't too many religions dancing around fires in this day and age, are there?"

"Then why are there soldiers about to murder them?" Greg muttered.

"Enough," Tom beckoned with his right hand and the sound of movement came from off camera, but our viewpoint didn't change. "We need to decide what to do."

"What's to decide? This isn't our mission."

"No, it isn't."

My heart was in my throat as Tom spoke.

"Which is why I'm asking for your thoughts instead of giving you orders. Your *quick* thoughts."

"We've got a perfect position to flank them," Greg nodded at the blurred outline of the ridge behind him. "Hit them from behind with the height advantage, no way they're expecting the attack."

"They aren't expecting the attack because we shouldn't even be here."

"Well, we are here."

"They're civilians, we have—"

"Not *our* civilians—"

"We can't risk the mission—"

It would have been comical, these bearded commandos whispering fiercely over the top of each other, if the situation wasn't so obviously serious.

"Enough," all talk ceased when Tom spoke. "Suppressors on. Hank, hit the BMP. Boys, numbers only from here on in."

The cameraman nodded, finally revealing his identity as Hank, the newest member of my husband's squad.

"And mate," Tom reached toward the camera, crooked grin on his face. "Camera off for this one."

The screen went black. The lights in the room pulsed and buzzed before finally coming back to their full, fluorescent brightness.

We didn't speak on the way home.

I pulled the car into the driveway and turned the key. Tom just stared into space.

"It was a good thing you did," I said after a long while. He didn't respond. "… That you *all* did; trying to save those people."

He said nothing.

"Damn it, Tom," I snapped, tearing open the car door. "You barely spoke for the rest of the session while that woman asked me all those horrid questions. I thought this was meant to be helping you! What is it exactly you are so ashamed of?"

As I moved to leave the car, he grabbed my wrist.

"You don't understand," he whispered. I was shocked to see there were tears in his eyes. "What we did…"

"You killed soldiers to save the innocent civilians they were going to slaughter. That is what you did!"

"We killed soldiers. We saved those people." He looked at me, his eyes cold, tears wiped away on the back of his hand as suddenly as they had arrived. "But what makes you think anyone is innocent?"

We went back to Olmstead's office seven more times over the next few weeks, each visit seeming to mark another low point in my relationship with my husband.

Each session began with the Doctor replaying the same footage over and over and asking me impertinent questions about our love life, whether 'the change' was coming on, whether our children were sexually active, and all sorts of things that seemed to have no connection to Tom's wellbeing; or, indeed, Tom himself, at all.

The only discussions that touched upon my husband were repeated assurances by Olmstead that the acts he had committed in war were natural and normal, and he should not feel shame nor regret.

For his part, Tom was relatively normal in the lead up to each session. Once there, however, he barely spoke, eyes glazed as he stared at the screen, and when we left he grew more and more sullen, not talking for hours, or flying into a rage over nothing. It was maddening. The footage, so exciting to see initially after years of not knowing anything about what my husband did, became a source of frustration. I found myself dreading the monotony of the visits, of the strangely inappropriate questions and the dark comments, the ghostly wartime footage and the incessantly irritating malfunctioning lights.

During the seventh session, I excused myself to use the ladies room.

As I walked, I tried turning the handles on the rows of unmarked doors surrounding me, but not one of them was unlocked. I had just begun wondering if the building was otherwise deserted when I heard a door click shut ahead of me. I rushed forward, coming to a single door identical to all the others. I placed my fingers on the handle and turned, gently.

It was unlocked! The door cracked open, revealing a room as dark as night, heavy blackout curtains obscuring the windows. A smell like rotten seaweed washed over me, pungent enough to make me retch. My eyes began to adjust slightly to the darkness. I thought I could make out a shape, moving slightly.

"Did you get lost?" Olmstead tore the door handle from my fingers and slammed the door shut.

I didn't bother saying anything. I was caught, and no amount of excuses would explain that away. Olmstead merely turned and walked away.

"I believe you are ready for the next film," she said, not bothering to look back over her shoulder.

I followed her, fear rising with every step.

I met with the wives of Tom's squad on Friday that week.

I had taken the day off from work and met the girls at a little cafe I'd frequented a few times with Hannah. I was surprised to see she was not there yet.

Greg's wife Sam sat chatting animatedly to a woman I did not recognize. I assumed her to be Hank's wife, whom I had never met before.

Diana and Lin—Leo's wife and Zac's partner, respectively—sat quietly watching as the other two spoke, seemingly content to listen and nod occasionally. Hannah was nowhere to be seen.

"Steph, it's good to see you again," Lin beckoned me to her end of the table, and rolled her eyes in Sam and the other woman's direction. "Those two are so busy debating the merits of therapy that I think they've forgotten why we are here."

"Well it *is* related," Diana frowned, taking a sip of her chai. "I mean, Leo has not been right since he got back. The therapy is helping."

"Is it?" The stranger cut in. "Helping with what, exactly? To come to terms with what they did?"

I gasped to see her face up close; the right side, obscured when I had approached, was a mottled purple bruise from brow to chin, poorly disguised by heavy makeup.

"That was your husband?" I didn't want to believe it.

"He took me to therapy with him. I told him I didn't like that pop-eyed freak telling him to 'give in to his urges' and 'accept his true nature'." She gingerly traced a finger along her blackened jaw. "This was the result."

Everyone stopped talking for a moment as the waiter returned, carrying more coffees with him.

"I'm so sorry, Bethany. Greg just lost it at me the other day as well." Sam said quietly. Tears welled in her eyes. "He was looking at his medal and I told him how proud I was of him. He threw the medal at me, started smashing photo frames of the kids, ranting about their future. He went to grab me, but I ran. I didn't want to admit it."

She raised her wrist from under the table, revealing a golden bracelet. It was so similar to my own as to obviously be from the same source "This was his apology."

"Leo has been distant, but he would never hurt me." Diana said, a little too quickly if I was any judge.

"Zac keeps talking about leaving the Army. He keeps telling me we are still young enough, and we can do something amazing with our lives." Lin gave a shake of her head. "He refuses to give me details, though. Anytime I ask him to explain, he just clams up or changes the subject."

"And what about you, Steph?" Bethany stared at me; they all did.

"Nothing," I replied.

"Nothing?" I could hear the disbelief in her voice.

"We've argued and he has been distant. When he talks, he seems...conflicted. Torn up, almost to the point of pain, and after that witch showed me that last video, I understand why." I let out a shuddering breath. "But he hasn't touched me, or the kids."

"So he hasn't hurt you?" Diana asked, her face screwed up.

"No, he hasn't hurt me."

No one said it to me, but even I could hear the unspoken *'yet'*.

had just pulled up to the traffic lights when I got the call.

"Steph, its Slavko." My friend's voice was almost unrecognisable. "I've been trying to call Tom. He isn't answering."

"Dobbo, what's wrong?" The car behind honked at me; the light had changed. I accelerated slowly. "Is it Hannah?"

"Steph, I..." He trailed off, but I heard it there; the anguish, like nothing I had ever heard in his voice in all the years I knew him.

"What happened?" I caught myself not paying attention, my big, lumbering SUV trying to slip into oncoming traffic. "What did you do?"

"I didn't want it to be like this, Steph. You need to understand, I did it to save her. It was all I could do."

"What did you do?" I yelled the words this time. My knuckles were white on the steering wheel.

"I, I'm sorry, Steph." His teeth were chattering. "I didn't want this, I didn't want to hurt her, b-but I couldn't put her through this. I couldn't fight it."

"What?"

He hung up the phone. It was all I could do to get myself home in one piece. I needed my husband. But when I got home, Tom was gone.

It was three in the morning. Again.

I still don't know why I just sat there, in the dark. The kids came home, whatever false smiles and empty words I offered seemingly enough for them to leave me alone. Perhaps they were battling their own demons.

So I sat, alone, too paralysed by fear of what had happened to take any steps to confirm if my suspicions were true.

Instead, I relived that day in Olmstead's office.

"You will want to pay attention to this, Stephanie." Olmstead activated the screen as she spoke, tone dry and not at all reflecting the anger she must have been feeling at my earlier trespass.

"—uck, I'm hit," the footage was the same grainy white, only now the camera was on its side. Hank sounded panicked.

"Get up, it just grazed your helmet." A hand came down and the camera feed turned to blurry nonsense, clearing when Hank was righted again, Leo's smiling face in front of his.

"They're done." The camera locked on Tom as he walked up to Hank, slapping him on the shoulder. "Let's secure the site and—"

"Sarge," I recognised Slavko's faint accent immediately. "You want to see this."

They advanced together down to the beach.

People in strange headdresses and robes stood upon the sand, forming a slow-moving circle, seemingly oblivious to the battle that had happened a mere hundred metres from them.

"What the hell?" Tom's sentiment echoed my own.

In the centre of the circle stood a woman, age indeterminate, screaming as she was shoved face first by two burly men into a pool of water.

The darkness around the pit writhed, revealing the presence of more people; dozens of them.

"Let her go," someone screamed. The order was greeted with static-laced, burbling laughter.

Then the gunfire started.

I had replayed it over and over in my head since that day. Tom had refused to talk about what else had occurred.

I was thinking about the drowning girl when Tom came through the door.

"Where have you been?" I was angry, suddenly. Fear turned to rage. "I needed you."

"I was busy," his face was pinched, more lined than usual. He was angry too.

"I needed you," I screamed it this time. I wanted to slap him. "Do you know what happened while you were *busy*?"

"Dobric beat his wife to death," Tom replied simply, eyes locked on mine.

The anger went out of me. I collapsed to the floor, knees to my chest. My body was wracked with spasms, the sobs unable to escape.

He stood over me, unmoving. My eyes were blurred, but I realised, in the moonlight, that there was blood on his clothing.

"Where were you, Tom?" I whispered.

"Doing what I needed to do." He was shaking too, but not for the same reasons. There was malice about him, a seething hatred I had never seen, even in his worst moments.

"Whose blood is that?"

I was on my back, my face on fire. It took a second for the stars to clear, and to realize Tom had hit me. He *never* hit me.

He looked as shocked as me for a moment, but then his expression firmed, a terrible sneer on his lips.

I kicked him in the side of the knee with my shin, as hard as I could. He grunted in pain, and I leapt to my feet and went at him. Every self-defence lesson I had ever had told me to take advantage of his surprise and put him down; I was an Army wife and an Army brat before that, and I had been doing one variety or another of martial arts since I could walk.

But in the end, all I could do was grab him and scream: "*Why?*"

"Because Hannah wouldn't stop asking questions," he grabbed my hands.

I kicked at him as he lifted me to my feet, a lucky knee taking him in the groin. It barely elicited a grunt; without the element of surprise, he was too tough and too well trained. If I had wanted to stop him or get away, it was too late now.

"Slavko was fine, but *she* kept asking questions." He forced me towards the wall, his nose pressed to mine. "All of a sudden he is questioning everything, too. He managed his little act of defiance with Hannah, and then I made him pay for it."

My back hit the wall, hard. He forced my wrists above my head, pinning me. His other hand stroked my cheek, almost gently, fingers still crusted with Slavko's blood.

His hand reached for my hair and I could sense he was about to wrap his fingers through it. I launched forward, hammering my forehead into his nose. I felt a wet crunch against my skin and he grunted, his grip on my wrists relaxing long enough for me to wrench my arms free.

I threw a punch at his temple, any ideas of restraint at him being my husband long since fled.

The punch connected, rocking his head back a step. His left hand came up, batting my fist away. His right hand came up holding a knife.

"It has to be this way," he mumbled as he slammed me against the wall, the service-issue combat blade against the side of my throat. I was on my tiptoes. "I don't want this, you understand? You keep fighting."

"Tom," I could barely get it out. "The kids."

It was all I could think of.

"The kids. You're right." He shifted the knife away.

I managed to take a deep breath before his fingers closed around my throat.

I kicked and punched and slapped and scratched. It made no

difference. I tried to scream, but no sound could escape his grip.

My vision greyed at the edges. His lips moved, but I couldn't hear anything over the roaring in my ears.

I think he said: "I'm sorry."

It was Danielle who saved me.

My daughter was hanging off her father's arm, prying at his fingers. A second later Jon was there too, grabbing Tom around the shoulders.

He should have been able to shrug them off easily enough, but he let them drag him away, his eyes glazed.

I fell to the floor, rubbing at my throat, coughing violently.

Tom was sitting on the couch, hands folded in his lap, completely still. Danielle held the knife in her hand like it was a snake, vaguely aimed in her father's direction, a look of queasy horror on her face. Jon stood protectively over me, tensed to defend me, as obviously terrified as his sister.

I stood, dragging myself up with the help of my son, and limped over to the couch.

"Danielle," I croaked. "Give me the knife."

I sat down next to Tom. He turned to face me and the mask slipped, just a bit. There were tears in his eyes again.

I leant against him, placing my arm around his shoulders. He sobbed once, resting his head on me.

I placed the blade of the knife against his thigh, directly over the artery. He froze when he realised what I was doing.

"Steph, I—"

"I'm talking right now, Tom." I pressed on the blade, harder still, for emphasis. "And not to you. Jon?"

"Mum?" he said, his voice a high-pitched squeak.

"In the bathroom above the mirror is a loose tile, third from the right. Behind it is a compartment your father thinks I don't know about. In that compartment is a gun and some bullets. Please bring them here and then take your sister to Aunt Lucy's, okay?"

He looked at me blankly, and then stumbled away, too dazed to question me.

"And Jon—grab my keys."

"**I** don't think I should be driving."

"Shut up, Tom. I need to think."

The car crawled around the corner with the kind of rigid, too-careful movements I'd always associated with those driving drunk.

"Steph, seriously, I am not up to driving. I need to—"

"You need to be quiet," I jabbed the barrel of the revolver into the back of his car seat for emphasis. I knew better, now, than to stay within his reach

"Pull over here," He nosed the car over, parking crookedly enough that any rangers working at four in the morning would have probably booked us. "Get out."

He stepped out of the car, stumbling forward, still dazed. I stood a few feet behind him, gun pointed at his back.

The glass monstrosity containing Olmstead's office loomed over us, glittering in the light of the few street lamps. Waves crashed in the background, cutting through the silence.

"Call her."

"I'm sorry," Tom's voice was an almost inaudible whisper. "I'm so sorry."

"*Call her*," I said back, harsher than I meant to sound; harsher than I thought I *could* sound.

"Why are we here, Steph?"

Tom walked ahead of me, pushing through the now-unlocked revolving door of the building. The lobby was completely unlit, but the glass allowed enough light so that we could find our way.

"Because *she's* the reason this has happened to us. You have all been seeing her since you got back. Tom, you've been more and more withdrawn, and then suddenly violent. The others too. Weird conversations with the kids, midnight visits to that woman's office you can barely remember or don't want to talk about."

He stopped and turned toward me.

"So, what are you saying?" he kept his distance, eyes purposely not looking at the gun in my hand. "You think we've been brainwashed?"

"That is exactly what I think."

"I would know if I was being brainwashed."

"Would you? Would any of you?" I gestured to my bruised throat. "Are you telling me *this* is you?"

I was greeted by silence.

The door opened soundlessly as Tom pushed through, plunging us into darkness.

"I know the way," Tom whispered.

Whispering felt appropriate. I followed behind him, gun still pointed at his back. We were perhaps a dozen steps in when the lights suddenly came on, bright enough to make me wince. In that moment, Tom spun around and ripped the revolver from my hand.

I stumbled as I turned to run, knowing I would not get away.

"I'm not going to hurt you, Steph," Tom removed the ammunition from the gun as he spoke, allowing the bullets to drop carelessly to the carpet before sliding the weapon into the back of his belt. "But we can't work this out with you pointing a gun at me the whole time."

"That wasn't your choice to make," I tensed, waiting for him to come at me.

"He was not the one who made it." Doctor Olmstead appeared behind Tom as if from nowhere, resting a hand casually on his shoulder.

"You," I wanted to lunge at her.

"Yes, Stephanie, me." She smiled, taking a step toward me, but not so close as to be within my reach. "I have only ever wanted you to understand the same truths your husband now embraces."

"By brainwashing him?"

"No one has been brainwashed," she stroked Tom's cheek, like a child petting a puppy. "Merely aided in accepting their choices."

"And what choices are those?" I snarled.

"Follow me and I will show you." Olmstead turned on her

heel and walked down the corridor, Tom following. "I believe you are ready to watch the final piece of film."

Fists clenched at my sides, I hesitated only a heartbeat before following. I needed to know.

The lights were already pulsating in that unusual way, the screen lit with the frozen, dull-white glare of the last footage she had shown me.

My eyes lingered for a moment on the image of the woman being forcibly drowned.

"Stephanie, please, sit down," Olmstead indicated the couch with a wave of her hand. "We have much to discuss."

I found myself sitting without quite understanding why I was still listening to this woman.

"Though you were the last of the wives and partners to see the second part of the footage, Stephanie," Olmstead placed her hand upon my knee, "I believe you are the first to be ready to witness the final element of your husband's journey."

"Let her go," screamed Zac's voice; it was definitely him, now that I heard it again. Laughter echoed from the screen, accompanied by the image blowing out as the gunfire began.

"*Cease fire, cease fire!*" Tom's roar ended a second before the gunfire did, leaving only silence.

Then the screaming began.

"See to the wounded," Tom ordered. The camera shook as Hank stood up, advancing with his rifle held before him.

As he approached the site where the woman had been drowned, Hank paused over the bodies of her killers, but paid them no mind. Instead, he stepped toward the corpses piled behind them; those civilians milling in the shadows who had absorbed the brunt of the gunfire after the initial target had been slain.

Before he could step closer, a figure stepped in front of Hank, in full view of the camera. Wearing a glistening, twisted tiara and a robe so dark as to appear almost invisible in the night vision footage, Doctor Olmstead placed a hand upon the barrel of Hank's rifle and slowly lowered it. She held a staff in her other hand, the rough-cut stone surmounting it glistening black and wet in the darkness.

"Do not seek to help these people, for they go to their sacrifice willingly." Her voice sounded the same; something about that surprised me.

"Bullshit," the camera bobbed backwards as Tom shoved Olmstead's hand away, Hank seemingly willing to step back and allow his leader to make the next move.

"It is true," Olmstead said, looking into Tom's eyes and smiling at him. The rock on her staff seemed to pulse with a dark light, punctuating each word. "It is through their sacrifice that we, the chosen few, might live forever."

The other soldiers surrounded Olmstead then, guns pointed at her.

"Those two bastards bleeding into the sand over there don't look too immortal," Slavko grunted.

"They had not yet undergone the change, it is true." She tilted her head sideways, looking back at my husband. "Ah, but you do not yet believe me. Allow me to show you instead."

She waved her hand and somewhere in the darkness a horn began to blow.

No, not a horn; a conch. The noise was ghastly, a deep, bellowing, discordant blast of unnatural power. The lights in the room pulsed eye-searingly bright for the duration of that eldritch note, and then dropped to utter darkness.

The cluster of prisoners, or human sacrifices, or whatever they were, dropped to their knees instantly, prostrating themselves on the sands.

The water began to froth and surge.

"No. No. *No. Nononono*—" I don't know which soldier it was that spoke, but I knew that I agreed.

The video footage flickered, becoming static-laced and unclear. Even so, I could make out the writhing mass rising from the waves. The camera was moving backwards, the soldiers scrambling away with little in the way of military discipline. It gave me a view of the creatures slumping their way up the sands that I immediately wished I had been denied.

Man-sized, but hunched over like apes, they seemed to hop their way towards Olmstead, surrounding her. Compelled as I was to watch, I still shied away from the detail of these things, making out little more than their pop-eyed stare and strangely glistening skin. They were chattering in a strange, braying cacophony, the noise making me desperately want to cover my ears. And there were hundreds of them, pouring from the surf.

Tom stepped toward Olmstead, rifle gripped in shaking hands. It was then that the horrible creatures brought forward great, oddly carved chests and dropped them onto the sand. Olmstead opened the lids, one by one. It was impossible to make out what the contents were through the static-obscured footage, but by the reaction of my husband, it was easy to guess.

"Jesus Christ," Hank's voice whispered.

"All of this and more can be yours," Olmstead whispered. "All of this and so much more,"

"W-what else?" Tom was visibly shaking as his eyes flicked back and forth between the treasure and the monsters that had brought it; the gun fell from his hands to the sand, unnoticed.

"*Immortality*," Olmstead whispered, "for your children and their children, for all eternity.

"For our children?" Leo this time. He too stepped into frame, hands outstretched, voice cracking.

"The Deep Ones have cities hidden all over the world. Modern times have not been kind to them, and so they seek to bargain with those with some manner of power." She smiled. "Those like you."

"Help them. Kill for them. Breed with them." She ticked each point off on her fingers, one by one. "And you will have wealth and power beyond your understanding."

The croaking got louder. Something larger seemed to shift in the dark, towering above the mass of Deep Ones crowding the beach. Blood filled my mouth as I bit down hard upon my tongue at that movement, knowing that to see any more of whatever that *thing* was would be to be driven utterly mad.

"Do these things and you will have children, thousands of

progeny, all of them coming of age and living forever beneath the sea, free of the weakness of failing humanity."

"W-what…" Tom seemed to be struggling, his mind fracturing from the sight before him. Every part of my mind was screaming for him to run away, to pick up his gun and shoot. "W-what would we have to do?"

"As I already said," Olmstead's smile glistened, her eyes unblinking. The stone atop her staff pulsed and seemed to suck the light from the footage, causing it to dim to a dirty grey. "Help them. Kill for them. Breed with them. Give to them yourselves and your kin, and they will give to you in kind."

My husband appeared to close his eyes as he leant down and lifted his rifle from the sand. I closed my eyes and sobbed. I could not bring myself to watch as my husband murdered hundreds of people.

"They sacrificed themselves willingly, Steph," I felt Tom's hand on mine.

"*You* sacrificed them willingly," I spat, recoiling from his touch.

"You saw what I saw," his voice cracked as he said it.

My head ached, my brain shying away from what I had seen lurking in the darkness of the footage. I could not imagine what it might have been like to witness that in person.

"And you heard what I heard."

"Glorious Pha-z'ph, the City of Ebony Coral, has lain almost entirely dormant off this coast for thousands of years," Olmstead's hand gestured in the direction of the harbour, "Now, through your husband and his brave men, the city has now received its first sacrifices in millennia."

"And how is that supposed to make me feel?" My voice rose in pitch, near hysterical.

"Forget that part," Tom interrupted before Olmstead could reply, a brittle smile on his face. "Think what this means for us; for our family."

I stared at him blankly.

"That bracelet I gave you," he pointed to the ugly lump of gold perched on my wrist. "Where do you think that came from?

We have thousands of them. *Thousands*."

"Money?" I almost laughed. "You think money matters to me compared to what you have done?"

"Not just money, Steph." The smile disappeared. "Power. Real power."

"I don't care about power, Tom."

"Doctor Olmstead says that they know things, ways to heal even the worst illness or injury. We could have more children, Steph, just like we always wanted, children who could live forever. Hell, *we* could live forever, and Jon and Danielle as well, and their kids, and their kids after them."

"The Deep Ones have ways, Stephanie," Olmstead spoke reverently, leaning forward to rest her hand on my wrist. "Imagine living forever, surrounded by countless generations of family, never wanting for anything."

I don't know what it was, but there was *something* there; something that appealed in a way no promises of power or wealth could have.

"Tom," I whispered, the ghost of a smile on my face.

"Steph," he smiled back as I leant toward him, my arms encircling his waist. "I love you," he held me close, squeezing me tight.

"I love you, too." My hands shifted against his back as I looked up at him. His eyes were still slightly glazed, but he looked almost deliriously happy.

"I am glad you have come to the correct conclusions, Stephanie." Olmstead watched on, eyes boring into me. "I had my concerns about your ability to accept your husband's path."

I ignored her as I held Tom's gaze. After a long moment the smile slid from his face. Even in his current broken state, he knew me well enough to see.

"Steph…"

I finished sliding the bullet I had snatched from the floor of the corridor into the cylinder and snapped it back into place. I drew the revolver from my husband's belt and brought it up, pushing away from him as I did so.

"I love you, Tom, but this isn't you." He was frozen, staring at me with his mouth hanging open. Olmstead had thrown herself out of her chair the moment the gun had appeared in my hand, running for the corridor.

"Steph, don't, please,"

"You need to wake up, Tom." I smiled, sadly. "You need to wake up, and as hard as I tried, I wasn't able to wake you."

He reached a hand toward me, pleading.

"Wake up from this nightmare, Tom. If not for you, then for our kids." I placed the barrel of the revolver against my temple, my hands shaking as visions of the Deep Ones inserted themselves into my thoughts once more. "Before it is too late."

I pulled the trigger.

DEPTH LURKER

GEOFF BROWN

Madness is the seed of knowledge; of that I am certain. I am obviously insane, but at the same time I know the truth. I know that we are but specks, less than motes in the eye of those great forces that move and slither through the many realities, immaterial in the plans of the cosmos. We swagger through life, unaware of how little consequence we hold. This is both a blessing and a curse.

I know too much, have seen too much.

I know the truth, yet it is so fantastic that if I were to tell anyone, I would be declared as insane as I truly must be. I would end up in an asylum, shaven-headed and classified for life. The truth, as it exists, denies all plausibility, all the natural laws as we believe them to be. It screams of madness and the existence of the impossible. It is utterly without reason, and I am aware of it in its entirety.

Victoria Hill, Sandhurst Town. The place it all began. The year was 1889, the area was full of gold, and the Bandersnatch Mine had just reached the depth of nearly four thousand feet. It was well on its way to becoming the deepest gold mine in the world. It lay near the Little 180 Mine, famously owned and operated by George Lansell's family.

My name is George Carlyon, and I was the foreman at the Victoria Hill Mine site. Now, after a lifetime of knowing nothing else, I have no desire to ever work in the mines again. Now, even a ditch is too deep for me.

When the Bandersnatch collapsed, amidst clouds of dust and a roar unlike anything I had ever heard, we thought it was the end of the world. For myself, it was the end of the world as I knew it. I cringe in the dark at the thought of where the event would lead me; the knowledge, the awareness of true reality; the awareness of true evil

I remember the day the Bandersnatch fell. The roar was like the end of the world. I'm sure it was heard all the way to Melbourne. I felt the earth shake as though The Trump and The Shout had finally arrived. For me, it may have well been the apocalypse, as it was the beginning of the end of my sanity.

Cold, windy, and dismal, it was more wintery than any winter's day I had seen, even in Sandhurst. It was barely half six in the morn, yet the surface miners, those who sought alluvial gold, had already left their shanties and moved to their own special areas on the creeks, panning madly to gain that elusive fortune.

Before I left the Goldmines Hotel, where the company kept me a room, I had partaken of a drop of whisky to stave off the chill. I felt slightly light-headed as I walked casually up the hill toward the mine entrance. I was within sight of the new diggings when an earth-shattering *boom* threw me to the ground. I thought I was having a conniption until I noticed other men around me trying to clamber back to their feet.

What the blazes was that? I thought.

The massive cloud of dust alerted me to the disaster that had just taken place at the top of Victoria Hill. People scrambled toward the source of the dust cloud, so I gathered myself from the ground and followed. Screams filled the air. The alert bell started to ring, heading toward ten to signal an accident. I knew deep inside that it would go past ten and hit fifteen, signalling a serious disaster. I knew because even though the dust cloud was thick, I should still have been able to see the poppet head, the wood-frame tower that stands above the shaft.

"It's gone down, it's gone down," someone screamed. "Bandersnatch has gone down."

The head of the morning shift staggered down the hill toward me, covered in dust and blood. I ran toward him.

"William. *William*! What happened?" I yelled. "What's happened to the mine?"

"Cave in," he managed to gasp as I drew near him. "The night shift didn't make it out."

"Get someone to contact the company," I said. "We need to start digging now, see if anyone is left alive."

"No-one survived that blast," William said. "Mark my words, no one will get out of that one alive."

"We still have to try, Will," I said. "We have to try."

"I know we do, sir," he replied sadly, his head hung low. He tried to rub his face clear of dust, but only managed to smear it further.

I grabbed Will by the arm and marched us both to the mine office. By now, the managers had started to gather, and the emergency crew had formed up outside, equipment ready.

"Let's get the poor buggers out," I yelled to the gathered men. "We need to do this quick, before they run out of air."

Harry Somers, the leader of the rescue crew, stepped forward. "We'll drill a hole down, until we strike open space, and put a hose through. With luck, it gets them enough air. After that blast, though, I don't expect much chance of them making it out."

I called the men to gather their equipment. "Follow me," I said. "Let's make this quick. I don't want no one dyin' on my watch if I can help it."

The rescue party grabbed shovels and such. If the covering dirt was more than ten feet, we'd have to dig fast. If it was more than fifty, we had no hope at all. The mob made its way up the hill to the Bandersnatch, through the dust cloud that was billowing forth. People stood around in a daze, staring at the remains of the now-collapsed poppet-head.

"Move aside, move aside," yelled Harry. "Get out of the damn way, you scurries."

As they neared the remains of the mine, I could see that the above-ground structure leant heavily to one side. The thick wooden posts that made up the framework of the poppet-head had sagged and fractured as the ground underneath sank. It would all have to come down before they could even attempt to dig down to the trapped men. Unless…

"William," I said, "can we dig across to the shaft from the side?"

William turned to me, speculation heavy in his eyes. "Yes, I think it can be done. 'Twould save time, too." He turned to the rest of the miners who would do the excavation work. "You lot, over the side of the gully. Now. It's only ten yards in to get to the shaft, and it should be low enough to pass most of the collapsed area."

The men ran over to a ridge of quartz that poked out of the ground, the edge of the reef Bandersnatch cut down into. The drop-off on the other side was a tiny valley thirty feet deep. *Low enough*, I thought, *to cut past the main collapse and possibly intersect with the mineshaft below the collapse to stage a rescue.*

It took nearly five hours to cut through the compacted earth and tap into the shaft of the mine. Five hours of darkness and fear for the men still down below. It was just past noon when we finally broke through into empty space. The men doing the digging turned away, choking and complaining about the smell. I was at the back, helping to scoop out the earth loosened by picks. At the news that the shaft had been reached, I dropped my shovel and struggled through the still-settling dust from the excavations. I noticed the smell myself as I drew closer to the breach.

"Careful there," said one of the other workers. "The edge is a bit unstable yet."

"I'll be fine," I said as I edged closer, the smell now almost over-powering. It reeked of earth and rotten flesh, and, surprisingly, a smell I knew well from my childhood. When I was younger, I used to love going down to the local dam to catch frogs and toads in a jar. I knew their stale, slimy odour well, and now I smelt it once again. In such a context it was mildly disconcerting.

The breach into the main shaft was big enough to move through, but the men had to take great care, as the ropes leading down to the ore buckets may not have remained in place after the cave-in. I moved back out of the newly cut tunnel and emerged to find the rescue team gathered around a pile of the oxygen tanks used deep underground when gasses could be a problem. Leather smocks, designed to be worn over clothing, lay in piles nearby. I found William standing nearby, directing the rescue effort.

"Five men," I said to him.

William turned to me. "Five?" he asked.

"Just five," I replied. "I don't want to risk too many more people until we know for sure what we'll find. There may be no survivors. Prepare a second team, though, perhaps thirty or so, and come down to Level Eleven. Wait there."

"I hope you're wrong, George." William turned back to the men sorting out the equipment.

"One thing, William," I said. "I'm going down as well."

"Are you sure, George?"

"I am," I replied. "Those men are my responsibility. Get Somers to arrange the main rescue party."

"You're the boss," said William.

Ten minutes later we were ready to enter the mine. We all wore leather smocks, and each had a small, square cage tied to our belts, about the size of a leather-bound Bible. In each cage was a canary, to ensure we were aware if the air grew too low in oxygen. On our backs were the air tanks, two woven hoses hung over our shoulders and down our front to join the facemasks. We made a professional-looking group, ready to save the lives of any surviving miners. There were over forty men down there, some possibly still breathing. Most likely not. Still, we owed it to the families of the lost miners to at least try to rescue any survivors.

Thanks be to God, the pulley cables still descended from the head of the mine, stretching down into the depths. We would need to climb down more than a hundred yards before we reached a safer place from which to descend further. At last report, the majority of the trapped miners had been working at the full depth of the mine—four thousand feet under the earth. I tried to avoid thinking about that.

We tied off some safety ropes and started down a cable, one after the other. The lead man, Jones, had his lamp lit, and the rest of us followed the yellow flare into the dark shaft. We belayed down two levels, suffering long minutes of cold-sweat terror. Down to the second level cross tunnel, where there was access to a hand-driven elevator. One by one, we swung over to the ledge leading into the second level. Outside the light from Jones' lamp, darkness encased us. The rest of us lit our lamps, each casting more shadow than light. A small, bright flame hung above the tip of each spout, burning acetylene from the reaction of water and carbide within the bodies of the lamps.

The five of us stood there for a second; Jones, Spooner, Hartnett, Barries, and myself. The small, rough tunnel surrounded us; behind us the shaft we had followed thus far, ahead of us the constricted and rock-filled way forward. Wooden supports held up the ceiling, and the floor held uncertain footing and loads of scree between the rails designed for mine-carts. In the light, veins of quartz flared white over the walls, like scribble from a mad child-god, placed at the dawn of time. At least we could walk upright, a benefit of being in the main tunnel. Once we moved deeper, that benefit would soon disappear.

We struggled in single file for what felt like an hour but could only have been ten minutes before we came across the barriers erected over a secondary shaft leading further into the earth. There were two small elevator cages, side by side, with a chain ladder descending next to them. The cages themselves were merely metal platforms with barriers around three sides, leaving the fourth open. I pulled a map from my pocket and checked. This was where we needed to be. This shaft dropped another thousand yards, cutting through the next eight layers and leading to Level Eleven. Once there, we could criss-cross through a series of smaller shafts that eventually led down to the very bottom of the mine.

The smell of toads seemed stronger here.

"Jones, do you smell that?" I asked.

"Aye, George. I do. Never smelt nought like that in the mines before."

"Keep an eye on the birds," I said. "We can't afford to get gassed."

"I am. They seem fine, if a little flighty," Jones said. "Normally they settle a bit once they get used to being in the mine."

I grunted and turned to study the elevator cage. It was just big enough for two men, so we'd have to make three trips to get us all down to the eleventh level.

"Harnett, Barries. You two go first. Signal for slow."

The two men nodded and grunted. They stepped into the cage and signalled the winder-room on the surface to lower the cage they were in. With a jerk or two, they started descending. The steam-powered winder was steady enough under a good hand, and only the best worked at Victoria Hill. Five minutes later the well-oiled steel cable gave a jerk, then smoothed out.

"What was that?" I asked, looking at Jones and Spooner.

"No idea, George," Jones replied.

"Who's on the winder today?" asked Spooner. "Is it Samuels?"

"It is," I replied.

"Well, he's the best one, in't he?" said Spooner. "No one better in any of the goldfields, I'd dare say."

Just as Spooner uttered the words, the cable shrieked and groaned, and then seemed to stretch. With a nasty *twang*, it snapped, just below our level. The remaining length whipped up and lashed Spooner, taking his head off with the ease of a giant razor. Blood flew, splattering all over me, and the rock wall behind. I don't know if I screamed, or blacked out, or merely lost my mind for a second, but the next thing I knew Jones was slapping my face.

"Snap out of it, George. Come on," he yelled at me, spittle flying into my face with each word.

"Wha...what happened?" I managed to slur.

"Cable snapped. Spooner's dead, and so are the other two. I heard the cage fall. It went all the way down."

"How could that happen?" I struggled to stand, still dizzy from the shock of it all.

"I don't know, but it did. I can only guess the mess it is up there, everyone running around wondering what happened."

"I should be there," I said. "I'm the mine manager. I should be there."

"Get a grip, man," said Jones. "Somers has got it under control, I tell you. He's the man for the job. We should be here. We're both trained in first aid, and can maybe make a difference if there are any survivors. We can at least get them to the eleventh level, ready for the main rescue party."

"We're just two men," I said. "You don't think there are any left alive, do you?"

"I'm sorry, but no. I think they're all dead and we're on a fool's errand, but I don't see what else we can do," said Jones.

"We'll have to take the ladder, you know," I stated. "No choice now."

We both turned to look at the chain ladder leading down the shaft into darkness. As we did, the smell we'd come across earlier strengthened, becoming almost noxious.

"What the blazes *is* that?" I asked.

Before Jones could answer, there came an odd sound. A long, low groan that built in volume until it was almost deafening, rising in pitch until eventually it just stopped, leaving behind an absence of sound I hadn't noticed previously.

"The question is," said Jones, "what the hell was *that*? And did it come from the shaft that leads down?"

We looked at each other, unable to answer either question.

An hour later, we were halfway down the shaft, clinging precariously to the chain ladder that led into the depths of the earth. We'd had to leave the breathers up top. There was no way we could climb down wearing those tanks on our backs. The sweat poured off me, making my grip more precarious by the minute. It took nearly three hours of climbing, interspersed with a rest at each level we passed, to make it down to Level Eleven. The shaft we'd been descending came to an end, the ladder swinging a foot above the rock floor. We jumped down, Jones first. A second later, I hit the floor beside him.

"Done it, Jonesy," I said, unhooking the lamp from my belt and placing it on the ground.

Jones looked disturbed, and it only took me a second to realise why. Where was the damn elevator cage that had fallen, taking two men to their deaths? I looked at the base of the shaft. All the signs of impact were there, but nothing remained of the cage itself. The floor showed the signs of a heavy impact: deep gashes cut into the rock, roughly the size of the cage floor; scrapes where the collapsed steel had impacted afterward, but not as deep as the initial gouges; dark stains on the rock that could only be blood from the two men. Alongside these marks, I noticed more gouges where the entire thing had been dragged away.

My head spun. All around the chamber, exits led off into inky-black tunnels, untouched by the light of the sun. As I took in the sights of the round elevator room, I noticed signs of a mining party: picks and hand-drills; a compressor over against the far wall, joined to the drills by cloth hoses. I also saw, to my horror, lumps of flesh that may have once been human. More blood-black in the current sputtering light from the bucket lamps spattered the walls of the chamber. I turned to Jones as he spoke.

"Something wrong here, George," said Jones. "Something very wrong indeed."

I opened my mouth to answer when that same shuddering cry we'd heard earlier burst out of the surrounding tunnels. It seemed to come from several different directions at once. I was unsure whether it was from one source, and the divergence was a trick of echoes, or whether it came from several different directions. Jones crouched, looking around in terror, and I couldn't blame him. The cry was ululating and unnerving, seeming impossible for a human throat. What the hell was it?

A clatter erupted from one of the tunnels, drawing our eyes as a figure stumbled out. A man—a miner—a survivor!

"Help…help me…" he stuttered as he approached, arms outstretched, beseeching.

I moved to him at once, Jones just behind me. I grabbed him by the arm, holding him upright. His face was a mess, covered in mine-dust and blood. A wound on his forehead, just below the hairline, explained the blood over his face and shoulders, but nothing explained the fear and madness in his eyes.

"Easy, man, easy," I said as I dragged him back into the light near the central shaft. I recognised him as one of the night shift. "What happened down here, Harper?"

"They came out of the tunnels, mate...they came for us all..." Harper shuddered.

He shook even more, eyes glazing and rolling back in his head as he muttered in some foreign language.

"...*fhtagn*...wait for it...the boundary...the boundary, man. *Ftaghugrah'n*...the lost one...Run for it, men...run for your lives!"

I couldn't make any sense of his words, and judging by Jones' face, neither could he. I laid Harper on the ground and drew a water canister from my belt. I poured a trickle over his face, hoping to revive him enough to find out what had happened. His eyes opened, and focused in fear on something behind me. I whirled to see two figures standing in one of the tunnels, staring at us. Chinese, I realised from their clothes, the ornate gold and red line work standing out even in the little light that reached them.

"Who's that?" I asked, reaching to raise the lamp.

"*Throd as uln*," one said.

"What?" I asked. I had some experience of their native language, and this sounded nothing like it.

"*Tharanak-yar*," the other said. "His time has come, as promised."

"What are you on about, man? Forget what you're doing. We need help here. Are you part of the night crew?" I asked.

"There is no more night crew," one of the Chinese said. "He is the last." He gestured at the man I held up. "You all must come, as blood offering. To become one with *Tsathoggua*."

"What the hell are you on about?" I asked. "What is this rubbish? Just get over here and help me. We need to get to the main shaft and signal that there are survivors."

As the two Chinese came into the light, I could tell that something was wrong with them. Grey skin. Shrunken eyes, almost hidden within folds of dry flesh. They looked drained, as though something had sucked all the water from their bodies. I gasped, and Harper stiffened. Strange shadows moved in the dark of the tunnel behind the two; inhuman shapes, impossibly tall and broad, with what seemed misshapen and swollen heads.

"*Fm'latgh ebumna*." Strange, bubbling voices carried to my

ears. The already-dark chamber seemed to darken even more, almost shrinking in upon itself. The air chilled, and streaks of light flowed over the rock walls.

The new shadows firmed into shapes that could not be human. Harper collapsed back to the ground. "No, no, no...no more... please," he begged.

The Chinese stepped further into the chamber, smiles on their desiccated faces. "You will all follow now," one said, voice rasping.

Discordant noises came from the tunnel behind the amorphous shapes. Clashes and bangs, the sound of chanting, and slithering noises, as though giant snakes moved over swamp grasses. None of this was possible. Was I hallucinating under the effects of underground gasses?

Harper stood, and took two stumbling steps toward the shaft Jones and I had come down. A shadow reached down from above him and dragged him into the air. I looked up. The roof was wreathed in darkness, but I could make out shapes. Most flowed smoothly over the stone, but two struggled together, one human, and the other...I couldn't make it out clearly, but it seemed to be a giant blob with arms—a lumpy head met a solid, oval body, with no apparent neck. It almost reminded me of a bloated, giant, frog or toad.

The smell, I thought. *The smell from earlier. Frogs.*

I'd forgotten Jones in all this mess, but I snapped my head around to look at him as he leapt at the two Chinese with a yell of defiance, pick in hand and swinging wildly over his head. The head of the tool slammed into the skull of the closest man, stabbing in through an eye socket and spearing out the other side of his face. Jones' momentum and the weight of the metal pick head literally tore the man's face off. Blood splattered, but less than I would have thought. Darker, too. Jones stumbled past the two, unable to check his movement, and something gigantic reached out of the tunnel, past the other shapes. It grabbed him and yanked him out of sight. A second later, a crumpled shape fell beside me; Harper, body torn and ravaged, eyes cloudy and unseeing. Dead.

I was alone. There was no one left but me.

I saw the two Chinese standing there; the one that should be dead showing no signs of dropping. I turned and pelted for the shaft, gasping for air, unable to believe what my own eyes had witnessed. I made it to the shaft without interference, thanks be to God.

I saw a shape land beside me and reach out, but I was not to be stopped. I sprang and grabbed the chain ladder, clambering up as fast as I could. I screamed as I felt rough hands grab at my legs, but I managed to shake them off before whatever it was could get a solid grip. My sight fogged, and my lungs felt empty no matter how much air I sucked in. I climbed that ladder faster than I thought possible, as though running from the Devil himself, and to be truthful, I knew I was.

Keeping an eye below me, I climbed for what felt like years, my body shaking and my thoughts clouded by what I had witnessed. The gas. It must have been some underground gas causing me to see things, I reasoned, but knew that wasn't true. I had seen it all. It was real.

A massive explosion sounded below me, followed by a thunderous rumbling. I knew the shaft had been blown, and I knew it had collapsed. I kept climbing among the rising dust, coughing and choking but desperate to get out of the mine.

I don't know how long I climbed, or when they found me, but I guess I must have reached the top of that shaft at the same time the second rescue team reached the main chamber. It was all a blur of faces and yelling. I was taken to the surface after I told them there were no other survivors.

I spent three weeks in convalescence. I pretended to not remember anything of the event, for I knew they would lock me away if I tried to explain what had truly happened in that mineshaft. The Bandersnatch was never opened again.

Thank God.

One morning, still in the local benevolent asylum, I awoke to a familiar smell. I thought my mind had snapped at last.

I opened my eyes to find three small, emerald-coloured frogs sitting on my bedside table, staring at me. I swept them to the floor, jumped out of bed, and managed to squash two underfoot before the third hopped away beneath the bed. I got down on hands and knees and lifted the sheets to see underneath. I jerked backwards, in shock at the sight that greeted me under there. Hundreds more of the blighters. Large, small, and every size in between. I grabbed the few clothes I had in the closet and ran from the room, still in my nightshirt. I ran from the asylum and never looked back. Later that day, I left Victoria behind me forever.

First, I tried Queensland, but there were too many damnable frogs in that state. I can't stand to be near frogs. Eventually I settled in far northern Western Australia. I drink too much, and I smoke too much. The locals in this tiny town think I'm crazy, and I haven't a friend in the world, but it's dry and it's dusty, and there are no damn frogs.

I hate to say that every now and then, I smell that damned smell. Of recent, it's been getting worse. And then things changed.

This morning, I saw the first frog I'd ever seen in that dry place.

Maybe it's time to move on once more.

THE SEAMOUNTS OF VAALUA TUVA

DAVID KURARIA

If you had travelled to the Solomon Islands that year you would have seen it on all the news feeds—hospitals filled to the car parks with Cordyceps victims, mushroom heads sprouting from their eyes, fruiting bodies dangling down by saliva-slick chins, children screaming on gurneys in reception. It was chaos. That was just the beginning.

For three years I had worked as an underwater rig welder off Australia's West Coast, when I snagged an open position offered by the Australian government. A few years back, the Australian Federal Police and other members of the Australian Defence Forces had formed RAMSI: The Regional Assistance Mission to the Solomon Islands. They were busy with the last straggling band of warlord militias, and also worked helping the indigenous peoples try to build sea walls to protect the lower-lying islands from inundation due to rising sea levels. I was to work with a small group to help police the illegal drag chaining and deep netting of protected habitats around the Solomon Islands. I jumped at the chance to escape the inevitable day when a welding accident thirty metres deep off a platform would claim my life or limb. It happened to the best of us.

I met the other members of my future team in the outer office of one Captain Buckmeister, an officious Navy-lifer, re-stationed from the naval base at Jervis Bay in Australia. I'd been standing alone—feeling stupid and trying to look inconspicuous—when

I felt someone step up next to me. I said nothing, but turned to look into eyes level with mine. She was tall, with smooth, light brown skin, showing small surgery scars around her collarbone. Lean and muscular, her black hair was shaved with a number two on the clippers. For some reason she reminded me of a volleyball player.

"I'm Jenna," she smiled and turned her head slightly to nod in the direction of a big guy studying a wall map of the Solomons. He turned and glanced at us, before turning back to the map, feigning nonchalance, but I could tell he was taking everything in. I'd seen that look out on the rigs, just before some bloke would put down his coffee and take out half the kitchen staff because they'd overdone his eggs. The man left the map, grinned back at us, and came over.

"Hey people, I'm Kerosene, Parks and Wildlife, South Australia — surfing represent."

He was wide for his height, like a rugby halfback, with the yellow-white hair of a surfer. He turned to Jenna: "Hey there you."

Jenna laughed and it sounded great. She reached out and forced this guy to take her hand. At once I could tell he was impressed with her grip.

"Sup, Kerosene?" she shot back.

He grinned and pumped Jenna's hand before letting go.

"Just Kero will do." He turned to me. "So, you're Rhys?"

"That's right."

"I was told to find you two here. It looks like we're going to be hangin' together for a bit."

I shook his hand. "Good to meet you. I see they have a staff shortage. Now they're bringing in civilians to help out about the place."

Kero gave a nasal snort. "Yeah, we're doing their old job. Those guys are more concerned with helping the government sort out rights to the gold these days. It's worth billions and there's shit loads of the stuff under a lot of the islands."

Jenna watched him. "Wouldn't that gold belong to the Solomon peoples?"

Kero scoffed. "Not if they're annexed. You get the major player in the South Pacific coming here with hundreds of millions of dollars in aid, Feds, the Defence Force and mining interests? Well, in ten years Solomon Islanders are going to be straight-up Australians. As for the gold—mining machinery is huge—little islands built on coral are an engineer's bad dream, but they'll find a way. You watch. The take-over is happening now."

I was sure it was going to be easy to get on with Kero; one cynic recognises another. A subordinate came out of Buckmeister's office and ushered us in. Once we were seated the Captain got down to business.

"Well, you already know what you are here for. I'll give you all the equipment I think you need, so I expect you to do your job and not come running to me with any little pissant problem you may come across."

He turned to me. "Rhys, I see from your papers, that you've been a professional fisherman in your time." He picked up a pen and began clicking the nib button up and down.

"Yeah, I worked around the rivers, mud-crabbing up New Guinea way a few years ago. Lost some good mates. Left a bad taste in my mouth."

He kept clicking that pen. "So now you're on the other side of the fence—conservation."

I wondered where this was going. "That's right."

Buckmeister nodded, looking unimpressed, all the while clicking that pen. "How old are you, forty? And still a diver? I'd have thought at your age...ahh never mind."

He paused, and then started up again, slowly, glaring at us. "I have to warn you, there's a medical condition spreading in the outer Western Chain. It seems there is a problem with children biting people. For reasons we don't know yet, the kids' saliva has been found to contain a shit-eating, disease-carrying enzyme. The toxicologist out on Gizo said it's some kind of neurotoxin. Now we have this goddamned biting going on, so you people are going to have to stay alert and keep a log book."

I wanted to ask if I could use his pen, just so he would stop clicking the damned thing. Buckmeister looked at each of us in turn, and that look said it all. He did not trust civilians.

"The kids out in Gizo hospital are frothing at the mouth," he continued. "They're deranged, trying to bite the staff. What a goddamned fiasco." The clicking of his pen was rapid. "There are nine hundred islands under our jurisdiction and we can't be everywhere. When you are in the field, I want you to keep an eye out for a bunch of folk called the Kõpura, who are coming in numbers aboard big-sailed outriggers. They seem to be taking advantage of the locals. I don't know what they want, but I don't want the bastards here. Apparently there's a woman who gives the orders—Pecan, or whatever the hell her name is. Some of these Kõpura women have been caught giving local kids a drink of something, and we think it is connected with the biting. If you lot see her or her cohorts skulking out past Ranongga or Imora, that will be the only time I'll want to hear from you. You'll get another shot from the doc on Gizo."

I was relieved when he finally threw his pen onto the desk. He handed me a sheet of paper with some instructions, a palm GPS, and a printout of a detailed map of the outer islands, then he glared at the ceiling, sighed and shook his head. "Goddamnit, as if I don't have enough on my plate already, now I've got my people helping shore up islands from sea inundation in the east, and out west I've got goddamned tsunamis and earthquakes and new islands rising out of the sea. I'm short-staffed and they send me civilians and geriatric divers. Ahh, hell." He looked at Jenna and nodded at Kero and me. "Just keep safe. Hit the local tarmac. I'll fit you three onto one of my flights in the next few hours. Your gear should be waiting for you at the Gizo docks, and they'll tell you where to go from there." He stood and we knew it was time to leave.

"So how come they call you Kerosene?"

We were at Honiara airport putting our gear on a plane for the trip out. Kero threw a bulky canvas sack up to the guy in the cargo hold and barked a short laugh. "My home brew vodka keeps exploding. Gotta get the formula right one day."

I looked at Jenna. She shook her head and led the way to the plane's entry stairs.

During the short flight to Gizo I looked out of the window, onto the scattered islands looking like so many heads of broccoli bobbing in a blue sea, and thought about how isolated we would be in the outer islands. I was glad that my companions looked capable of handling themselves. That would be useful once we got west of Ranongga Island, beyond Gizo, where we were to rebuild a broken down hut and put up a shower for our base.

First, though, we stopped at Gizo's well-equipped hospital and went to get our inoculations. On the way through reception, I tried not to stare at the people on stretchers crying in pain, but it was hard to ignore those freakish facial growths—especially at first sight. After locating the doctor's office where we were to receive our shots, I left Jenna and Kero briefly, wanting to find out more about exactly what we were letting ourselves in for. I cornered the toxicologist in his office after bluffing my way in. I told him who I was and who had sent me. He told me what to expect if a child bit us.

"When this enzyme enters the bloodstream it produces a fungus called Cordyceps, a parasitical growth which sprouts in 'bunches' from the skin. In insects such as ants and beetles, it actually pierces the skull from the inside, driving the insect insane. I've never heard of it inhabiting human hosts before now. We have traced it back to the saliva of children who have been infected with a rare cone shell neurotoxin—lethal for anyone unfortunate enough to be pierced, and very toxic when taken as a small amount orally. We still don't know who is feeding these kids this stuff. Anyway, you have to watch yourself out there. Don't get bitten. I would rather you don't go at all, but I understand you have a job to do."

Now seriously concerned, I sought refuge with the others back at the doctor's waiting room. Jenna had already been jabbed, and Kerosene walked out of the office rubbing his arm as I arrived, so it wasn't long before I was called up. Seeking more info, I told the doctor what the toxicologist had passed on. She didn't seem surprised and took this as a sign to educate me.

"Mr Rhys, this Cordyceps gives off its own enzyme, producing a rare condition called Urbach-Wiethe disease." The doctor swabbed my arm and inoculated me casually, then recapped the needle and threw it into a hazard bin. I rubbed my arm. She cleaned her hands.

"Urbach causes skin lesions, and the build-up of calcium deposits on the brain destroys part of the amygdala," she pointed to the base of my neck, "here. The amygdala processes emotions, particularly fear. You may have heard of the 'fight or flight' response? That's the amygdala. But it doesn't just deal with immediate threats. It also manages the smaller signs which curb our social behaviour and keep us safe, such as the ability to read cues in facial expressions."

I raised my eyebrows to indicate that the conversation may be about to breach the limits of my own brain's capacity. She seemed to understand.

"You see, a normal brain can recognise joy, pain, or sadness with barely a second thought, it's kind of automatic, but when the amygdala shuts down, a person not only can't recognise fear or danger, for example, in some cases they can't even *experience* it. Does that make sense?"

I shook my head.

The doctor shrugged as if dismissing a wayward student. "Look, my patients are stacking up. Our *Doctors Without Borders* staff are being treated for stress. All I am asking is for you and your colleagues to be extra-aware of what is happening around you, okay? When you are in the field be wary of all physical contact with people, especially the children."

That much, I already understood.

At the docks we hooked up with some Navy personnel and told them Buckmeister had sent us. Their expressions said everything. They set to helping us without delay. They showed us to a six-metre runabout that had a small cabin and an Evinrude 120 outboard motor, with a few spare jerry cans of fuel on board. It was ours, they said. We were loaded up with axes, shovels, hammers and a machete, plus a crate-load of canned food and drink. We were to head to Imora, an uninhabited teardrop-shaped speck that was five hundred metres wide by a kilometre long on the edge of the Solomon Deep. Though I'd never been there before in person, this was familiar territory to me. Solomon Deep sunk to seven thousand metres, while the long, wide Planet Deep goes more than nine thousand metres down to the sea floor—one of the deepest known places on earth.

From Gizo we headed west across the Gizo Strait, south of Vella Lavella Island and around the northern tip of Ranongga. Passing Ranongga we saw the surround of raised coral, now bleached and dead under the sun. Scientists had flocked here after the 2007 eight-point-one earthquake, when Ranongga was raised three metres leaving the coral reefs around the island exposed. Now, in the shallows, we could see coral-encrusted planes and sunken boats from the WWII Pacific Campaign. It was a reminder that the island chain hasn't changed much since the US landed and ousted the Japanese in 1942. The western group that borders the Solomon Sea has several hundred small islands. Out there justice falls only to local communities and village chiefs.

After many hours and with the help of the GPS and a refill from one of the jerry cans, we arrived at tiny Imora. We hauled our gear ashore: axes, shovels, diving equipment, food supplies, and our backpacks.

Together we set to making our camp using discarded poles from the back yard of an abandoned shack. We plaited Sago palm for the roof, and as the locals did, made palm raincoats to protect ourselves from the daily downpours.

It was during a break from getting the campsite built and putting our gear under the still partially-built roof when Jenna told me about some of her ancestors who had settled in the Solomons back in the nineteenth century. Jenna was part Pacific Islander—Tokonu blood—and had been born in Port Moresby over in Papua. She knew the waters bordering the Solomon Sea well, and had had a few run-ins with illegal boats deep netting the protected seamounts in the area. She took a big knife from her carry sack and strapped it to her waist. It was not long before I realised she was an accomplished scuba diver; she knew how to fillet a fish and dive for shellfish and pry it off the rocks. She said she was bought up in Papua killing and skinning wild boars. I found it easy to believe.

We started a small fire on the beach down from the hut so we could cook some of the fish Kero had speared. Kero, however, was in no mood for a story.

"I'm gonna check the waves, have a bit of a body surf." He put some cooked fillets in a piece of palm leaf and left us. Jenna and I settled on the sand with our fillets on the end of a stick.

"A few of my ancestors joined a group of Kanakas—South Sea Islanders—who were shipped to the Queensland cane fields in the 1890s. They were taken on as day workers, on the promise of good food, good hours and comfortable beds. They got nothing they were promised. The rest of the world was already abolishing slavery, but Australians were still going hard at it—of course they didn't call it slavery."

I wondered if this was a rebuke and she was trying to shame me, but as she continued her story I realised there was no malice in it. In fact, she seemed quite distant from what she was actually saying.

"It was during this time when people started to see the Kōpura again—they're the people Buckmeister wants us to watch for. The locals round these parts call them The Blistered Ones, on account of their skin pigmentation. I've been close to them many times. They came to my home in Tokonu before moving on to here in their outriggers. Local oral traditions have it that they originated from far out in the Solomon Sea, at a place called Vaalua Tuva. Every time there is a conflict or a catastrophe, such as an earthquake or a tsunami, the Kōpura would arrive. It is rumoured they kidnap people. Many here do actually go missing; but these are mainly put down to fishing accidents at sea."

She seemed to drift for a moment then, long enough for me to wonder if she, too, had lost someone close to her, but before I could ask she continued.

"They came again during the chaos of the Pacific war. Before that, Catholic missionaries were talking about them back in the nineteenth century, writing about how the Kõpura came and claimed land that was not theirs, even forcing frightened locals to live out of their canoes, to sit it out and wait for the Kõpura to return to where they came from. And that is the problem: to this day no locals know where the Kõpura call 'home'. "

Jenna finished her fish and drank some water from one of the plastic bottles we had bought along. The sun was low in the west, an orange ball that lit the wave tops of the sea. I stared at a seashell between my feet. Jenna wiped her mouth.

"The Kõpura men don't say much. Mostly they sit in groups waiting for whatever it is their women have to do. The women can be creeps, playing with local kids when their parents aren't around. If some local mother ever caught one of these women with her child, she would start shouting and drag the kid away. The locals never speak to the visitors, they don't even look directly at them."

I remembered what Buckmeister had mentioned regarding a woman who was supposed to be a leader.

"What about this leader—what's her name—Peequad?"

Jenna grinned. "She's called Pecan. There's been talk that her skin is the brown of Melanesians but her features—her nose and forehead—are Caucasian. Pecan must be in her seventies by now. They all wear volcanic obsidian plugs in their ear lobes and as flesh inserts on their foreheads," she used her knife to scrape fish bones from the sand into the fire. "The women's throats are mottled with big freckles, only more orderly, with stripes running from under their ears down to their breasts. The men have scarred foreheads, running V-shaped from the hairline to the nose-bridge. They wear western clothes—shorts and shirts—clean, but ragged and faded as if each person has only one set. What's weird is you never see them with weapons or tools for harvesting or fishing. The women are friendly enough, but they have no sense of personal space and it can make you uncomfortable. You know when they are close, even before you see them. It's as if they are concentrating so hard you begin thinking of them even before you realise they are close."

The sun had reached the horizon and twilight approached. Somehow this made me more aware of the sound of the small rollers swishing up upon the sand.

I had been diving with Jenna out on Imora shoals next to a big drop-off into the deep. Here were a couple of flat-topped seamounts rising five thousand metres from the seabed to within twenty metres from the surface. Fish and molluscs and king crabs swarmed across these underwater peaks. We had left Kero for the day to mind camp and to finish putting up the temporary shower. We sat in the runabout, the swell rocking us, and unshackled ourselves from our tanks. During our dive we had not seen any sign of recent drag-teething or deep netting, so we packed up our gear and headed back to base. We were only halfway back to Imora when we met two Solomon men in an outboard runabout. They came alongside and kept their motor running. One of them shouted at us in the local Ganongga language. They looked furious. They spoke in halting English.

"Your friend has done a bad thing," they shouted. "He has been with Kōpura women!" Then, with hateful stares at Jenna, and me, they spat out more words in their own language. Jenna's eyes told me she understood. They steered their boat eastward. I looked at Jenna.

"What did they say?"

"You sleep with animals, you are animal."

Back at Imora, we beached and looked for Kero, but we couldn't find him. He had left his work on our temporary hut unfinished. Jenna could not find any tracks in the sand and we assumed he had gone bush. I knew, by the way we had been treated, that we were in trouble. Kero had been screwing, literally, one of the unwanted strangers. It was a weird night to be on a remote speck of land, with the knowledge something bad was about to go down. The rain started. It pelted down and we were glad that part of the roof of the shack had been finished.

We sat under cover and ate from tins of baked beans and

drank bottled water. Jenna was troubled and rightly so. I spoke what I assumed she was thinking.

"Doesn't he listen to anything being said? What the hell was he thinking?" I moved further back away from the rain slanting in through a sagging driftwood window opening.

"Look, we don't know what went on," Jenna said. "It may be nothing."

I knew she wasn't even convincing herself. "He banged one of them, okay? I get the point. There's going to be some local men here in the morning, beating the crap out of us, isn't there?"

Jenna nodded. "Seems likely. We can't go anywhere in this weather — won't be able to see a thing."

I couldn't argue with her. "Okay, what do we do?"

"When the rain eases, we're out of here."

"Fine," I said. "We still have to take Kero with us."

Jenna growled. "It's a small island, we'll find him."

It was a long night. I was no longer hungry. I found a spot to rest and lay awake for some time listening to the rain smash down onto the weakening plaited roof.

The next morning I was walking along the beach with Jenna as the sun was rising. We saw Kero sitting in the sand. As we approached we saw he had his hands up against his temples, effectively hiding his face. He saw us and croaked out a statement, which sounded muffled, as if his mouth was packed with something. I felt a punch to my shoulder and turned to see Jenna pointing out to sea. I saw the outrigger. Expecting to see some of the locals I was surprised to find that it was one of the big sailed outriggers of the Kōpura. Kero was whining and began rubbing his fingers against the corners of his eyes. I stood on the sand with Jenna, waiting for the Kōpura to walk up onto the beach. They stepped through the waves to stand metres from us. There were a dozen of them, and nearly half were the taciturn men. The group parted to allow a tall woman to walk ahead of them up the beach towards us. I knew I was looking at the one called Pecan.

I looked back down at Kero. He lifted his head and returned my gaze. I stepped back a few paces in shock, bumping into

Jenna. Kero was staring insanely, his head nodding as if he was suffering from Parkinson's. His eyes bulged, as if there was some massive pressure behind them, pushing outwards. His voice was croaky and weak.

"She gave me a drink, Rhys. She gave me a drink."

The Kõpura surrounded us. I found myself unable to move, as if these people had somehow sapped my will to resist. Afraid, I let my shoulders drop as three of the men came to me and took hold of my arms. Jenna too seemed to lose any fight. She spoke a sentence of Ganonggan to several of the women. They ignored her and grabbed her arms—one even took Jenna's knife from its sheath.

Kero was still whining like a thrashed dog. I heard him huff with exertion as he was dragged to his feet. Without a fight from any of us, the Kõpura led us down the beach to the outrigger.

It wasn't until I was actually thrown into the bottom of the craft that I began to fight back. While the women and the rest of the men were standing alongside in the waves, two of the Kõpura, a man and a woman, jumped in and thrust their knees onto my chest. All the wind went out of my lungs. Totally controlled by their grip, they released a little of the pressure, allowing me to breathe. They leaned down close to me, and I noticed two things. First: the carved strips of volcanic glass inlaid into the man's forehead, with old-growth flesh holding them in place; second was how calm these people looked, in spite of their exertions. The man reached down and, with a serene stare, yanked my head up. He held a half shell level and I could tell it was full of something.

The woman kneeling beside me also had obsidian inlays, but hers were small and round, forming broken circles surrounding her big eyes. Calmly, with a half-smile—almost as if she were doing nothing more than ruffling a child's hair—she held my chin and forced me to drink. It all happened so fast that it was some seconds before I recalled what Kero had said on the beach.

"She gave me a drink."

I began to panic, but it was only permitted for a few seconds.

The woman kneeling on my chest held up a spongy thing. I smelled a sickly sweetness, and the sponge was pressed down, covering my face. I struggled in vain for a moment and breathed deeply trying to gasp in oxygen, then I felt myself going under the sweet nectar and my struggles seemed a waste of time, so I gave up and let things happen.

I swam up out of a stupor and became aware I was lying with the lower half of my body along the bottom of the outrigger, my chest resting against the gunwale and my throat and chin over the edge. Without moving my head I saw sand forming a beach. A metre directly below, but a little away from the outrigger I saw a series of flat, interlinked rocks, seeming to form a kind of roadway. I turned my head and looked up the beach along the length of the road, and saw that it sloped gently upwards and in under Sago palms. Then I realised that the same paved road ran past the outrigger down into the water. Turning further I saw it ran downward under the surface until I could no longer see it amid the green depths. It looked like some kind of ancient boat ramp. Yet I wondered why it would need to run so deep. Somehow I was sure there was much more to its length further down, leading into the darkest depths.

I was properly conscious now. I dragged one of my arms up to grab the gunwale and to take the pressure off my throat. Above me I heard seagulls. My eyes began to itch and a pain arched across and behind my eyeballs. Putting my hand over the edge of the outrigger I gripped it and sat up. Seeking the source of pain I touched the edge of my eye, near my temple. There I felt a lump in the outer corner. I must have shouted, because it drew attention to me. The hair on the back of my head was grabbed roughly and another soft sponge was thrust across my face. Again I fell away into sleep.

I woke to the feeling of sun on my face, which would have been pleasant had it not been for the pain behind my eyes. I managed to sit up, and looked upon an earthen floor packed down hard. I glanced about and saw a waist-high stone wall surrounding me. I regained my senses and realised I was in an enclosure that was open to the weather. I could not see over the top of the wall, but noticed the stones fitted together neatly, cleanly, without mortar. I was reminded of the walls in South American Incan towns. To one side there was a gap in the wall the width of a normal doorway. I shifted and heard the clatter of something I had disturbed. I realised I was sitting amid a scattering of bleached white bones, many of which were oddly shaped and twisted. Some had the overall look of ribs, but were deformed. Some femurs and shinbones had growths branching off like a second stunted leg. With rising disgust, I swept my arms about and shoved the nearest ones away. They clacked into each other.

I heard the sigh behind me, a kind of wet gurgling exhalation. Twisting I sucked in a deep breath. It was Kero, lying on his side. I blinked and saw him smile in my direction. Looking closer I realised he was not seeing me. When I leant forward the pain in my head sharpened, causing my eyes to water. Wiping them, I looked and saw that Kero had his hands wrapped in what looked to be bark strips, with the tips of his fingers protruding. With one bark-covered hand he was clumsily playing with something at the corners of his eyes. There were stalks, much like gangly field mushrooms. I sat up and leant back in an effort to get away from him. He had spittle dangling from the corner of his mouth nearest the floor. Deformed white bones lay close to his face. I leaned forward again and saw the fungus growths flop against one of his cheeks when he turned his head to look upwards. He was still obviously not seeing me. I knew I was looking at the fungus, Cordyceps. The stalks exiting from the corners of his eyes were a pinkish grey, and from this were growths looking like sickly baby lettuce with soft curly edges. I felt ill.

Without warning Kero began to cry out. But they were weak calls, again, wet and gurgling, as if his throat was filling with mucous. His cries soon lessened and finally became a soft, laughing, coughing sound. I was exhausted from my treatment and from the time I had been drugged. In spite of my growing fear and the thought of what might happen to us, I could not stay awake. I slept amid the bones.

Days must have passed because my time in the enclosure seemed interminable. Sunlight and darkness came and went many times. I slept most of the time, only waking occasionally to feel a woven piece of bedding across me, or waking to daylight to see nothing but stone wall, white bones, and Kero's back as he lay with his face away from me. I only knew he was still alive because of his irregular, gurgling breaths. One time I awoke with the sounds of screams fading away from some fevered dream, only to find they were continuing as I fully woke. I lay on my side with a plaited palm raincoat covering my shoulders. Still the screams continued in short bursts. Again they were incorporated into my nightmares. Daylight came and went and came. The sun burnt me during those days.

The lethargy left and I sat up for the first time in what seemed ages. I ached and felt pains on my hips. Checking them I found I had pressure sores. Immediately I realised how hungry I was. I felt weak and could hardly hold myself upright. Because of this, dizziness had come over me. Finally I managed to turn to face Kero. He was sitting among the bones, staring as if blind. He was filthy and emaciated. From his eyes and from out of his head grew a massive growth of greenish grey fungus that nodded and flapped against his cheeks as he shook his miserable head. He moaned and lifted his hands to look at them. I saw the bark bandages had been removed. I stared in disbelief. Bloodied and smeared with soil from the floor of the enclosure I saw what had been done to him. I could tell his fingers had been broken, because they were crooked and a couple bent a little backward in a way that would not be possible on a normal hand. But the worst thing was seeing evidence the Kōpura had sewn the fingers of each hand together. My friend now had two crude paddle-like appendages where he should have had hands.

For a moment I lost reason. Then, regaining clarity, I thought of Jenna. But my body was rebelling at its ill treatment. I vomited up some bile into the back of my throat. It stung and I gasped, swallowing the acid. I began to tremble. All the while I sat there in the dirt among the bones, listening to Kero's gurgling mucous and still thinking of Jenna, wondering what horrors she was being subjected to. I realised we were being purposely starved, in order to completely break us.

I did not have long to contemplate all this. I saw a group of the Kōpura leaning across the enclosure wall. They came through the open part of the enclosure, their bark-sandalled feet crunching upon the twisted bones. I was forced to eat a foul-tasting puree. When I saw one of my captors holding a wet sponge, I knew what was about to happen, but was too weak to resist.

I woke on a woven flax mat, which sat upon a grassy expanse, some way up from a beach of sand and shingle. I raised myself and sat and realised I was no longer hungry.

I looked up at a cloudless sky. I lowered my gaze and saw a small bay of turquoise water almost surrounded by two finger-like projections of jungle-draped land spits. Out in the bay, some way from the beach, three big-sailed double outriggers rocked in a light swell. I heard birdcalls sounding from some distance behind me. Palms lined the beach, dividing sand from grass. It was beautiful.

Some distance to my right was a pyramid, ancient, and flat-topped with a walkway of massive steps on the side facing the bay. Much of the structure was under water. I peered with my hand up against my eyes to stop the glare of the sun. I saw the sand had encroached upon the massive lower blocks of the structure and that part lying in the water appeared to reach down into the green depths, and I knew it went down further than I could see. I wondered at the millennia that must have elapsed since its erection, for tectonic plates to move, allowing the ocean to climb this high up the structure.

The sun felt good upon me. I felt strength unfamiliar. It was as if I had eaten a substantial meal. I looked about and upon turning my head I felt something soft brush against my check. Raising my hand I felt the soft edges of the fungus. I did something then, which, a short while ago, I would not have been capable of. I smiled. Again, I touched the growths. To my mind they seemed the most natural thing in the world. I heard a sound behind me, the one place I had not yet looked. Turning upon my flax mat, I saw one of the Kōpura women. She was sitting upon a large rock that looked to have been chiselled to form a seat. While she regarded me, her form shimmered under the glare of the sun. She smiled and I could not make out the shape of her mouth. It altered even as I looked at it. She was topless. I saw the mottling on her breasts flash a different colour—green to brown, to scarlet and back. I blinked and stared stupidly at her. My gaze was drawn back to her face. Her entire head had for a fleeting moment changed shape. For an instant it elongated and took on a light brown colour. And for a second there seemed something familiar, but as well something unearthly about the shape. I stretched open my mouth and worked my jaw. Looking again at the woman's face I caught a glimpse of bright yellow spots ringed by deep blue, flash diagonally up across her face from chin to forehead. It looked like an octopus changing colour.

I sat on the mat feeling confused, looking again at this extraordinary woman who now appeared completely normal. Behind I heard the sound of feet squeaking on hot sand as someone walked towards me. I turned with renewed strength and saw to my astonishment Kero striding purposefully across the sand toward us. I looked at his face and was surprised to see none of the pain and horror I had seen only recently. It occurred to me I had no idea how long ago that had been. His transformation was miraculous. He appeared to be now taller and thinner, but it was still his face. Gone was the fleshy, nodding, grey fungus of the Cordyceps. In its place, circling his eyes, were incisions not yet healed, tracing a V-shape from his forehead down to the bridge of his nose, inside of which sat freshly inlaid shards of volcanic black glass. I stared and wondered how long had elapsed since we had lain in terror amid the bones inside the open stone enclosure.

To my surprise, the man whom I had once known as Kero, looked down at me and smiled faintly, as if he did not recognise me. I could think of nothing to say. But I caught one thing in his look and it was as if he pitied me. Remembering his hands, I looked at them as he passed me and walked towards the Kōpura woman seated on the chiselled boulder. He was swinging his hands by his side as he walked, like a man supremely confident in himself. It was on those swinging hands where I saw the most change. There was no longer any dirt or blood. The hands were clean and there were no fingers. As he strode past me I saw there were no longer any stitches. The skin had grown seamlessly together and all he now had were two thumbs and one seamless expanse of flesh on both hands. I watched his back, and he reached the Kōpura woman, bent down and kissed her on her mouth. She responded enthusiastically, the bare flesh of her arms rippled as if the muscles underneath were tightening and relaxing, bulging with stubby, extended pseudopods looking like a blind worm smelling the air. Colour flashed up and down the lengths—blue, emerald green, red and purple. They stopped kissing and the woman leaned out from behind Kero's shoulder. She smiled and winked at me. She spoke and I recognised the voice.

"Your growths will wither and pain will come and then go. It will be lost and you will no longer care. Your vices will be many and you will feed on the terror of our guests."

It was not what she said, it was who said it. I realised I was looking at Jenna. What had once been Kero, and what had once been Jenna, looked down at me sitting on the mat. It was as if they were thinking of me as a child. Again, I remembered Kero's words on the beach at Imora: "She gave me a drink".

Then I knew. He had been talking about Jenna. She was Kōpura. They had sailed to her home of Tokonu all those years ago and had taken her, changed her. There were those marks across the flesh covering her collarbone—not surgery, but makeup, where her pigmentation had been covered in order for her to walk unsuspected among the Solomon peoples. Even before she had met us, she had been planning our abduction.

I felt no anger at this. Something had been lifted from me, some sense of responsibility for my existence had been removed and there was nothing to ever worry over—others could now make all my decisions. I felt light headed and strangely safe.

In another moment of clarity, I realised it had never mattered that I had not been bitten and had escaped the enzyme from the saliva of infected children. The hospital at Gizo had been harvesting it. That was what was in the syringe when I had my shot. When the doctor had given me the needle and had explained things, she was shutting down my amygdala, by infecting me with Urbach disease. Realisation came to me. Jenna had been sitting in the chair in the waiting room, because she had never needed a shot. The doctors at Gizo, the navy; RAMSI, the entire lot of them were creating a weapon. I laughed at the genius of it all.

I pulled my knees up to my chest and held them together with my arms. I watched my old companions watching me, smiling with their oddly shaped mouths. Colours flashed across Jenna's flesh. She and Kero stood and walked to me, one each side. They held down their hands for me to take and I did so. To my new way of thinking, Kero's surgical enhancements seemed now quite normal.

They led me up the beach towards a group of people waiting for us on the sand. As we got closer, Kero and Jenna let go of my hands. I looked at Jenna in her splendid form and she smiled and nodded to me. I turned and faced those others. I heard them give a collective sigh. I wondered what they might smell like. I knew, of course, that creatures so powerful would smell sweet. I went forward on shaky legs, still a little weakened from my incarceration, but gaining strength with each step. I crossed the expanse of sand and shingle. For a moment their forms jerked in unison, like a faulty hologram. Then, as if a veil had dropped, I was allowed to see beyond, to the true reality that was hidden from humanity. I knew I would soon be seeing things as they really are, and I would gaze upon my brethren and marvel upon their terrible majesty. I laughed and stared in wonder at the sight of the flashing and brilliant colours as their subsurface chromatophores relayed their many emotions. With a happiness I felt would burst out of me, I walked into the arms of my new family.

BIOGRAPHIES
(IN ORDER OF APPEARANCE)

STEVE PROPOSCH, CHRISTOPHER SEQUEIRA & BRYCE STEVENS are the co-editors and creators of the Cthulhu Deep Down Under (CDDU) concept. Their recent decision to collaborate on a rolling series of anthologies under the group moniker 'Horror Australis' reflects their belief that the most exciting opportunities for southern equatorial genre fiction lie ahead. Works by the members of this team in collaboration include co-editing Terror Australis: The Australian Horror and Fantasy Magazine; Bloodsongs magazine (published internationally) and horror comics under the Sequence Publications banner that included contributions by each of them. One further CDDU volume, as well as Cthulhu Land of the Long White Cloud, are set for release in 2018-19.

STEVE SANTIAGO became a fan of all things weird at an early age and that attraction has never stopped. He graduated with a BA in Graphic Design and has over 20 years of experience working as a full-time graphic designer in California. The past few years he has been able to devote most of his time to illustrating and photoshopping covers and interior art for anthologies, magazines, ezines, CD covers, board game art and concept art for a Lovecraftian film. As a freelancer, Steve has created art/designs for clients from as far away as Australia, Germany, Hungary, U.K., and the Netherlands—illustrator-steve.com

ANDREW J. MCKIERNAN was once an award winning writer and illustrator. These days, he mainly just sits on his back porch sipping whiskey and playing the blues—www.andrewmckiernan.com

PETER RAWLIK is the author of more than fifty short stories, the novels *Reanimators*, *The Weird Company*, and *Reanimatrix*, and *The Peaslee Papers*, a chronicle of the distant past, the present, and the far future. As an editor he has produced *The Legacy of the Reanimator* and the forthcoming *Chromatic Court*. His short story *Revenge of the Reanimator* was nominated for a New Pulp Award. He is a regular member of the *Lovecraft Ezine Podcast*, which in 2016 won the *This is Horror* Non-Fiction Podcast of the year award. He is a frequent contributor to the *New York Review of Science Fiction*.

KIRSTYN MCDERMOTT is an Australian author of two award-winning novels, *Madigan Mine* and *Perfections*, as well as a collection of short fiction, *Caution: Contains Small Parts*. Until recently, she produced and co-hosted a literary discussion podcast, *The Writer and the Critic*, and is currently undertaking a creative PhD at Federation University with a research focus on retold fairy tales. She can be found online at www.kirstynmcdermott.com

Over the years **ROBERT HOOD**—once referred to as "Aussie horror's wicked godfather"—has published many short stories in the genres of Horror, SF, Fantasy, Crime and other generally weird mutations of these, appearing in Australian and overseas magazines and anthologies, as well as in several personal collections. He has also written novels, including the award-winning epic fantasy *Fragments of a Broken Land: Valarl Undead* (Wildside Press, 2013). His most recent book is *Peripheral Visions: The Collected Ghost Stories* (IFWG Publishing Australia, 2015), a kaiju-sized tome that won the Australian Shadows Award for Best Collection. Some people believe he long ago disappeared into some dark, chthonian dimension and has been replaced by a number of demonic alter egos. If this is true, only time will tell. His websites can be accessed from www.roberthood.net

LEE MURRAY is a nine-time winner of New Zealand's prestigious Sir Julius Vogel Award for science fiction, fantasy and horror. Her titles include the bestselling military thriller *Into*

the Mist and supernatural crime-noir *Hounds of the Underworld* (co-authored with Dan Rabarts). She is proud to have co-edited eight anthologies, one of which, *Baby Teeth*, won her an Australian Shadows Award in 2014. She lives with her family in the Land of the Long White Cloud.

JASON NAHRUNG is a Ballarat-based writer, editor and journalist. He has four novels and more than twenty short stories to his credit, all on the dark side of speculative fiction. He is undertaking a creative writing PhD investigating life in a climate-changed near-future Brisbane. He lurks online at www.jasonnahrung. com.au

BILL CONGREVE is an award-winning writer, editor and independent publisher (MirrorDanse books). His stories have appeared in a number of countries in publications such as *Faerie Reel, Tenebres, Event Horizon, Terror Australis, Aurealis, Borderlands, Bloodsongs, Intimate Armageddons, Monstres*! and *The Year's Best Australasian Fantasy & Horror*. His recent collection of vampire stories is *Epiphanies of Blood*. His most recent collection is *Souls Along the Meridian* (2010). He won the Peter McNamara Achievement Award in 2012 and has acted as judge for the Aurealis Awards on nine occasions. He works as a technical writer and editor in the emergency services sector.

J. (JOHANNES AKA JAN) SCHERPENHUIZEN is a writer, artist, editor and publisher. His comics, illustrations and prose pieces have appeared in Australia and the United States. Jan has collaborated with other talents but also acted as both writer and illustrator on projects, ranging from the picture book series *The Wild and Crazy Dinosaurs* to the gritty horror graphic novel *The Time of The Wolves*. As an editor and manuscript appraiser he discovered Nancy Kunze, Christopher Ride, Anthony O'Neill, and the late Martin Chimes, all of whom have credited him with playing a significant role in their becoming professional authors. Jan recently contributed several stunning, full-page black and white illustrations and a short story to the well-received *Sherlock Holmes: The Australian Casebook*. You can find out more about Jan's activities as agent, manuscript assessor, writing mentor, etc. at www.janscreative.com and his art can be viewed at www. jscherpenhuizenillustrator.com

SILVIA BROWN describes herself as a creative writer with a dark soul. She is a volunteer for the Australasian Horror Writers Association and TEDx Melbourne. Silvia writes dark fiction, film reviews and everything else in between. You can check out her website http://silviabrown.me for more details or join her on Twitter @SilvBrownWriter

T. S. P. SWEENEY is a dashingly roguish public servant by day and a roguishly dashing writer of fantasy, science fiction, and horror by night. He is the author of numerous published short stories, ranging from a Sherlock Holmes mystery set in the Australian bush through to a story in which a demon dismembers Nazis during the fall of Berlin. He dwells within the dank confines of his Sydney, Australia abode with his gorgeous and entirely-too-tolerant and supportive wife Sam and their collective menagerie. Information on his published and upcoming works can be found on his blog at www.tspsweeney.com. He can also be reached on Twitter @TSPSweeney

GEOFF BROWN is an award-winning Australian writer and Australian Shadows Award finalist-editor raised in Melbourne's gritty Western Suburbs. He writes fiction across various genres, and is the author of many published short stories, a novella, and a memoir. He has had numerous articles published in newspapers, both regional and metropolitan. He is the past president of the Australian Horror Writers Association (2011-2013), as well as the past director of the Australian Shadows Awards. He owns Cohesion Press, an award-winning Australian publishing house focused on fast-paced military horror anthologies, and currently works with Tim Miller, director of *Deadpool* and the

upcoming *Terminator* movie, as a senior story consultant. He is also the owner of Asylum Ghost Tours in Beechworth, and he's sometimes not a big fan of people.

DAVID KURARIA was born on the island of Ranongga in the Solomon Islands. He attended Kingsland Intermediate School in Auckland, New Zealand, before reuniting with his family in the Solomons' capital, Honiara. "The Seamounts of Vaalua Tuva" is David's first published story and is one of a trilogy of tales describing a malign, marine-dwelling race named *Kōpura*. Kuraria also wishes it be known he has a pet coconut crab named Ping Pong, and that he is currently employed in habitat protection by the Honiara Department of Fisheries.

There are a number of sides to **DAVE HEINRICH**. By day, he is currently working as an art director and internationally recognised medical illustrator at a university hospital, following extensive experience in graphic design, web development, advertising, game design and webcam animation. But he's probably best known as a comic book artist and cartoonist. His credits include *Phantom: Ghost Who Walks*, *Batman: Legends of the Dark Knight*, *Conan The Barbarian*, *Elvira* and *Mad*. In recent years Dave has also enjoyed producing art for car-shows and editing *Torqueback* magazine, as well as revisiting his indy/underground comic-book roots as a collaborator on *The Universe Gun*, *Weird Wild West*, *Savage Bitch*, *Weird Sex Fantasy* and *Decay*.

Printed in Australia
AUOW01n0855070818
301146AU00002B/2

9 781925 496994